D1523138

A LAZARUS RISING STORY

HOLD ON
TIGHT

New York Times and USA Today Bestselling Author

CYNTHIA EDEN.

PART ONE

"I trusted the wrong man once. I don't ever want
to make that mistake again."

—Savannah Jacobs

PROLOGUE

"Get in, get the woman, and get her out alive. Simple enough?"

Nothing was ever simple. Especially not a rescue operation. Jett raised one brow at the terse orders that had just been issued by the team's handler. "How many hostiles are we talking here?" He'd just been hustled into the briefing room with two other members of his team. Two that he had to trust with his life — Maddox and Andreas. They'd worked other missions before, and they knew the routine. By this point, they all knew the fucking drill.

Complete the mission. Do whatever it takes. Failure is never an option.

"We don't have an exact number on the hostiles," their handler said. The guy was sweating in his white lab coat, and he kept pushing his glasses higher on his thin nose.

Maddox gave a low whistle. "So you want us to go in blind?"

"The target is the daughter of a very important man."

That meant they were dealing with someone who had political pull and plenty of cash.

"Politician?" Maddox asked. "Or some fancy CEO?"

"Her father is the senior senator from Mississippi."

Maddox gave a knowing nod.

"The abduction has been kept out of the papers, and we want to continue keeping this situation quiet."

"Gonna be a bloodbath," Andreas said, his voice flat and his blue eyes glacial. The guy never showed any feeling. Jett wasn't sure he *could* feel. "That's why you're sending us in there."

The handler — what was the guy's name? Sometimes, it got hard to remember. There were so many bozos in white lab coats in the facility. So many who liked to keep their hands free of blood and death.

Jett looked at his own hands. They'd be stained with blood forever.

"Uh, it's…" The handler coughed. "Your special skills are needed here for the extraction."

Maddox laughed.

Jett didn't. Their "special skills" made them all freaks and perfect killing machines.

"No one can see you when you retrieve the woman," the handler continued. "If you're spotted by the hostiles, then they must be taken out. Recovering the target is the top priority."

Jett exhaled. "Let's just get the show on the road, all right?" He snatched the manila folder off the table. Flipped it open—and saw her.

Dark hair. Golden skin. Eyes a hazel mix that seemed to smile up at him.

"Savannah Jacobs," the handler said. "Age thirty. Last seen in Biloxi, Mississippi. She was taken from one of the casinos. She's being held for a large ransom, only these particular kidnappers have a habit of taking the money and still sending back their victims in pieces."

Jett was still staring at her picture. Her face was oval, her mouth curved into a grin—one that flashed the dimples in her cheeks. She looked happy. Innocent.

Jett wasn't sure if he'd ever been innocent.

Or fucking happy.

Mostly because...he couldn't remember a damn thing about his life. At least, not before he'd woken in the Lazarus facility. And since he'd been part of Project Lazarus, his life had been nothing but a series of dangerous missions. Project Lazarus was called in when no one else had a chance in hell of pulling off the operation.

This woman... *She's real. A person who needs help. And I'm the weapon that will be used to free her.* He made sure Maddox and Andreas saw her picture, then he returned it to the file.

"The ones who took her won't be expecting a team like…" The handler cleared his throat. Pushed his glasses up higher. "Like you three."

No, no one ever expected them. Who the hell would? Or could? You didn't expect the dead to show up for a battle. But that was exactly what the Project Lazarus members were…

Dead men.

"Get her out, eliminate anyone in your way, and then contact me for pick-up," the handler instructed. "Saving Savannah is mission priority. She must be recovered, no matter what it takes."

Maddox nodded. Andreas looked bored. And Jett…he wondered if Savannah was scared. If the men holding Savannah had hurt her.

Eliminate anyone in your way. If they'd hurt her, if they'd hurt the woman with the sweet smile and warm eyes, he'd make absolutely sure their deaths were as painful as possible.

"Black Ops rules, as always," the handler muttered. "Make sure anyone who sees your, uh, special skills, doesn't live to spread the story."

"When do we leave?" Maddox asked.

"Right now. We have a tentative location on the hostiles. Getting inside their base will be your job."

"It will be child's play," Andreas muttered.

Yes, it would be.

Jett's gaze slid to their handler. He was balding, and his forehead was slick with sweat.

Mathaway. Silas Mathaway. That was the guy's name. "You're not telling us everything." He could hear the guy's heartbeat racing. And the sweat—talk about bucket loads.

Mathaway's eyelids flickered.

"What are you holding back?" Jett pushed as he pulled out one of his knives. He polished the blade against the side of his shirt as he waited for an answer. He wasn't walking into a trap.

"They...they've had her for over forty-eight hours." Mathaway swiped at the sweat on his forehead. "By this time, they've usually sent the first piece to the family."

The first piece? Jett's jaw locked.

"They haven't," Mathaway rushed to add. "That worries...some people. People who think that the kidnappers could be changing their plans. People who think that something different is going on with Savannah." He swallowed. "She's very important. Critical, in fact. You have to retrieve her."

Andreas grunted. "Don't we always get the job done?" A rough laugh escaped him. "Or die trying?"

An absolute truth. If they didn't succeed, they died on the missions. They never gave up.

Luckily, they *did* come back from death.

Jett slid his finger over the edge of the blade, kept his eyes on the handler, and demanded, "Anything else you're holding back?"

"N-not a thing."

Total lie.

But the team was waiting. The woman was in danger. And the idea of anyone cutting into her and sending *pieces* of Savannah back...hell, no. Not happening. Not on Jett's watch.

Time to get the woman and kill anyone who got in his way.

CHAPTER ONE

She didn't want to die.

Savannah Jacobs jerked against the rough rope that bound her wrists behind her back. She was sitting in a hard, wooden chair, with her ankles tied to two chair legs. She'd been in that room — that dark, cold room — for hours. A gag filled her mouth. She'd almost choked on it when she'd tried screaming before. Not that her screams had done any good.

No one had come to help her. She was starting to think that no one would.

Her eyes strained to see in the darkness around her. The only sliver of light came from the right, from beneath what had to be a door. The light shone near the floor. So small.

Her wrists twisted again as she tried to fight free of the ropes. No give. The rough hemp dug into her skin, cutting her.

A creak reached her ears, and the sliver of light...it got bigger. *Bigger*. Her heart thundered in her chest because when the door swung open, she could see the outline of a man standing there. Tall, broad shoulders. And his face—

For just a moment, she glimpsed his face, and real terror filled her.

She wanted to shut her eyes. Wanted to pretend that *none* of this was happening.

The floor groaned as he closed in on her. She tilted her head back. The gag nearly choked her again.

"Oh, Savannah…" His voice was familiar. Just as his face had been familiar. Just as everything about him was familiar. Terribly familiar. "It's time, sweetheart."

A tear leaked down her cheek.

"I've got to send them proof that I have you." His hand brushed over her cheek, wiping the tear drop away. "Don't worry. It will be something small. How about we just start with your pinky?" Then he moved behind her.

A moan broke from her, one that was muffled by the gag. Inside, she was screaming, begging…*No, no, please don't! Don't cut me! Don't do this! Please!* But only that weak moan emerged from her.

Then she felt the edge of a knife against her hand. Felt it press to the base of her right pinky finger.

Oh, God. Oh, God…

***

"I'll cover the sound of your approach," Andreas announced in his low, dark voice. "They'll never hear your coming."

Andreas was speaking literally. They weren't just normal soldiers. As part of Project Lazarus, they all had special powers, talents that their prey would never expect. Andreas had the ability to cloak sound — to distort it. The bastards waiting would never know that they were being hunted.

Jett stared at the small house that waited up ahead. A house cradled in the middle of a swamp. "I'll make sure they never see me, too." Because that was *his* power. Part of it, anyway. For this mission, he was the one going in the house. He was the one getting the woman.

Maddox would take care of the armed guards on the outside. Andreas would hide all the sounds — dying men could be freaking loud. Or they could never make a sound. These men would never have the chance to make a sound.

I count ten men. Five outside. Five in. The voice didn't speak out loud. Instead, Maddox's voice reached Jett and Andreas on the psychic link they shared. A link that few outside of Lazarus would ever understand.

There was a reason why Project Lazarus was kept off the books. A reason why no one without the highest classification of security clearance knew about the group. Most folks wouldn't believe what Project Lazarus could do.

It was better that way. Safer.

Do we have a visual on Savannah? Jett asked, using the same psychic link to push the question at Maddox.

Negative.

Shit. So, she might not even be inside, but…

With ten men there, the guys were sure guarding something.

Search the house, Maddox directed. *If you find her, Andreas and I will have the extraction vehicle ready on the south side.*

Fair enough. Time to get moving.

Jett gave a little salute to Andreas, and the Greek slipped away.

Jett exhaled slowly and called up the strange, dark power that he'd discovered shortly after waking up in a Lazarus lab. He'd opened his eyes and found a bright light overhead. He'd been strapped to a gurney, buck-ass naked. The room had been cold as ice. For a moment, he'd thought he was dead.

Then he'd realized…then he'd learned, he *was* dead. A dead man brought back to life.

A man without a past.

A man with no future.

A man whose soul seemed to be gone — or at least, a soul that seemed to belong to the US government.

Jett kept to the shadows as he advanced on the house. A quick glance showed him that

Maddox was closing in, too. Maddox reached the five exterior guards first. Maddox lunged for the first bastard just as Jett—

"No!" A woman's scream cut through the night. *"Someone — help me*! Please!"

***

She'd managed to spit out the gag. Managed it because she'd been so terrified that she'd knocked her chair over. The blade had been pressed to her pinky, and Savannah had freaked the hell out. She'd shoved her body — with all of her might — away from the blade. She'd crashed face-first into the floor, but the gag was out. And the chair had broken. She twisted and heaved and managed to get her upper body away from the chair, but her legs were still tied tightly and —

A knife pressed to her throat. "Savannah, what in the hell are you doing?"

Her breath heaved in and out. Her mouth was cotton dry. She licked her lips, but that didn't help the dryness. Or the terror. "L-let me go." She'd screamed just moments before. Had someone heard her screams? Would someone come to help her?"

"That's never going to happen." The knife stayed pressed to her throat, but she felt his fingers on her cheek in a chilling caress. "You're mine now. You don't get to leave me."

No. She was going to get out of here. Somehow. "Don't cut me. M-my father will pay —"

"Oh, I have no doubt that he will. He's going to pay everything that I ask...and more." Rough laughter. "But guess what, Savannah? I'm not going to give you back. Even when he pays, even when I take every cent that he has...you won't ever go back."

He meant those words. She knew it, with utter certainty. He was going to keep her. Kill her. She would die in this room.

"I don't like it when you cry," he muttered.

And she didn't like it when he put a knife to her throat. Or when he threatened to cut off her pinky. Or when he kidnapped her.

"I have to send in proof. It's part of the process. Don't you get that?"

"Please..." She was begging and she didn't care. "Don't hurt me."

Silence.

Then... "I'm sorry, but it has to be done."

No, no, it didn't. She braced her body, ready to fight with every bit of strength that she had. It had been a while since he'd brought her food or water. *When was the last time?* Nausea rolled through her, her body was shaking, but, dammit, she'd *fight*.

Footsteps thundered toward them. Then a voice blasted, "Boss! Boss, dammit, something is happening outside! The men — they're gone!"

And she was released. Shoved back toward the floor.

"What?" A lethal fury vibrated in that one word. "The cops know better than to get involved with my business."

What did that mean? Were the local cops on his payroll?

"Someone is here. Someone is fucking with us." The words tumbled out with a nervous fury from the man who'd just raced into the room.

Savannah didn't move. She barely breathed. But she did hope. She hoped like crazy.

"Stand guard at her door. No one comes in or out until I return, got me?" And then the "boss" was leaning toward her once more. "Don't worry, sweetheart. I'll be back for you."

She wasn't his sweetheart. She didn't want him anywhere near her.

He kissed her cheek.

She shuddered. Hated him. Wanted to take his knife and shove it into his heart.

But her hands were still tied behind her. Her feet were still roped to the chair legs and he — he was leaving. He hurried toward the door. Slammed it shut. She saw just the tiny sliver of light and...and the shadow that came from the guard he'd left on the other side of the door.

The gag was gone from her mouth. He hadn't bothered to shove it back in. He hadn't bothered to pull her off the floor. She was sprawled with chunks of the broken chair, her shoulders hitched up, her arms burning. Savannah rolled, trying to get free. If she got free, she could use one of the broken pieces of wood as a weapon. She could slug the guard outside and run.

She twisted again and jerked hard, biting back a cry of pain as more wood broke but the ropes didn't give and—

A hand flattened over her mouth. A hand that just came right out of the darkness. She stiffened, every muscle in her body clamping down as fear drove straight into her heart. Then she erupted, heaving, straining, wanting to *fight* whoever the hell this new bastard was.

"I'm here to help you. Not hurt you." His hand was still over her mouth, and his voice was whisper-soft. "I need you to calm down."

She was way past the point of being calm. She was in extreme hysteria mode. A man had been in the darkness of her room? Just hiding? How long had he been there? How long had he been watching her? Oh, God, oh—

The last of the chair broke away. She rolled and the rope cut into her legs. Her shoulder nearly popped from the socket, and she cried out in pain and fury, but the sound was muffled by his hand.

He cursed. "Have to do this the hard way, huh? Shit."

Did he think she was going to make this easy for him?

But suddenly, he was on top of her. A big, heavy, muscled form that crushed her. His hand was still over her mouth. Her arms were lodged behind her, and the position hurt. Tears pricked her lashes.

"Don't cry," a rough rasp. "Give me a second. I'll cut the rope."

What?

But...he rolled her. She felt the sharp blade of a knife between her wrists. She remembered the other man's promise to take her pinky finger, and she shuddered. *Don't! Don't!* But this fellow didn't cut her finger off. Didn't slice her wrist. He just sawed through the rope, freeing her hands. She hadn't realized just how tight the rope had been, not until feeling came flooding back to her fingertips. Feeling that started as pinpricks of pain then erupted into a full-on burning.

He hauled her up toward him, pulling her onto his lap and still keeping a hand over her mouth. "I know it hurts, but don't make a sound. I'm trying to figure out our escape plan here, okay?"

An escape plan? Then he...he really was there to help her?

Savannah clamped her mouth shut behind his hand, not letting the pain-filled sounds escape. She'd choke down the pain. She'd do just about anything to get out of there.

"If I move my hand from your mouth, do you promise not to scream? Because if you do, only the bad guys will be running in here. Then I'll have to kill them, you'll have to watch, and you'll probably freak the hell out."

She was already freaking out. Had he missed that part? But Savannah nodded quickly to show him that she promised. That she wasn't about to scream.

His hand lifted from her mouth.

She didn't scream.

"Good." His voice was so low. It had been low the whole time. Just a gruff whisper that barely reached her ears. In the darkness, he was nothing more than a big shadow. She couldn't see his face. Savannah could only feel him, all around her.

Him…and his knife. The knife that was now sliding near her ankles.

"Gonna cut you free," he breathed the words in his rough, dark voice, "it will hurt at first. The same way your fingers are hurting. Just don't cry out, okay?"

Okay.

He gave a little jerk, as if she'd somehow just caught him by surprise.

Then he was cutting through the rope at her ankles. Finally freeing her legs and yes, it hurt, but she didn't care.

"I need to check you for injuries. I'm going to run my hands over your body, all right?"

She nodded. Wait, could he see her nod? She couldn't see him. Surely, he couldn't —

His hands slid over her body. A quick, thorough search that seemed totally impersonal. She had bruises, scrapes, her shoulders felt like they were on fire, but Savannah didn't think she had any broken bones. And she still had all of her fingers. Major win.

"Can you walk?"

If they were getting out of there, she could handle a marathon. "Y-yes…" Her voice was scratchy and low.

"Good." He pulled Savannah to her feet. And her knees immediately gave way.

So…no marathon.

She would have crashed right back to the floor, but he held her tight. Her body was flush against his. She realized the guy was strong — very, very muscled. Tall.

"My team is taking care of the guys outside. But there were a few men Maddox missed when he did the first check." His mouth was at her ear, and his breath slid over her lobe, making her shiver. "Not like him. Maddox never makes mistakes this way."

She didn't know who Maddox was.

"I counted eight men inside the house. Three of them ran out when they discovered the guys outside were missing. We have to play this scene carefully. If bullets start flying, I don't want anyone shooting you."

She'd prefer not to be shot, too. *Thank you very much.* "Don't want…you hurt, either."

"I can handle the bullets. Don't worry about me."

What was he? Superman? No one could handle bullets. But maybe he just meant that he was wearing a bullet proof vest. That could be it. "How did you get in?" The windows in that room were still boarded up, at least, she thought they were.

"Snuck in when the guy came to collect his boss."

He had? Wow. That was impressive.

"In a moment, I'm going to need you to scream for me."

Do what? Hadn't he been the one demanding that she *not* scream?

"When you scream, the guard on the other side of the door will rush inside. I'll take him out, and then I can take out anyone else who comes in after him. I'll control the entrance, so only one hostile will be able to enter at a time."

A hostile? Did he mean the men who'd taken her?

"Can you scream for me?"

"Yes."

"Good." He let her go. Stepped back — and the warmth that she'd felt emanating from him vanished.

She spun around, straining to see in the darkness, but he was just gone. No, not gone. Hiding. Waiting.

Her bare foot hit a broken chunk of the chair. She picked it up, wanting a weapon. Wanting to have some kind of protection for whatever was about to happen next.

"Scream, Savannah."

She sucked in a breath — and then screamed. Over and over.

The door flew open. Banged against the wall. A man stood there, the light spilling in from behind him to fill the room. He was thick in the middle, and his right hand gripped a gun.

"How the hell did you get loose?" He rushed into the room.

He'd left the door open. Light filled the space. She could see the broken chair. She could see the angry asshole rushing toward her. But she couldn't see her rescuer. Where had he gone? *Where*?

She lifted the chair leg. "Stay away from me!"

He didn't. He ran right at her, snarling and —

He was hit from behind. He stumbled, whirled, and then his head was jerking back, whipping with the force of an attack. Two seconds later, he was on the floor.

And there was still no sign of her rescuer. He had to be there, in the shadows, right? "Where are you?" Savannah whispered as she stepped over the downed jerk's prone body. She dropped her chair leg and took his gun. A way better weapon.

There was no answer.

Savannah peered around the room. The light didn't reach every corner. Her rescuer had to be in those shadows. Still hiding. Why —

"What did you do to Wayne?" a voice blasted.

She spun around, facing the open door, and saw another man standing there. Tall and thin, he had his gun pointed at her. Only fair — she had her gun pointed at him, too. But his gun wasn't shaking. Hers was. "Get out of my way!" Savannah yelled.

"Hell, no. You're not going anyplace." He stormed toward her. "You're —"

Crack.

He howled in pain. Howled because it looked as if his right hand had just been broken. The gun fell from his fingers, and when it hit the floor, it discharged with a loud bang. Savannah screamed, pure reflex, and she fired her gun, too. Blood poured from the guy's shoulder.

Holy shit. She'd just shot him.

"You bitch!"

He lunged at her.

She got ready to shoot again, her finger squeezing the —

Her rescuer appeared. He grabbed the other man from behind. Sliced up with a blade and…

Blood. So much blood.

Her eyes squeezed shut. This couldn't be real. She opened her eyes.

It was real. Horribly real. Her rescuer had just killed a man with a knife, slicing the bad guy's throat, and she was about to vomit. Right there. The gun slipped from her suddenly nerveless fingers and hit the floor.

Her "hero" wiped the knife on his pants. "You good?"

Uh, very much nope. But she nodded.

"Then let's get the hell out of here."

He caught her hand in his. Then he was rushing into the hallway and pulling her behind him. He looked to the left, to the right, and then they were bounding toward stairs.

They raced down those stairs in what had to be record time. Hope was making her breath come fast and hard. Or maybe that was fear. Whatever. They were almost at the bottom of the stairs. Almost —

"She's mine!" The bellow came from above. And so did the gunshots that blasted at them.

Savannah expected the bullets to tear into her back, but her rescuer—he was there. In a lightning fast move, he yanked her down and put himself in front of her. When more bullets erupted, she felt his body jerk. *The shots are hitting him!* First one, then the other. And…

"It's going to be okay." He stared into her eyes. They were in the light, and she could finally see his face clearly. He had beautiful, coal black eyes. Pure black hair. A face that was hard and fierce, a jaw that was—

"Run…" He gasped out the one word before he fell.

He just—he fell right there. Collapsed on the stairs. And she could smell blood.

"Savannah!" Her head whipped up. The shooter—the familiar bastard was smiling at her. He offered his hand to her. "Come back to me, sweetheart."

Sweetheart. He called her that often, because they'd known each other for a while. This man—the man who'd kidnapped her and threatened to cut off her finger—wasn't a stranger. They'd been friends. Lovers. And now…now they were this. *Captor and captive? Would-be killer and victim?*

Savannah shook her head. "Stay away from me."

His lips thinned. He was handsome. Dark blond hair, green eyes. A perfect, chilling grin. He still gripped the gun in his hand, but as she stared up at him, he moved down a few stairs — and he aimed that gun at her rescuer's head.

"Is he still breathing, Savannah? I think he is. I think I can see his chest moving."

Her knees had locked.

"But if you don't get your ass over here to me, the next bullet will go in his brain. Do you want that, Savannah? You want me to put a bullet in his head? You want me to kill him in front of you?"

No. "You'll do it, anyway." She knew this with certainty. He'd kill the man who'd tried to save her. Yes, the fellow was still breathing. She could see his chest rising and falling. He was bleeding, though. He was hurt. He was —

He had a knife in his left hand. She could see it.

She forced her legs to bend. She grabbed his hand, as if she was holding on tight to him.

"Savannah!" Fury blasted in that word. "Come to me, now!"

"Come and get me," she whispered.

Did he hear her? Did it matter? He rushed down the stairs, still holding his gun, and then when he was close —

She surged back to her feet and drove the knife at him. It hit him in the side, sliding deep, and he bellowed. He bellowed even as he fired his weapon.

I'm going to die right here. This is how it ends for me.

But the bullet didn't touch her.

Just as he'd fired the gun, the house had plunged into total darkness. She heard the thud of flesh hitting flesh, a grunt, and—

"I told you to run." His voice. Her rescuer. He was talking.

And he was reaching for her hand.

"Said run...not steal my knife."

A wild laugh escaped her. He was okay? He was—

He scooped her into his arms and raced down the remaining stairs. "This place is about to blow. Maddox said the fire is coming."

What? When had this magical Maddox said anything? She hadn't heard a word—unless...was her rescuer wearing some kind of mic? Were they communicating via—

"I only had five minutes before the detonations were scheduled. Time is up, Savannah." His hold tightened on her. "But I've got you."

He had her, but what about the "boss"— what had happened to him?

Her rescuer kicked open the front door. They ran into the night.

Bam! Bam! Bam!

More bullets were flying. Were they flying at them? Were they—

The house erupted behind them, sending flames shooting high into the sky and sending Savannah — and the man holding her — hurtling forward.

I've got you. His words filled her mind right before she slammed into the earth.

CHAPTER TWO

"You want to stop holding her?" Maddox asked as he glanced into the rear view mirror. "I mean, we're safe now. You can put her in the seat next to you."

Jett didn't want to put Savannah in the damn seat next to him. "She's still out cold." His fault. When they'd hit the ground, he'd tried to cushion the fall, but he hadn't done a good enough job. Savannah had been knocked out, and she still hadn't opened those gorgeous hazel eyes to look at him.

"That's probably for the best. This way, she doesn't freak out because we left an inferno in our wake."

It wasn't for the best. She was hurt. Jett growled.

"Uh, buddy? Everything all right back there?" Maddox pressed.

It was just the three of them in the SUV. Andreas had stayed back at the house. Once he was sure the scene was clear, Andreas would head out on his motorcycle and meet them at the rendezvous location.

"She needs a doctor," Jett announced. "She's covered in bruises. And now she's got a knot on her head. She needs—"

She moaned. Turned in his hold. Rubbed her cute little nose against his neck.

It got harder to breathe.

"How much did she see?" Suddenly, Maddox's voice had gone low. Cold.

Jett swallowed. "I turned things dark." A talent he had, one that came in very, very handy on covert missions. "I don't think she saw anything but, well, me taking a few bullets."

He was wearing a bullet proof vest, so most of the bullets had never reached his skin. One had torn through his upper arm, bleeding like a bitch, but he'd only faked the whole near-death thing. The plan had been for Savannah to keep running. He'd figured she'd leave him on the stairs and get to safety. Maddox had been waiting outside to swoop her up.

Jett had intended to keep playing dead/severely injured on the stairs until the ring leader came down those steps. Then taking the guy out would have been easy as pie. Only Savannah had surprised Jett.

And she'd taken his knife. She'd stabbed the man coming to take her.

She'd also impressed the hell out of Jett.

That had all been *before* he'd gotten her hurt.
Shit, *I'm so sorry.* He didn't like to ever see a
woman get hurt. And definitely not her.
Definitely not—

"Why are you sorry?" Savannah's voice was
a little slurred. "You got me out."

Jett stiffened. He hadn't spoken out loud. No
way should she have just heard what he'd said.
No, not what he'd *said*. What he'd *thought*.

Her lashes fluttered open. Jett found himself
staring into wide, hazel eyes. He had perfect
night vision, a Lazarus bonus. All of his senses
had been enhanced courtesy of Lazarus. The
program came with lots of bonuses, and some
extreme negatives.

"You're holding me."

He felt his lips twitch a little at her low
words. "I think you may have a concussion."
And who the hell knew what else? He'd searched
her for broken bones and hadn't found any, but
Savannah could have other injuries. They needed
to get her to a hospital. They'd drop her off, and
he'd vanish from her life.

The way he always vanished after a case was
done.

"A concussion." Her gaze stayed directed up
at him, and Jett wondered just how much she
could see of him in the dark. "That would explain
the throbbing in my head."

His smile wanted to stretch.

She didn't get up, just remained curled on his lap, against his chest, near his heart. A heart that was beating a little too fast. Probably a side effect of the adrenaline. It had been one hell of a night.

"You saved my life."

He realized he was stroking her arm. He should stop. He didn't. "I think you saved mine, too. Didn't realize you were handy with a knife."

"I totally am not," she confessed in her husky, sensual voice. "But I was desperate, and the knife was handy."

Her hair smelled like flowers. Fresh. Light. He found himself leaning even closer to her.

"Who are you?" Savannah asked him.

"Jett." Just a first name. Not a last. She wouldn't ever need to know his full name. Within the hour, he'd be walking out of her life.

"I'm Savannah."

"I know."

He heard the faint click of her swallow. "How did you find me? Who sent you?"

He couldn't answer either of those questions. Or he could, but if he did—he'd just be lying. As he stared into her eyes, he realized he didn't want to lie to her.

From the front seat, Maddox cleared his throat.

Savannah immediately stiffened.

"Easy," Jett soothed. "That's just Maddox."

"Ma'am," Maddox called, "you're safe now. We'll take you to a local hospital so you can get your wounds treated."

"I'm fine," she answered immediately and she slid off Jett's lap.

He didn't like that. He'd been enjoying having her close.

But when Maddox had spoken, she'd seemed to shut down. Now she hunched in the far left seat, pulling a seatbelt across her body.

"I don't need a hospital," Savannah added quickly.

"The concussion says otherwise," Jett muttered.

"It's not a concussion. It's just a bump on the head." Her fingers fluttered in the air, and he grabbed her hand, turning it over, inspecting the bruises and the cuts on her wrist.

Rage filled him. A dark and twisting fury, but his fingertips were light as he traced the marks on her.

"It's just from the rope," she whispered to him. "I was trying to get away. The rope cut me. They — the men — they didn't hurt me. Only at the end…"

Her voice trailed away. He reached for her other wrist. Saw the same wounds.

"It's so dark in here." Her voice had gone higher. Gotten nervous. "How can you even see —"

"Jett can see like a cat in the dark," Maddox replied blandly. "One of his talents."

A talent that Maddox shared.

"What happened at the end?" Jett demanded. Because her words were nagging at him.

They didn't hurt me. Only at the end…

Maybe he should have sliced every one of those bastards into little pieces.

"He was going to cut off one of my fingers. Said he had to do it. Had to send proof." Her breath rasped in and out. "But then you came. One of the men told him…said the guys outside were missing. He stopped." Her hand turned in his grasp. Held Jett's. "Thank you. Thank you so much. I will *never* be able to repay you for what you've done."

"I don't want payment." She wasn't the first they'd saved. She wouldn't be the last. His team was sent all over the world on missions. Often, they were sent in for extractions — when normal channels weren't going to work and a rescue was vital. And sometimes, they were sent for kills. To take out targets that were imminent threats. They always worked outside of the law, and they never left evidence behind.

As far as the rest of the world was concerned, they were ghosts.

Actually, that was fucking true…considering that his team was composed of the dead.

Every single one of us died. Me, Maddox, Andreas…all of the other test subjects at the facility. We died, but they brought us back.

"Do you know who took you?" Maddox asked quietly.

Jett's gaze cut to the front seat. Maddox wasn't using headlights — the better to not attract the wrong kind of attention. They were on an old, graveled road, rushing back to town. To safety.

Maddox didn't need the lights to spot trouble coming. Neither did Jett. The road around them was dead silent.

"I…I know," Savannah said quietly.

This was new. And it was the development that their handler had hoped would happen.

"He was — the leader was Patrick Zane. I, um, I knew him. He was the one who came to take my finger." She gave a long, tired sigh. "A few days ago, we were out together…at a bar in one of the casinos near the beach. He must have slipped something in my drink because when I woke up, I was in that room, tied to the chair." Her words came quickly. Her fear pulsed just beneath the surface as she said once more, "I knew him." A pause. "We'd been friends. We'd been dating."

Fucking sonofabitch.

"And he was still going to hurt me." She pulled her hand away from Jett. "I thought I could trust him. I thought I'd found someone safe."

Maddox was silent, and Jett didn't know what the hell he was supposed to say. It pissed him off that she'd been hurt. Made him want to destroy something — or someone. Too bad the fire had beat him to the punch.

"He was the one on the stairs," she said after a moment. "He was the one I stabbed."

***

Andreas stared at the flames. Bright orange and gold, stretching into the dark night. The house had erupted, and when the fire exploded, the glass from the windows had shot in all directions. Maddox knew how to place his detonators.

No one appeared from the wreckage. The men outside had been taken care of — knocked out, tied up, and left for the collection crew who'd eventually be coming for them, once Andreas was gone. And all traces of his team were gone.

The blast would burn hot and fast. He'd stay until it sputtered out, making sure that it didn't spread anywhere else. Nothing was close to the old house, and there was no wind that night. The fire should die away, it should —

He heard the faint roar of an engine.

What in the hell? His head whipped to the right. A motorcycle shot out of an old shack, what he'd thought was just a storage building. It erupted into the night and surged right past him.

Then…

Another. Going just as fast. Only Andreas was leaping forward, roaring his fury because no way, no damn way should anyone have gotten out of that house. Not unless…

Sonofabitch! An escape tunnel. He should have considered that. They all should have considered it. These guys were professionals. They would have had a way to cover their asses, and a tunnel that led from the house to the shack — to the place where their motorcycles were stored…

Smart. Fucking smarter than he'd anticipated.

The second bike was close enough that he might be able to leap up and knock the driver off the cycle. With a burst of speed, Andreas attacked —

Only the bastard driving the bike just lifted his gun and fired right at Andreas. One hit to the chest. *Bullet proof vest will cover me.* Andreas didn't slow down —

The second bullet hit him in the neck.

Fuck.

Andreas felt the blood burst from his neck. He fell on the ground, his hand flying up to his neck in a futile effort to stop the blood flow. It was pumping out too fast and too hard. This shit wasn't good. He knew he was dying. He knew it.

But before the whole world bled away, he sent out a desperate call on the psychic link he shared with his team members.

Two men...got away. The warm blood poured down his neck, his chest. *And I'm dead...*

***

Two men...got away. The message blasted through Jett's mind. *And I'm dead...*

"Fucking hell," Maddox growled from the front seat. Jett knew he'd just gotten the message from Andreas, too. "Change of plans." He slammed on the brakes.

Savannah lurched forward, but the seatbelt grabbed her and heaved her back.

Maddox spun to face them. "I'll go back for Andreas. Stay with him until he..." Maddox didn't finish. He didn't need to. *Until Andreas comes back.* Because unless he'd taken a shot to the head, Andreas would be coming back. There was pretty much only one way to keep a Lazarus soldier down.

They were rather zombie-like that way.

"Get her to a doc. Get her checked out, and then keep her safe." Maddox was the team leader, and the guy always loved to blast his orders. But Jett didn't need to be told these things. He could figure shit out for himself.

"I'll stay with her until I hear back from you," Jett said flatly. Two men had escaped? That shouldn't have happened. No damn way. He wasn't about to risk Savannah. He'd guard her until those SOBs were caught.

With Lazarus on the job, it shouldn't take long.

Maddox nodded once, grimly. Then he was gone. He jumped out of the SUV and raced into the dark.

"Uh…" Savannah coughed. "Did he just run away? I mean, I—"

"He had to go back for a team member." Jett jumped out of the SUV. Hurried to the driver's seat.

Savannah hopped from the back and climbed into the passenger seat. As she slammed her door, she turned to him, frowning, "On foot?"

He couldn't tell her just how fast Lazarus super soldiers were. "He's good at recon."

He turned the key. Shot them forward.

"This other team member…" Worry whispered through her words. "Is he okay?"

No, he was dead. Hopefully, though, that was just a temporary condition. "Two men got away from the house." Might as well tell her that part.

"How do you know?" Then he felt her hand on his cheek. Her silken fingertips. "Are you wearing a radio? One of those super tiny devices in an ear? All spy-like and covert?" Her voice dropped. "*Are* you a spy or something?"

"I'm something." His hands tightened on the wheel.

Her fingers slid away from him. Why the hell did he miss her touch?

"Those two who got away…they won't come after me." Her words weren't a question, but they also weren't very steady. "They'll run, won't they?" Ah, now that was a question. A rather hopeful one.

"If they're smart." If they had any sense, they'd run as far and as fast as they could.

"You didn't tell me if your other team member is okay."

Lie. It was the only way. Though he hated to do it. "He's fine." He would be, maybe. Jett had tried contacting Andreas again, but only got darkness. Shit. It wasn't the first time a team member had been killed on a mission. Jett had been taken out before, too. But it didn't make things any easier.

How many times could you really cheat death?

They were almost back to the old highway. When they'd planned the retrieval, they'd originally intended to drop her off at a nearby hospital. With those two guys on the loose, there wouldn't be any dropping off now, but Jett would damn well get her checked out. He'd stay at her side. Every single moment.

"Um, where, exactly, are we?"

"About an hour outside of Biloxi."

"I should call my family. Let them know—"

"You can't call them. Not until I have a secure line for you to use." The SUV hopped onto the highway. "We don't know what we're dealing with, and my priority is just you. Your safety has to come first. These bastards have gotten away with attacks before, and I have to make sure that they don't come after you again."

The road stretched before them. Long. Dark. Winding.

"Is my...my family is safe, right?"

They should be. "You're the target."

"You said 'before'—that the men who took me had gotten away with attacks before." She pulled in a deep breath. "I wasn't the first victim?"

Hell. "No."

"How many other victims?" Jett could hear the strain in her voice. "How many times has Patrick done this?"

"You're victim number six."

Her breath expelled in a gasp. "Those others—they all went home, didn't they?"

He didn't speak.

"Jett?"

"No, baby, none of the others ever made it home." He risked a fast glance at her. "But you will. I swear it. Just trust me, and I'll keep you safe."

CHAPTER THREE

"I need a doctor, *now.*" Jett's booming voice filled the small ER.

And his shout got immediate action. A nurse leapt up from behind the check-in desk, and she rushed forward. Of course, the security guard was rushing forward, too. Probably because Jett looked so dangerous.

He wore all black, and his dark hair was heavy and thick. He was covered in ash, and Savannah realized that they both smelled like smoke.

He'd taken off his bullet proof vest at some point—she'd seen it in the back of the SUV, and now he stood there, glaring at everyone.

"Sir, what are your injuries?" The nurse's eyes were sweeping over him.

And over Savannah. Because Jett was currently holding Savannah in his arms. Even though she'd insisted that she could walk. Her legs were fine.

"Her injuries. Her injuries are what matter," Jett gritted as he carried Savannah to a nearby

gurney. "I think she has a concussion. She's also got lacerations on her wrists and ankles."

She had scratches. Not deep lacerations. Savannah started to correct him but—

More nurses and some orderlies were rushing from the back of the ER. She and Jett were the only patients in the place. Must have been a slow night.

"We'll take her back," the nurse assured him. Her gaze was still mostly on Jett, and Savannah understood. In the light, she could see him clearly and he was...

Sexy.

In a hot, dangerous way. In a good way. In a way she'd really be appreciating if she weren't currently in the middle of a nightmare.

"You're injured!" The blonde nurse suddenly called out as she put her hand on Jett's arm.

Savannah saw the blood there—and she remembered the bullets that had been flying on the stairs. The way Jett had fallen like a stone, utterly terrifying her because she'd thought he was dead.

But...

He'd said he was fine.

"You were shot?" Savannah gasped.

Jett's dark eyes instantly flew to her. He stepped closer to the gurney. "Barely a graze." He tucked a lock of her hair behind her ear. "I'm already healing."

How could he be already healing? No one just magically started healing from a gunshot wound.

"I'll take care of you," the nurse assured Jett. "You come this way—"

He gave a hard, negative shake of his head. "No, I'm staying with her."

"But—your injury! And there's paperwork—"

"I'm staying with my wife." His voice was low and lethal, but he leaned forward and pressed a tender kiss to Savannah's cheek. "Once she's safe, once I know she's okay, then I'll handle the paperwork."

Savannah didn't think that was usually the way things worked.

"But I need to know her allergies!"

The others were wheeling Savannah back. Jett stayed at her side.

"Penicillin," Jett threw back.

Savannah stiffened. How did he know that?

"And latex," he added. "Otherwise, she's good."

Savannah blinked up at her "husband" in confusion. How did he know those things?

The ER treatment room doors swung open. A young doctor with close-cropped hair and glasses smiled at her. She didn't smile back. Her heart was racing, and she found herself grabbing tight to Jett's hand.

Someone shined a light in her eyes.

Someone else took her blood pressure.

Someone else barked, "What happened to her? How did she get these injuries?"

"Check her out first," Jett growled. "Then we'll explain everything."

She looked down at her wrists. In the glaring light, the bruises appeared extra dark. The scratches were long, red. Her two wrists matched exactly. So did her ankles. And to her, it seemed pretty obvious that she'd gotten those injuries because she'd been tied up.

The team checking her out suddenly went quiet, and she knew they'd reached the same conclusion. The doctor nodded to a petite, dark-haired nurse. The nurse slipped away.

Probably to go call the cops.

"My head hurts," Savannah murmured.

All eyes flew to her.

"Could you please check my head?" Because it was the only injury that worried her. "And can you do it…fast?" As in…before the cops arrived. Before the whole scene went straight-up crazy.

"Sir, you'll need to step outside," the doctor told Jett in a firm, authoritative voice.

Jett still held one of her hands. His head turned, and he stared at the doctor. Smiled and said, "Not fucking happening."

The doctor swallowed. Started to sweat a bit.

"My wife," Jett prompted. A lethal edge of command entered his voice as he snapped, "*Now.*"

The doctor jumped — and he got busy checking out her head.

***

"You have a mild concussion," Dr. Francis Harris explained to Savannah after way too much poking and prodding. "You'll need to take it easy and avoid strenuous activities for the next twenty-four hours. If your vision becomes blurred or if you have trouble speaking, you should immediately come back to the ER."

She flexed her wrists. They'd been bandaged up. So had her ankles. She now wore a too-thin, paper hospital gown.

The doctor patted her hand. "You're going to be—"

Jett growled.

The doctor snatched his fingers away from her. "You'll be just fine, ma'am." A nervous glance at Jett. "Just fine."

"Thank you," Jett murmured. "You can go now."

The doctor blinked. He probably wasn't used to being dismissed. He probably also wasn't used to a woman appearing at — well, the clock said it was nearly 3 a.m. — with rope burns on her wrists and ankles.

The doctor hurriedly backed away. They weren't in a private room, but were just in the open area of the small ER's exam space. There were about six beds in that area, and she was the only occupant.

"The cops are waiting outside those doors," Jett murmured as he moved closer to the bed. "They'll want to question you and me. Now that the doc is done, they'll be coming in here any moment."

"What do I tell them? Do I tell them about Patrick? About—"

He scooped her into his arms again. "We're not telling them a damn thing."

"But—"

"Money will be sent to the hospital. They'll be compensated for your care." He was hurrying her toward a green door. Was it an exit door? "We're getting the hell out of here because I'm not going to let the cops separate us."

He kicked open the door without even slowing his steps. Behind them, though, she heard a voice call out, "Stop! You can't go in there! Wait!"

He didn't stop. He did go in there — into what turned out to be a narrow hallway, not the exit. He rushed down the hallway. It twisted to the left, to the right, and then they hurried through another doorway. This one led them back to the ER's waiting room. Actually, it spit them out right next to the check-in desk.

Cops were there, but the cops were heading for the swinging double doors that would take them back to the exam room. Their backs were turned to Jett and Savannah. Maybe she and Jett would be able to make it out without even being seen—

Then the blonde nurse erupted from the exam room. The double doors shot outward. "He's taking her away!" She pointed toward Jett and Savannah.

So much for their sneaky get-away.

Jett cursed. And then he ran. Really, really fast. So fast that everything seemed to pass Savannah in a blur.

Wait, is this the blurred vision that the doc talked about?

In the next instant, she was in the passenger seat of the SUV. Buckled up. Jett had jumped into the driver's seat. Cops ran out of the hospital. A security guard rushed in front of the SUV and tried to block their escape.

Jett just swerved around the security guard. He left the cops in his wake, blasting out of that parking lot with a squeal of his tires.

She glanced back. "They're going to follow us." Her heart was about to burst right out of her chest.

"They're going to lose us," he replied with utter confidence.

She realized he wasn't using headlights. And that he seemed to know exactly where he was going. He drove fast and hard, pulling a total Vin Diesel, and in moments, there was nothing behind them but darkness.

"Wh-what if they got the tag number?"

"It's a stolen tag. Won't do them any good. They won't find you."

Goosebumps rose on her arms. Was that what the good guy was supposed to say? That he was using a stolen tag? That the cops wouldn't find her?

Was a good guy supposed to rush her out of a hospital and not stop to answer the questions that the cops had?

Cops were…they were safe. They were the ones you were supposed to turn to when things got crazy. Or when you'd been, you know, kidnapped.

She took a deep breath. Then four more. And tried to think this mess through.

Jett *had* saved her from those jerks at the old house. He was the good guy, wasn't he?

He wouldn't let me call my family.

He never left me alone at the hospital so I couldn't talk privately with anyone.

And we may be rushing away in a stolen car.

"Why are you afraid?" Jett's voice filled the interior of the vehicle. "I'm not going to let anything happen to you."

She swallowed, twice. She was afraid...of him. "I think you should put me out at the nearest police station."

"Not happening."

Shit. Not good. "Why not?"

"Because that wouldn't be safe."

"The police aren't safe?"

"You are too damn trusting," he rasped.

Yes, she'd figured that out when her lover had *kidnapped* her. And maybe she'd jumped on the Jett bandwagon too fast. "How do I know you're good?"

Silence.

He turned the vehicle to the left. She could see nothing but darkness. "I saved you," Jett spoke in a flat, hard voice, "didn't I?"

Right. Yes. But... "Why won't you just let me go?"

"Because I can't."

That wasn't a very good answer.

Her fingers slid toward the door handle.

"Baby, if you jump from this car, you will hurt yourself. Then I'll just have to go back and threaten that doc again so he can patch you up." His fingers drummed on the steering wheel. "And I'll get really pissed if you're hurt. Really, really pissed."

She was sweating, her heart was racing, and the idea of slamming into the pavement while wearing a paper gown wasn't exactly high on her list of fun activities, but she wasn't about to trade one hell for another. "I want to talk to my family. Right now." She had to get some proof that she could trust Jett. "If you don't mean me any harm—"

"If I meant you harm, would I have taken you to the hospital?"

Uh—no—

"If I meant you harm, would I have busted you out of that house in the first place?"

"You killed a man. I saw you do it. You killed without any hesitation." She wasn't backing down. "I don't know you. The only thing I know about you—it's that you can kill really, really well." Yes, she'd just thrown his *really, really* back at him.

"I can kill well because I'm a former Navy SEAL. I was trained by the best." He turned the SUV again, and they headed toward what looked like an old garage. A security gate blocked the garage. He rolled down his window and reached out toward a keypad.

Navy SEAL. Should she buy that? Or should she run? Savannah fumbled with the door handle—

His hand flew out and circled around her wrist. "I know you've had one hell of a week."

Understatement.

"And I'm sorry about killing the guy in front of you. That was probably bad."

Probably?

"But he would have killed me. It was a survival situation. He was the bad guy."

The gate was opening.

And Jett was still holding her wrist, above the bandages, being careful not to touch her bruises or to hurt her anymore.

"My mission is to protect you. I don't know who all is involved in the kidnapping ring. I don't know who I can trust. It's suspected that the local authorities may be involved because *no one* has made any progress catching these assholes. Until I know who I can trust, until I know you're safe, I have to keep you close."

He drove forward. The gate closed behind them. A moment later, the garage door was sliding open, and he drove the SUV inside. When the garage door closed behind them, the sound seemed very, very loud.

He was still holding her wrist. Still touching her. Still absolutely unnerving her.

"There's a phone inside. It's untraceable. My team set it up—they secured this whole place for us. You can use that phone. You can call your family, but you can't tell them where we are."

Easy enough. She wasn't sure where they were.

"I need you to trust me."

He didn't get it. She'd trusted Patrick — then she'd woken up tied to a chair. With her past, it had never been easy to trust anyone.

He flashed her a quick smile. "I know that you've been through hell, but I promise you, my only goal is to keep you safe."

"You're the good guy, right?"

His smile slid away. "I'm the guy who will destroy anyone who tries to hurt you."

Did that count as a yes or no?

"Fresh clothes are waiting for you inside."

She opened her door and felt a distinct breeze against her ass. Wonderful. Now she was probably giving Jett a show, on top of everything else. Savannah threw a desperate glance over her shoulder.

Jett wasn't staring at her bare ass. He exited the SUV. A moment later, he hurried around the front of the SUV, and he took her arm, helping to steady her. She'd been plenty steady, but she didn't protest. Just, well — because.

They walked toward a set of stairs. The place was one hell of a lot bigger on the inside than the exterior had led her to believe. After biting her lower lip as she thought for a moment, Savannah asked, "Is this a safe house?"

"Of sorts." He didn't let go of her on the stairs. Her feet were covered in socks that they'd given her at the hospital, and she could feel the cold metal of the steps through the thin material. "We're off-grid here. Maddox and Andreas will be rendezvousing with us soon."

Andreas. "I don't remember seeing Andreas." He must have been the team member that Maddox had gone back to get.

"That's because he was working outside the house when I went to secure you. Don't worry, he'll be here soon enough." The door in front of them had a keypad instead of a lock, and Jett typed in a quick code. There was a soft click, and then the door opened. He ushered her inside. "The bedroom is to the right. There are clothes in there. Or, if you want, you can just put on a robe and ditch the hospital gown."

"You bought clothes for me." *Before* he'd rescued her? Something else odd. Something else that unnerved her.

"No, we picked up clothes from your place for you. We thought you'd prefer *your* stuff."

She did. Her gaze cut toward him. "What about the stuff at the hospital?" Her bloody, dirty clothes. "They'll probably turn all of that over to the police, won't they? They'll —"

"They can't turn over something they don't have. Don't worry. I took care of things there."

She was worrying, a lot. But she was tired of wearing paper so she headed for the bedroom he'd indicated. She walked through what looked like a small den. Saw a kitchenette to the side. A bathroom.

"Do you need help dressing?" His voice stopped her when she was at the bedroom door.

Her hand rose and gripped the door frame. "I'm good." Even if she wasn't, Savannah wouldn't be getting naked in front of Mr. Tall, Dark, and Dangerous. She looked back over her shoulder at him. "When I'm dressed, I *will* be calling my family."

"Absolutely."

Right. She stepped forward—

And felt another draft.

"Baby, you have got one killer ass."

She slammed the door shut behind her.

***

He probably should have kept that last comment to himself. But her ass truly was stellar.

And this isn't the time to go lusting after the mission target.

Jett raked his hand through his hair. There was just something about her. He'd felt a connection from the moment he saw her photograph. And when he'd actually gotten close to her, when he'd touched her...

Desire had ignited. A consuming, white-hot lust that he'd never expected. One he sure as hell shouldn't be feeling when he was in the middle of a mission. She had a concussion, for shit's sake.

She didn't need him lusting after her on top of everything else.

He could hear the faint rustles of sound from the bedroom. She was changing. Sliding out of the hospital gown that had revealed far too much, and, God willing, covering way, way up.

He hadn't heard from Maddox or Andreas yet. And that wasn't a good sign. They should have checked in by now. With every moment that passed, more tension slid down his spine.

He tried reaching out on the psychic link he shared with Maddox. *Can you hear me, buddy? What in the hell is happening?*

Silence. Emptiness. No response at all. Just—

The bedroom door flew open. "What do you mean, what in the hell is happening? I'm changing, you knew that." Savannah frowned at him. "Why were you yelling at me?"

She'd put on jeans and a white t-shirt. Her feet were bare, her toes curling against the floor. Her hair was loose over her shoulders, her eyes wide and deep, and—

Problem. Serious fucking problem. No one had bothered to brief him on the fact that Savannah Jacobs was psychic. And since she'd just somehow picked up on the link he'd formed with Maddox—shit, she might be able to hear all of the team's psychic communication.

Going dark. He shot out that psychic message hard and fast. *Line is not secure.*

She rubbed her temple. "What line isn't secure? What are you even talking about?"

She thought he was talking. Did she not understand her own powers? Or was something else at play? He'd never met anyone with psychic skills, not outside of Lazarus. Suddenly, this mission was looking a whole lot darker. He stalked toward her, caught her hand, and pulled it away from her temple.

"We're not as secure as we thought," Jett murmured. His fingers stroked along her wrist, just above her bandages.

"What?" Her gaze darted around him. "Is someone else here? Are we in danger?"

He didn't know what was happening, not just yet. But his inner alarms were blaring, and he realized that Savannah's wide, innocent gaze might actually be hiding plenty of secrets. "I will protect you," he promised, "but you have to be honest with me. Understand?"

She gave a quick nod.

"No secrets."

Her gaze slid away from his. And his suspicions deepened.

"I, um, I really need to call my family," Savannah told him. "I need to make that call now."

He let go of her hand. Backed away. In silence, he took a secure, burner phone from the nearby desk. As he handed it to her, Jett said, "Call them. But don't tell them where we are. Don't tell them anything about me."

Her fingers trembled a little as she took the phone. She dialed quickly and put the phone to her ear.

"No, baby." The endearment slipped out. "On speaker."

She lowered the phone. Her finger swept over the screen, and a ringing filled the room.

One ring.

Two.

Thr—

"Hello?"

"Dad?" Savannah's voice broke, her happiness apparent.

Jett rubbed his chest.

"Savannah? Baby, Christ, you're okay? Tell me that you're—"

"I'm okay." Her gaze was on Jett. "I'm safe."

For the moment.

"Where are you? What happened? What—"

"It was Patrick. He took me. I-I woke up in some room, tied to a chair."

A low, vicious curse came from her father. Then… "He's dead." There was absolute, cold determination in that one word. "I swear to you, he'll be a dead man." A stark pause. "Where are you?" he asked again, voice roughening. "I'll come for you. Right the hell now."

Jett shook his head.

"I'm — I think I'm in a safe house. A…a team got me out." She gave a nervous laugh. "They seem all Black Ops, very fancy. Did you use some government pull to get them?"

Jett reached for the phone. She'd said too much —

"I haven't contacted anyone about your abduction. I was told that if I did, you'd die." Her father's voice had turned ice cold. "No one was sent by me, baby. *Get the fuck away from — "*

Jett snatched the phone from her. Horror had flashed on her face. She backed away, putting space between her and Jett even as he crushed the phone in his hand. Pulverized it with a strength that a normal man wouldn't possess.

"You weren't supposed to mention me."

She swallowed. Retreated again. Her gaze was on the phone. Or rather, the chunks of the phone he'd just tossed into a trash bin. "I didn't — just said that you were — "

"Black Ops." Because he'd told her that he was a SEAL. His mistake.

"My dad didn't get you to come for me." Her breath came in and out. Fast, desperate pants.

Hell, was she about to run? It sure looked like she was about to run. He moved, deliberately placing his body between her and the exit.

"I…I would really like to see some ID," Savannah added, notching her chin up. "Something that says you're a cop or—"

"I never said I was a cop." He was trying to keep the lies to a minimum. "Not like I carry some kind of SEAL ID in my wallet." Despite everything, a smile tugged at his lips. "That's just not a thing."

She didn't smile. Her eyes narrowed. "My dad didn't arrange for you to rescue me."

Now that he thought about the instructions they'd gotten from the handler before taking this mission, the guy had never said the senator had requested Lazarus assistance. Interesting.

"So how did you know about me?"

This wasn't going to be an easy one to explain. "Maybe you should just be happy that you're free?"

"I'm not free. I'm in a warehouse—or garage or whatever the hell you want to call this place— with a man I saw *kill*. And I'm trying to hold my shit together."

He thought she was doing a pretty stellar job of that.

"Give me something."

Fine. He closed the distance between them and stood right in her path. Staring straight into her gorgeous eyes, he sent her a message. *I know what you can do.*

"What I can do? What the hell does that mean?"

Look at my mouth, Savannah.

Her gaze dropped and focused on his mouth.

You're psychic. You're reading my mind. Because I'm not speaking right now.

"Oh, shit." She backed up. Hit the wall behind her.

He stalked toward her. *What other secrets are you keeping?*

CHAPTER FOUR

An alarm started beeping, a low warning sound that put Jett on high alert. He whirled, his gaze going to the monitors that sat on the desk. Monitors that clearly showed him the "company" who had just slipped into the garage.

Maddox. Maddox was there, and he had a man slung over his shoulder. *Andreas.*

Andreas didn't appear to be moving.

"Go into the bedroom," Jett ordered Savannah flatly. "Get in there, now." Because she didn't need to see this scene.

Seeing a dead man coming back to life would be the kind of thing that freaked out a person.

He stepped forward.

Her fingers slid down his arm. A surge of warmth filled him, like a shot of straight electricity that zipped along his nerve endings. "That's the guy who helped us escape." She frowned at the monitors. "Maddox, right?"

"Yeah, but we've got an injured man." Injured, dead. Semantics. "I need to help Maddox with him, so…get some rest, okay? I'll check them out, and we'll finish our talk later."

He hurried away from her.

"Bullshit."

Jett spun around.

Her eyes gleamed as her chin lifted and she faced off against him. "That guy is hurt because of me. He was part of the rescue op. I want to help him."

The guy was past the point of *helping*. "You don't need to see this."

Her lips trembled. "What?"

But he could tell by a quick glance at the monitors that Maddox was already at the inner door. "Savannah, please, just wait in your room."

He hurried to meet Maddox, and, luckily, he heard the bedroom door shut behind him. A swift glance showed him that Savannah had retreated. Just in time. He let Maddox in, immediately understanding by the grim look on his friend's face that the situation was dire.

He grabbed Andreas. Put him on the couch. Didn't feel a pulse. *Too much blood.* "Shit."

"I tried communicating with you the whole fucking time," Maddox gritted out. "But it was like some kind of wall was in the way, blocking my message."

What?

Jett's gaze whipped to him.

"Someone was blocking me," Maddox added. His body was tense. "There's another player in this mess. Someone with psychic power. That would sure as fuck explain why this mission got top priority, and we were yanked off the other jobs. We've got a very dangerous perp here, someone that has to be eliminated."

Jett squared off with Maddox. "We're not eliminating her."

Maddox's eyes widened. "Her?"

"I tried to send you a warning a few minutes ago. Savannah…she's been picking up on my thoughts."

"That's not fucking possible."

It was more than possible. He tried to figure this shit out. "If she can read my thoughts, then maybe she was blocking our psychic link, too." He raked a hand over his face. "Because she could sure as hell hear me when I tried to communicate with you on that channel just a few minutes ago."

"We have to report this. Report *her*."

Before Jett could respond, Andreas let out a long, rough groan. Jett's attention snapped to him just as the guy's body started to tremble. Andreas shook, moaned, and his eyes flashed open.

"Welcome back to the land of the living," Maddox drawled. He strode closer to the couch. "Now tell us what in the hell happened back there."

Andreas's hand flew to his throat. Blood still covered his neck, but the wound had closed. The wound that had killed him.

Hello, Lazarus. The Lazarus world — the world where no one stayed dead, not unless you took a bullet to the brain.

Andreas had just literally come back from the dead, the same way all of the test subjects did.

"Fucking bastards…there was an escape tunnel." Andreas sat up slowly. His skin was too pale, and a tremble shook his body. "Got out…two survived the fire."

Shit. *Shit.* "Who survived the fire?" Jett demanded. "Did you see their faces?"

"No…on a motorcycle. Shot me." Anger rumbled in his voice. "Got away."

Maddox started to pace. "This simple mission is getting too damn complicated."

Yes, it sure as hell was.

Andreas slumped back against the couch. "Feel like I've been hit…ton of bricks."

No one said coming back from the dead was easy.

Maddox cast Andreas a worried stare, then said, "We need to check-in. Need to figure out what to do next."

They did. They —

Jett turned toward the bedroom door. Something was wrong. He could *feel* it inside. An emptiness had just settled in his gut.

He took a step forward.

Maddox grabbed his arm. "Hey, focus, man! We need to check in at base. Tell them about Andreas and this psychic block. If it's coming from the woman, they might want her brought in. For all we know, she could be one of us."

One of us. Lazarus. Was it possible?

"Do *you* know anyone else with psychic power like we have?" Maddox pushed.

No, he didn't. Jett had never met anyone outside of Lazarus with any sort of gifts like that. When they'd come back from the dead, the Lazarus soldiers had quickly realized they had enhanced senses. Better vision, better hearing…but the advantages hadn't stopped there. They were faster. Stronger. And each test subject had some very handy psychic gifts.

"I'm calling this in," Maddox told him flatly. "And if we need to take her back to base, we'll do it."

Jett nodded grimly. But the thick knot in his gut told him something was wrong, and he found himself heading for the bedroom. Toward the shut door.

"Jett? What are you—"

He ignored Maddox's voice and twisted the bedroom knob. It opened easily in his hand. But as it spun open—

Another alarm began to sound.

He rushed into the room. Savannah stood in front of the window — the *open* window. That was why the alarm had sounded. She'd tripped it when she shoved open the window. Her eyes were huge as she glanced at him, and then she lunged for the window.

They were on the second fucking floor!

He grabbed her, moving fast, faster than she ever would have expected, and he locked his arms around her waist. He pulled her back against him. *"What in the hell are you doing?"*

"Trying not to be eliminated!" Savannah snapped right back, and then she elbowed him, hard. "Get away from me!"

Shit, she'd *heard* them? Their voices had been low, deliberately so, and with her in the next room, he'd thought they were clear to talk but...

Maybe she didn't hear us. Maybe the woman is still in my head.

He tried to block his thoughts. Tried to put a shield in place, a stronger one than he'd had before. "We aren't going to hurt you."

"*You* don't want to hurt me." She twisted hard in his arms. "You're the one who said they weren't eliminating me! But I don't know what those other jerks are planning to do!"

Play this right. Think. He forced himself to let her go. To step back.

She whirled toward him.

"We're on the second floor, Savannah. If you'd jumped out the window, you would have been hurt."

Her brows lifted. "I wasn't jumping. I was going to climb. There's a ledge out there, and then a long pipe that slides down the building." Her hands fisted at her sides. "I want to go home, okay? I want this nightmare to end." Her breath came faster. "You were saying something about taking me in…In where? I don't want to go *in*. I don't want to go anyplace but home!" Tears filled her eyes. "It's been a really shitty few days. I need this mess to be over."

He didn't like her tears. Didn't like the pain and fear he heard in her voice. He found himself moving closer to her. He wanted to pull her into his arms. Hold her tight. But…*Focus. Get the job done.* "What does Lazarus mean to you?"

She blinked. "What?"

"Lazarus."

"Uh…isn't he the guy who rose from the dead? You know, they went back to his tomb, and he was walking around…"

He waited.

"Am I supposed to know more?" Her head turned as she glanced longingly toward the open window. The alarm was still beeping.

He moved around her, his body brushing against her shoulder, and Jett closed the window.

A few moments later, the alarm stopped. He remained in front of the window, his back to her.

"Jett." Her voice was soft. Her hand touched his shoulder. "I'm scared."

Something inside of him seemed to break and give way. He found himself spinning toward her, and this time, he did reach for her. *She shouldn't ever be afraid when I'm near.* He pulled her into his arms. Held her tight.

"I just want to go home," Savannah whispered.

"It's not that simple." What all had she picked up? Had she just been reading his thoughts or everyone's? "My team hasn't found the two men who got away. Those men are a threat to you."

She gave a little jerk.

He held her tighter. "It's okay, Savannah. I won't let anyone hurt you. I swear it. But we have to figure out where those men are. We have to find them." He needed to hunt the bastards.

Destroy them.

He eased back so that he could stare down at her face. "But you can't keep secrets from me."

He saw the faint flicker of her lashes.

Baby, I can feel your secrets.

Her lips parted. God, he loved her lips. Full, plump, and—

Maddox cleared his throat.

Jett glanced up, glaring. His buddy had poked his head into the room and was staring straight at them.

"Need a moment." Maddox nodded. "Really need that moment with you right now."

Savannah was upset. She needed him then. "I'll be out soon."

Maddox blinked. "Uh, Jett…"

"Soon," he snapped.

The guy backed out, shaking his head.

Jett realized his whole body was tense. He also realized that if Maddox hadn't interrupted, he would have kissed Savannah. What in the hell was that about? He never got attached to mission targets.

But then again, mission targets didn't tend to slip into his head. She had.

He had the strange feeling that she might never leave his mind. *This woman could haunt me.*

"We need to get something clear." His hands were around her waist. "I will not hurt you. And I will not let anyone else hurt you, either."

She stared up at him.

"But you can't go climbing out windows. You need to trust me."

"The last man I trusted kidnapped me, tied me to a chair, and was getting ready to cut off my pinky finger." She delivered this news flatly. "Trust is hard for me."

Uh, yeah, it would be. "My job is to keep you safe. Until that job is done, I'm going to be your shadow."

"Like my personal bodyguard?"

If that was what she wanted to call it. "Yeah, consider me your personal bodyguard."

Her smile was slow, and it was damn beautiful. He found himself unable to look away from it. "You've got dimples." He'd noticed them in the photo, but seeing them up-close like this was a whole different thing.

"Um, two of them."

Cutest damn dimples he'd ever seen. "And you're psychic."

Her smile faltered. "Look, I—I'm not sure what you mean."

"I mean you were reading my thoughts, Savannah. You were in my head."

Her gaze lowered. She seemed to be spending a whole lot of time staring at his throat. "People think I'm crazy. I was...I was told never to talk about that."

Now they were getting someplace. "Who told you?"

"My father. The doctor. All the people in the white lab coats at the psych facility I stayed in when I was sixteen years old."

What the fuck?

Her gaze lifted. "I was in a car accident. My mom died. My twin brother died. After that, I found out that sometimes…I could pick up thoughts. Every now and then, I mean, it wasn't constant or anything. But when you suddenly start telling people that you've got voices in your head…" Those dimples of hers flashed, then vanished. "Well, I think you can figure out the result. If you can't, then I'll tell you…you get sent to a really plush facility where the doctors want to talk about how you feel and why you are crazy."

He needed her to understand this. "I don't think you're crazy."

"Jett—"

"I can pick up thoughts, too, Savannah." He could do plenty more than that, but, for now, they'd stick with the basics.

Hope lit her eyes. Made her even more beautiful. "You're like me?"

Only if she was dead.

"I've never met anyone…anyone like me before." She licked her lips. "It's nice to not be alone."

"You will never be alone again." The words just came out, but dammit, they were oddly true. He didn't want to imagine her alone. Didn't want to think for one second that she was scared or hurt or feeling like a freak because someone didn't understand her. She'd been put in a psych ward? For how fucking long?

He would be finding out. He'd be finding out everything about her. For now, though, he needed to step back. Mostly because he liked the way she felt in his arms far too much.

And because Maddox was on the other side of the door, probably about to flip the hell out.

"You're safe," Jett assured her as he forced his hands to slide from her waist. "I'd give my dying breath to keep you safe." Then he'd wake his ass up again after he died and destroy anyone after her.

"I don't want anyone dying for me, but thanks for the offer."

He found himself smiling at her. Something was happening, he knew it. Could feel the connection between them. Once more, his gaze slid to her lips.

He wanted to taste her.

The woman had been through hell, and he was lusting after her. He was fucked up. *Walk away. Don't kiss her. Walk away.*

He headed for the door.

"But what if I want to kiss you?"

No, hell, no. He stopped. "Savannah, you slipped into my head again, didn't you?" She was strong. Very strong. Strong enough to get past the shields he'd put in place.

"Does it count if it honestly seemed like you were screaming the words?"

His lips wanted to twitch. Instead, Jett spun toward her. This wasn't the time to laugh. But something about her made him feel good. This wasn't the time to lust, but he did. He sure as all hell did.

Slowly, she closed the distance between them. Her hand rose and pressed to his chest, pressed right over his heart. He lowered his head toward her. She rose onto her tip-toes and brought her mouth to his. Their lips met in the briefest, lightest of kisses. "Thank you for saving me," she whispered. Another soft, light kiss. One that only made him yearn for more. "And thank you for not making me feel like a freak. I don't tell many people my secrets."

"You can tell them to me."

Her gaze searched his. "I tell you my secrets, and you'll tell me yours?"

If only. But, no, that wasn't the way it worked. He couldn't tell Savannah his secrets. That was a line that he wouldn't be able to cross.

She started to pull away. His hands curled around her shoulders. "More."

Her lips parted.

Perfect.

This time, he was the one to initiate the kiss. He put his mouth on hers. Dipped his tongue into her mouth. Tasted her. Savored her. Didn't demand. Didn't push. But, fuck, he *craved.*

Lust beat through his veins. A powerful desire, more powerful than he'd ever seemed to feel before. Maybe it was the adrenaline still humming in his veins or maybe—hell, maybe it was just her. But he wanted. He needed. And because he needed so much, he kept his hold easy on her.

He treated her like the fucking precious thing she was.

And he slowly eased back.

Her breath came faster as she gazed up at him.

He should say something important. Reassuring. But the words that came out were, "Don't climb out any other windows."

She smiled at him. Those sweet dimples winked.

And his chest felt lighter. He left her, before he gave in to the urge to pull her into his arms again. To kiss her again.

Concussion. She has a freaking concussion. Keep your hands off her.

Her laughter followed him. "My head feels better. But maybe we'll try again *after* the freaking concussion…"

He had to guard his thoughts one hell of a lot better.

Jett shut the bedroom door.

Immediately, he felt Maddox and Andreas staring at him.

Andreas was still on the couch. Still looking like, well, death.

Maddox stood across the room, with his hands crossed over his chest. "You fucking having fun?"

He didn't like the words. Didn't like the tone. Didn't like the implication that he was just screwing around with Savannah. Not her, she was...

More.

Without a word, he headed for the exit. He'd go downstairs and back into the main garage. For this talk, he wanted to put some space between him and Savannah's bedroom. Maybe if he was farther away, she wouldn't pick up on his thoughts. Or maybe his shield would just be better. "Andreas," he said, as he passed the guy. "Keep watch on that bedroom."

Maddox followed him out. As soon as they were clear, Maddox growled, "While you were making time with Savannah Jacobs, I checked in at base. She's *not* one of ours."

His hands were fisting. Unfisting. And a twisting rage filled him. "Not making time. Don't fucking talk about her that way."

Maddox blinked. "What?"

"I know she's not one of ours. I asked her. That's what I was doing in there. *Asking*. When I mentioned Lazarus, she had no reaction. No increased heart-rate, no breathing changes, no sweating. The name meant nothing to her."

Maddox gave a low whistle. "You told her about Lazarus? Are you crazy?"

"I didn't tell her what we can do. I just asked if Lazarus meant anything to her. It didn't." He rolled back his shoulders. "But she is psychic. Savannah woke up that way after a car accident. So we have to guard our minds around her. She said she can't hear everything. That she just picks up some thoughts." Though she'd sure picked up a hell of a lot of *his* thoughts. Jett exhaled. "She heard me when I tried to communicate with you on the link our team uses. So, we stay away from that shit for the foreseeable future."

Maddox rubbed the back of his neck. "Our orders are to take her back to her father."

"Right." Jett nodded. "We'll do that, as soon as the perps who escaped are caught and—"

"No." Maddox shook his head. "You misunderstand. I was just told that we have to take her back at dawn. Apparently, her father is raising some hell right now, creating a stink with the government because he was told a Black Ops team had her."

Uh, yeah, about that... "Savannah may have the wrong impression about what we do. I, um, told her that I was a SEAL."

Maddox squeezed his eyes shut.

"So, when she called her dad to check in, she may have told him—"

Maddox's eyes flew back open. "You let her call to check in? That wasn't part of the plan."

"Of course, it was. We had a burner phone here."

"For emergencies!"

In a sense, it had been an emergency. "She *wanted* to talk with her family. I used a secure phone. It was fine."

Maddox shook his head. "This woman has got you wrapped around her little pinky."

"The fucker who took Savannah was going to cut off her pinky." The angry words blasted from him. "He was going to hurt her. And two of those assholes are still out there. You think I'm just going to turn her over and walk away when she's in danger? You think that's the option I'll be taking?" *Think again.*

Maddox put up his hands. "Easy there, big guy. I get that you're, ah, feeling something here for the target."

She wasn't just a target. She had a name. Savannah.

"Never seen you like this before." Maddox appeared mildly worried. "This isn't you."

"How would you know?" Jett demanded. "How would anyone fucking know? We don't remember life before Lazarus. Don't remember a damn thing about what we were like or what we weren't like." For all Jett knew, he'd been a cold-blooded killer in that other life.

His handlers had told him that he'd been a former SEAL. Flashed him some copies of his service files. They'd showed him videos of himself volunteering for the Lazarus program. But…that was it.

He had their word to go by. Some grainy videos. Papers that could have been falsified. Nothing else. Everything he'd had before Lazarus was long gone. Everything he'd experienced was gone.

And now he was supposed to just turn Savannah over? To walk away? Another thing gone. "I said I'd keep her safe," he snarled. "If the threat to her is still there…"

"Relax. You *will* be keeping her safe. The orders are for you to stay with her. Andreas and I are to hunt the men who got away. You keep her close, you make sure nothing happens to her, and when we've got the bastards in custody — or they are dead — that will be our cue to fade into the shadows."

Breathing got easier. The thick tension Jett had felt slowly vanished. He wasn't leaving Savannah. Not yet, anyway.

Good.

"Jett?" Maddox paced closer. "Man, are you okay?"

No, he didn't feel okay at all.

"If you need to be pulled off this mission, if something is going on, then you tell me."

Because, despite everything, Maddox was his friend. In this twisted world he lived in, Maddox was probably his best friend. "I...react differently to her."

Maddox gave a grim laugh. "That's obvious."

No, he didn't get it. It wasn't just lust. He'd felt lust plenty of times. Fucking was natural. But when he was close to Savannah, something else was happening. Something he didn't understand. Something he sure as hell couldn't explain. "I'm not being pulled from the mission." There was no way he could walk away. "When she's safe, when those men are caught, *then* I'll leave." The way he always had to leave. He'd slip from Savannah's world, and she'd never see him again.

Unfortunately, he had the feeling the woman might just haunt his dreams for the rest of his life.

CHAPTER FIVE

As soon as Savannah walked through the massive front doors of her father's house, she was swept into his arms. He held her tight, his body shaking.

"I thought you were going to die." His words were gruff. "I was trying to get the money ready. I would have paid *anything*."

Behind her, Jett cleared his throat. "Wouldn't have mattered what you paid, sir. This particular group of kidnappers never released their victims alive. But then, you know that."

Her father let her go. No, he stopped hugging her. He kept a tight grip on her wrist, as if he was going to chain her to him.

"Who in the hell are you?" her father demanded.

"Senator Jacobs." Jett inclined his head. "You know who I am. You should have received a dossier on me this morning."

"I *never* requested any sort of Black Ops help with her—"

"And you fucking should have." Jett's voice cut like a knife.

Savannah gave a little shiver. He sounded absolutely deadly.

"You have pull," Jett continued grimly, "why the hell didn't you use it? Why didn't you use every connection you had to get her home safely?"

The senator's face flushed. Her dad—Senator Phillip Jacobs.

"I was told," her father said flatly, "that if I contacted any of the authorities, my daughter would die. I didn't want her dying. So I did what those bastards ordered me." He straightened his thin shoulders. "Thank you for bringing my daughter home. I appreciate—"

"You're not kicking me out." Jett was dressed from head to toe in all black, and his dark hair gleamed. His eyes—cold, angry—raked over her dad. "I'm staying with Savannah until the bastards who took her are apprehended. Two of those men got away from the crime scene."

"But—the local cops, I haven't—"

"Right. You still haven't called anyone. You don't have to. My team is taking care of things. We've got people back at the crime scene at this very moment, and those men are the best damn trackers you will ever encounter." His body seemed rock hard. "Until I am certain that Savannah is safe, I'll be sticking to her like glue."

She felt the tension in her father's body. "Son, I'm sure you are—"

"I'm not your son," Jett cut in flatly. "I'm Jett Bianchi. I'm in charge of your daughter's safety. But you know all of this. Like I said, it was in the dossier you were given this morning. It should have been delivered by courier."

Her father patted her hand. He wasn't looking at her. She hadn't said a word to him yet. Did Jett notice that? Did he have any idea just how screwed up her relationship was with the man standing so angrily near her?

Probably not.

When she'd told Jett that she'd wanted to go home, she hadn't meant to the mansion. To the cold, mausoleum-like place that her father lived in for a few months out of the year. No, she'd meant her place. Her little cottage on the beach.

"I have security members who can watch Savannah." Her father jerked his head toward the two men and one woman who stood nearby. They were all in dark suits, white shirts.

"Yeah," Jett drawled. "They did a bang-up job before. Good thing I'm on the case now." His gaze swept the foyer. A gleaming chandelier hung over the black and white floor. "I'll be in charge of her security until the case is closed."

"Now listen here…" her father began.

"No, you listen." A muscle jerked in Jett's jaw. "I brought her to you, and I can take her away. Savannah's safety is my number one priority. I can take her out of here faster than you can blink."

"You aren't taking my daughter *anywhere*."

"Dad." Now she spoke because she was just tired of this BS. It was making her head ache again.

Her father's gaze snapped to her.

"Jett is staying. I feel safe with him. I want him here."

"But…but you don't know anything about him." He squeezed her hand. "I barely got any details on this man in the so-called dossier I was sent."

"He was a SEAL." She glanced toward Jett. "He can kick ass. And he got me out of a nightmare. All of that means…" Her stare slid back to her dad. "He stays with me."

"Savannah—"

"And I'm not staying here." She could never stay there. Not in that cold house with all of the memories of the dead that surrounded her. She could hear her mother's voice in that house. Hear her brother's laughter. "You know I can never stay here."

Pain flashed on his face.

Her father couldn't stay there, either. She knew there was a reason he spent so much time in D.C., and, no, it wasn't just for the job.

"I had to see you." Because whatever else happened between them, there was love. She knew he loved her, just as she loved him. Now she hugged him again. "I'm okay," Savannah whispered into his ear. "But I want Jett."

"I always give you what you want." His voice was gruff. Low. "You know that."

No, he hadn't always given her what she'd wanted. When she'd been sixteen, and she'd begged him to believe her stories about the voices she heard, he'd locked her up. He'd stared at her with anguished eyes, and then he'd left her in the facility. Left her with the shrink who'd seemed to turn her in to his own, personal experiment. Dr. Anthony Rowe. Sometimes, she swore she could still feel his icy blue eyes on her.

When she'd gotten out, she'd sworn to never be a prisoner again.

She'd kept that promise, until Patrick had locked her up. Tied her up.

"Savannah!" Her name burst out as a cry of joy, and she pulled back from her father. Pulled back so she could see her cousin Sam come running down the stairs. Sam was just a year older than her own thirty years. Tall, with broad shoulders and a quick grin, Sam had always helped to keep her sane.

He was being groomed to take her father's place as senator. Sam was the heir apparent.

Because she'd never been interested in that spot.

Sam scooped her into his arms. Held her in a bone-crushing grip as he spun her around.

A growl sounded behind her. "Put her the fuck down." Jett's lethal voice. Only Jett didn't wait for Sam to let her go. He pulled her from her cousin's arms. Carefully but firmly. "She's got a damn concussion," he added, his voice a hard rumble. "You don't yank her around like that."

"Concussion?" Her father's voice rose. "Savannah—"

"I'm okay." She glared at Jett. "Really."

But Sam had caught her hand. He stared at her bandaged wrist, obviously seeing the dark bruises that extended out from the bandages, and an angry curse tore from his lips. "The sonofabitch is dead."

Her father flinched.

"Not yet, he isn't," Jett said, voice so cold that Savannah actually felt a chill slide down her spine. With a careful touch on her, he eased her away from Sam. Kept her in his arms. "My team has been scouring the scene, and we have reason to believe that the ring leader of the operation— the guy Savannah identified as Patrick Zane—is still out there. He had an escape plan in place, and the guy hauled ass. He was accompanied by one of his men."

Her father was sweating. Sam was glaring. And the knot in Savannah's stomach was just getting worse. Jett had told her — before they entered her father's house — that Maddox believed Patrick had fled the scene. She had thought Patrick might have burned in the flames, but Maddox had apparently searched the scene and determined that Patrick had escaped. She didn't know what Maddox had found at the crime scene that led him to that conclusion, but Jett seemed certain of his friend. Maybe Patrick had left a trail of blood courtesy of his knife wound? Didn't really matter. The only thing that mattered was that Patrick was alive and on the loose.

Savannah was scared.

"Will he come after her again?" Her father's voice was low.

But Sam shook his head and answered before Jett could. "The guy is probably on his way to Mexico. Why the hell would he bother — "

"I think he will come after her again." Jett's voice cut right through Sam's blustery words. "And that's why I'll be staying at her side until he's either locked in a cell — or he's a dead man."

Her father's gaze met Savannah's. She could see his fear. He usually hid it from her, but this time, it was different. This time, she could see the same fear in his eyes that she'd seen so long ago. When she'd woken in the hospital room, when she'd opened her eyes and found her father staring down at her, the same terror had been in his eyes.

"Baby, what do you remember?"

Screams. Pain. Death.

"Let's take this into the study," her father murmured. He turned and led the way, and when they entered his study, he went straight to his bar. Right to the whiskey. His fingers were shaking as he poured the amber liquid, sending it raining over the edge of the glass.

She'd followed, Sam had followed, and Jett — but Jett had stopped her father's security team from entering. He'd shut the door very deliberately as he closed them out. And now…now Jett came to her side.

Was it strange that she felt better when he was near her? No, he'd saved her. Perhaps she was getting some huge hero complex where the guy was concerned. Maybe she was starting to think he was invincible.

No one was, though. No one.

"I'm sending you out of the country," her father announced after he drained the whiskey way too fast. "If this freak is coming after you, if he's really killed all of those other women like it said in that damn dossier — "

"He *has* killed those other women," Jett interjected flatly. "Five other women. And as I said, I do believe he will come after her. He made it quite clear that he feels Savannah belongs to him. I'm not a fucking shrink or a profiler, so I can't tell you some clinical BS about his behavior."

Her father turned to face him. The whiskey had made two bright spots of color appear on his cheeks.

"But I can tell you what I think." Jett's body was tense beside her. "I think he's obsessed. Obsessed with killing. Obsessed with money. Obsessed with your daughter. A man like that won't stop on his own. He has to *be* stopped."

Her father glanced down at his empty glass. "That's why I'll send her away," he murmured. "Out of the country. You can go back to Paris, Savannah. You always loved it there."

She'd studied in Paris a year during college. Yes, she did love it there, but—

Jett shook his head. "Leaving the country will put her at greater risk. She'll be in an uncontained environment. We don't know how big this guy's network is, and I can't allow her to be placed in additional danger."

At those words, at Jett's tone, Sam surged forward. "*You* can't allow, buddy? Seriously, where the hell do you get off? Who do you think you—"

"Sam, stop," Savannah told him quietly. "Jett has helped me. He got me out before Patrick could hurt me." She swore she could still feel his blade against her skin. "Jett knows what he's doing in these situations, all right?"

Sam gazed at her, his expression hard. "You trust this man? A guy you just *met?*"

He was a guy who'd gotten her out of hell. "I trust him to keep me alive."

"You also trusted Patrick. That didn't exactly work out for you, did it?" As soon as the words left his mouth, horror flashed on Sam's face. "Oh, shit, Vannie," her old nickname burst from him. "I didn't mean that." He hurried toward her. "I've been scared as all hell, and I didn't mean—"

Jett placed his body in front of her. A protective pose. "You trusted the bastard, too. So, don't throw that shit off on *her.* I've read the intel reports on you, Sam. You're the guy who is supposed to clear everyone this family comes into contact with. The guy who is supposed to make sure scandals don't happen, that lying, dangerous SOBs like Patrick never get touching close to Savannah. But *you* were the one who introduced them."

Those intel reports must have been very, very thorough. She wondered when Jett had read them. And he was right. Sam had introduced her and Patrick at a gallery opening.

"He'd donated to her father's campaign." The faint lines near Sam's mouth deepened. "He looked fine on paper."

"Did he?" Jett crossed his arms over his chest. "You were asking before…I believe the question was *who do I think I am*?"

Sam hadn't finished that actual question but…

"I think I'm the man who found Savannah. I think I'm the man who got her out. And I think I'm the man who is going to keep her safe from the bastards out there." He glanced at Savannah. Held her gaze. "I swear, I will keep you safe." His voice had lowered, softened, just for her.

She had to swallow to clear the lump in her throat.

He turned his head and seemed to focus on her father and Sam once more. "Any other fucking questions?"

***

She was too quiet.

Jett had finished the search of Savannah's home. The only cameras and security devices in the cottage were his—the ones he'd installed because no way would anyone get the drop on them. She stood in front of the floor to ceiling windows in her den, windows that looked out at the pounding surf of the Gulf.

She hadn't spoken since they'd left her father's house. She'd been right beside him in the SUV, but seemingly a million miles away. She still seemed so very far away, even though she was right there.

He didn't like that. He didn't like feeling that if he reached out, his fingers would just slide right through her. "Savannah."

She didn't move when he called her name. Just kept staring at the waves.

So he moved closer. Lifted his hand. Touched her shoulder. His fingers didn't pass through her skin. He touched *her*. Felt her warmth and felt the long shudder that slid over Savannah's body.

"I don't want to die," she whispered.

"You won't." Not on his watch.

She looked over her shoulder at him, and there were tears in her eyes. "You said I was victim number six. All of those other women — they really all were killed?"

He wouldn't lie, not about this. "Yes."

She sucked in a quick breath.

He wasn't going to tell her that those women had been cut into pieces. She didn't need to know that shit. Once you got some images in your mind, you could never get them out.

"And…you truly believe Patrick will come after me again?"

"I do." Because if there was one thing he knew, it was a predator. He'd heard the obsession in the man's voice when Patrick had raged that Savannah was his. "I'll be here."

She turned to fully face him. "For how long, though? You have a life waiting, I know you do. What if it's days, weeks, what if it's—"

"I'll stay as long as you need me." She was the mission. Top priority. His team hadn't ever handled a case quite like this one. Usually they took out targets. Retrieved people of importance. Then disappeared into the wind. Minimal contact. A protection detail wasn't normal Lazarus work.

But this wasn't a normal case.

His hand lifted, and he tucked a loose lock of hair behind her ear. "I'll stay with you until this is done."

"Don't you have a life waiting? People who need you? Family? A lover?"

He didn't have a life waiting. He had a fucking cell. Because when they weren't on missions, the Lazarus subjects didn't just get to come and go as they pleased. They stayed at a government run facility. They were studied. They were trained. They were monitored.

He was being monitored right then, Jett knew it. Their handlers always knew where they were because a tracking device was implanted beneath the skin of Lazarus subjects.

He wasn't free. The handlers made frequent promises, though, said that maybe one day—*one day*—he and the others would truly get their lives back. Jett just wasn't sure if he believed them.

"No one is waiting. My family is gone." That much, he knew. The lab coats had showed him records of his parents' death. His mother...the dark-haired beauty from Hong Kong. She'd been a celebrity there, a star in the Cantonese opera. And then she'd met his father...an Italian with a dark past. With secrets. A man who'd taken her to a whole new world.

A world that had been filled with pain.

His mother had died from cancer a few years back. According to the paperwork he'd read, Jett had been with her at the time.

His father was another story. The crime boss had been murdered twenty years ago. And, once more, according to the damn paperwork, Jett had been with him at the time. He'd been found, holding his father's hand, after the guy was gunned down in the streets of Chicago.

"What about a lover?" Savannah's voice was hesitant. "Someone who is waiting —"

Since he'd woken up in Lazarus, there had been no lovers. The other test subjects — sure, they'd hooked up with civilians on missions. Their handlers encouraged the hook-ups. Wanted the test subjects to let off some of the dangerous, dark tension that could gather within them. But he hadn't gone for the fast encounters. Hadn't wanted the women who'd been placed in his path.

Not like I want her.

Because he did want Savannah. He should just be focused on protecting her, but he kept thinking about fucking her. "No lover," he rasped.

Her gaze fell. Her shoulders trembled. "I…have a secret."

So did he. Too many of them.

Her hands curled around her stomach. "I slept with him."

Jett's muscles clenched.

"Before — before Patrick took me, before I knew what he was. I-I thought he was a good guy. He seemed to care about me. We'd been dating for two months. Two months." She bit her lower lip. Shuddered. "While I was dating him, he was killing those other women, wasn't he?"

Yes, he had been.

"I fucked a killer. And he's all I can feel right now." Her lashes lifted. She stared at him with desperate eyes. "I can feel his hands on my skin, and then I can feel his knife. *I fucked a killer,* and now he's going to keep coming after me. He's going to kill me."

"No." Patrick would be the one to die. Jett would make absolutely certain of that fact.

"I-I have to shower. I have to wash away…"

But she didn't finish. She'd already turned. Rushed toward her small bathroom. The door shut behind her with a soft click.

Savannah wanted to wash away the other man's touch. The lover who'd betrayed her.

He's all I can feel right now.

That situation was going to change. She needed time to heal. Jett was going to keep his hands the hell off her until she had recovered. And then, only then...

I'll put my hands on you. I'll make sure you forget how Patrick Zane made you feel. I'll give you so much pleasure that you forget the pain.

And then he'd kill the bastard who'd made Savannah afraid.

CHAPTER SIX

Three days had passed. Three days spent constantly looking over her shoulder and wondering when Patrick would show up. Three days spent knowing that she was being hunted. Only...

There had been no sign of Patrick. There had been no attacks. No contact at all from the guy.

Today...*today* was the first day that she'd gone back to her small shop on the edge of Biloxi. A place that sold local art and crafts, a spot that had quickly become popular with tourists looking to take a bit of the beach home with them. Her assistant Megan had been running things, an assistant who knew nothing about Savannah's abduction.

The cops still didn't know — at least, not the local ones. Jett had assured her that authorities higher up the food chain were investigating. But no one had come to her. No one had asked her a single question.

In fact, she hadn't even seen Maddox or Andreas again. It was just —

"He never seems to take his eyes off you."

Her assistant's voice made Savannah jump. Savannah glanced over and found Megan with her hands propped under her chin as she leaned across the counter. Megan's eyes were on Jett.

And Jett—

Savannah shot a quick glance his way.

His dark stare *was* on her.

For a moment, she almost got lost in his stare. Almost…then…

Focus. It's business. He's doing his bodyguard routine. Nothing more. Settle your ass down, woman.

Sighing, Megan glanced back at her. Megan's close-cropped, bright blonde hair framed her pixie-like face. A face dominated by unusual, deep gold eyes. "If a man looked at me like that…"

Megan's voice was too loud. Savannah had to fight the urge to shush the other woman as she hurriedly went back to wrapping up a lighthouse painting that needed to be shipped to a customer.

Megan gave a rough purr. "I'd probably just strip right then and there."

Savannah ripped the paper.

Crap.

"Oh, hey, sorry…you need some help?" Megan asked as she came closer.

What she needed was for Megan to *not* make sexual references that Jett could overhear. Wasn't it bad enough that Savannah had told him that she'd fucked Patrick? After her big confession, she'd been crying and she'd been so desperate to jump in the shower and wash away the other man's touch.

When she'd come out of the shower, Jett hadn't said a word. He'd just watched her.

He seemed to watch her all the time.

"I've got it," Savannah muttered as she started wrapping the painting again.

"Sorry if I embarrassed you," Megan said, her voice — finally, blessedly — low. "It's just, I think your new guy is hot. He's got this bad ass vibe going on—"

"He's standing against a wall. Literally, just standing. Not kicking any ass." Her voice was also low. But when she risked another glance at Jett, Savannah found a faint smile curving his lips.

No way he could hear them. They were almost whispering now.

"I know but he's got this intense, coiled snake thing going on."

Coiled snake? She almost asked Megan if the woman was drunk.

"Did I ever mention that I have a huge crush on Bruce Lee?" Megan asked. "Because he could kick ass. So much ass. And I bet your guy could do the same. It's that look in his eyes. The whole, I-get-shit-done confidence. No one fucks with him, not unless they wanted to get fucked over."

Savannah stared at her assistant. Just stared. "What?"

Savannah cleared her throat. "I think I can handle closing up today. You've been working extra hours this week, so you know, you deserve some time off." *Leave, now.* The woman needed to stop ogling Jett.

"When did you meet him?" Megan murmured. "Where?" Her attention was on Jett once more. "And does he have a brother?"

I met him three days ago when he burst into a dark house, kicked ass, and saved me from kidnappers. If she said that, well, Megan would just like the guy all the more. She'd probably pounce on him. "We've known each other a while."

Another sigh from Megan. A wistful one. "I want a man to look at me that way."

Savannah finished wrapping the painting.

"Like he can't wait to eat me up."

She didn't tear the paper.

She *did* pull down the sleeves of her shirt though, making sure that Megan didn't see the bruises on her wrists.

Megan touched her shoulder. "You okay?"

Savannah could feel her cheeks flushing. Okay wasn't the way she felt. "Jett and I are just friends." Now her voice was too high. "You are reading this all wrong. He's just hanging out with me while I finish up a few things."

Megan lifted one brow. "No, you aren't friends." She leaned closer to Savannah. "You just aren't lovers...yet. But trust me, you will be." She gave Savannah's shoulder a quick squeeze. "Glad you're back. Sorry the work trip took longer than expected."

Work trip, right. That was the cover story she'd given Megan.

"I will head out early, if that's okay with you." Megan eased back, but frowned. "You sure you don't want some help?"

"I'm here," Jett announced. "Anything she needs, I'll give her."

There was just something in his deep voice...Savannah had the terrible, sinking feeling that somehow, he'd overheard every single word they'd said.

A few moments later, the bell over the entrance door jingled as Megan made her way out. After one more wistful look at Jett, she was gone.

"Your assistant is interesting."

She put the finished package to the side, leaving it in her out bin. It was scheduled for a shipment the following week.

"She's got nice tats."

Yes, Megan had some interesting tats on her arms. Beautiful, detailed flowers. Twisting thorns. "We went to the same tattoo artist,"

Savannah confessed. She put away the packing supplies. Glanced up—

Jett had moved to stand right beside the counter. "You've got a tattoo?"

Two. "Yes."

His gaze seemed—hot. Very hot. "Where?"

Like she was going to lift her shirt and show him. "In places you probably won't see." There. Let him wonder. The location wasn't really that risqué, but he didn't need to know that. She was actually surprised he hadn't noticed her tats when she'd been wearing the thin hospital gown.

She headed to the register. Started tallying the sales.

"Won't see them, huh? Don't bet on it."

Her fingers froze. Then she looked up at Jett. And his gaze—okay, yes, maybe it was intense. Maybe it was lustful. Maybe it was just downright sexy. But in the last three days, he hadn't made a single move toward her—well, not a sexual move, anyway. He'd been very much hands-off.

"How's your head?" he murmured.

"Fine?" Yes, she made it sound like a question because she wasn't sure why he was bringing up her head and—

He reached across the counter. Caught her hand. Pushed up the sleeve of her blouse. "The bruises have faded a lot."

Yes, they had. She'd ditched her bandages, too.

His fingers — long, strong — slid over her inner wrist. She sucked in a sharp breath, wondering just when her wrist had turned so incredibly sensitive.

And wondering when she'd become so attuned to Jett.

Hurriedly, she pulled her hand back. "Any word yet? I mean, any sign of Patrick?"

"Not yet. He's gone to ground. But we'll find him." He sounded absolutely confident.

A shiver slid over her as her gaze darted to the windows in front of her shop. She knew that Jett's friends, his "team" had searched Patrick's house. His business. Unfortunately, they'd turned up nothing useful. He'd said the guys were the best trackers out there. If they couldn't find Patrick, did that mean that no one could?

Could she really spend the rest of her life always looking over her shoulder? Always searching the crowd for Patrick? Looking for his dark blond hair?

"What did he do with all of the money?" she whispered. Money that Patrick had taken from the families of his victims. Jett had told her about that, too. The families had paid the ransoms for their loved ones, only to have to bury the bodies.

"The payments were wire transfers to off-shore accounts."

"Then maybe…maybe he's off-shore, too. Maybe he fled the country." Her gaze returned to Jett. Found him staring right at her.

"I don't think so."

"How long can we continue like this?" She hated the faint tremble that slipped into her voice. She hated being afraid even more. She'd been happy, before the abduction. Living her life, following her dreams. Thinking she had all of the time in the world for everything.

Then her time had been up.

"As long as we need to." He flattened his hands on the counter. Leaned toward her. "I'm not going to let anything happen to you."

Now she smiled at him. "It's not like you're indestructible, you know."

His eyelashes flickered.

"You can be hurt, too. And have you considered that I don't want anyone taking a bullet or getting hurt because of me? You have a life, too, and I don't want it stopped because you're trying to save me."

His gaze slid to her mouth. "I wouldn't mind getting shot for you."

That was—that was crazy. So, she told him. "That's crazy. You don't—"

He leaned forward and brushed his mouth over hers.

It was a light, fleeting kiss.

"What are you doing?" Savannah whispered.

He laughed. Low, deep. Sexy. "If you don't know, then I must be doing it wrong." He started to pull back.

Her hands flew up and locked around his upper arms. *Hello, nice muscles.* "Why did you kiss me?"

"Because your assistant was right…" He smiled at her. "I can't wait to eat you up."

The sound of her heartbeat was very, very loud in her ears. Like, thundering loud. She could feel the flush on her cheeks. She could feel her nipples tightening. This was wrong. So— "I'm pretty sure you told me no before."

"Sweetheart, that's something no sane man would ever do."

The way he was looking at her…

"But you were hurt," Jett continued, his voice oddly tender. "And I had to make sure you'd recovered before anything else happened."

Anything else? So, he was saying—what? That he wanted to sleep with her? Quick, dirty sex? She didn't want that, did she? Not right now. Not in the insanity of her life. Totally not something she wanted.

Wasn't it? Or was it *exactly* what she wanted?

"Don't be scared. It's just a kiss."

It had been too light. Too brief.

She leaned across the counter this time. Her mouth took his. An open-mouthed, hot kiss. Her tongue slid into his mouth. Licked. Teased. Stroked. He growled.

When she pulled back, it was Savannah's turn to smile. "That was a better kiss."

His gaze was hot with lust. So hot she felt singed.

She also wanted more.

No, wrong. Don't do this. Savannah jerked back. "I should—"

Glass shattered. Her front window splintered—

One moment, Jett was in front of her. The next, he was over that counter, on top of her. He'd tackled her to the floor and put his body over hers.

Her heart raced too fast, her breath heaved in and out, and he was crushing her. *"Jett?"*

His head lifted. He didn't get off her. His face was tight with fury. With fear? "Are you hit?"

Hit? She'd been hit by him when he'd tackled her—

"Sniper shot. Heard it coming too late. Was too focused on you." His hands flew over her body. "Dammit, baby, I'm sorry."

Sorry? For what? She was fine. "I'm not hit." How had he heard anything coming? The only sound she'd heard had been the breaking glass.

There's a sniper in the area.

Jett's voice blasted through her mind. She was staring right at his face, and she never saw his mouth move. *Maddox, get over here. Someone just took a shot at Savannah.*

She swallowed.

"Yeah…" His fingers brushed lightly over her cheek. "Don't even pretend you didn't just hear what I said to Maddox."

"You didn't say anything." Her voice was hoarse.

"But you still heard me. Something else we'll have to talk about soon." He gave a hard shake of his head. "Not right now, though. Not while you're in danger."

Because someone had just *shot* at her.

"Stay behind the counter. Don't make a move until I get back."

Back?

He pressed a quick kiss to her lips. Fast, hard, possessive. "I'm going after the bastard."

"Jett—"

Too late. He was gone. He'd rushed from behind the counter, and she wanted to yell after him to come back. To be safe.

Instead, she hunched down behind the counter. Her gaze darted to the left, to the right, looking for some sort of weapon. Not finding a damn thing.

Jett, watch your ass! It should have been impossible. But…she still sent that psychic message to him with a wave of fear and worry. Maybe he wouldn't hear her, maybe he couldn't get the messages she sent in some wild projection out to the world, maybe it was—

Don't worry about me. His voice rolled through her mind. Deep. Dark. *I'll come back to you.*

Savannah sucked in a deep breath. And she stayed hunkered down behind the counter.

***

He'd heard the bullet coming. The whistle of the wind that a normal man would never have been able to pick up. Even as the glass in the front window had started to shatter, Jett had been moving. He'd leapt over the counter, grabbed Savannah, and shoved her down.

Too close. Too fucking close.

If he hadn't been there, if he'd been slower, she would have died.

He'd been distracted. He hadn't been focused enough. The too-close call was on him. It couldn't happen again.

Jett raced across the street. From the angle of entry, from the trajectory path he'd *heard,* Jett knew where the shooter should be. He bounded up the stairs of the nearby building, a killing rage filling him as he headed for the second story.

He kicked open the door. Rushed inside—

Empty.

The space was completely empty, except for one lone chair that sat in front of the partially open window. He advanced, his hands clenched. From that window, he could see right into her shop. The attacker had sat there, waiting. He'd—

"You're a dead man, asshole," a voice snarled and Jett's gaze jerked up—and to the right. To the small, black box that was attached to the ceiling. A speaker? And was that a damn camera, too? *"This time, you burn."*

Jett realized he'd run straight into a trap. He didn't even try to make it to the door. Instead, he turned and hurtled right through the window. The glass broke around him even as an explosion burst from the room behind him. The white-hot flames followed him down as he fell to the pavement.

***

The explosion seemed to shake the whole block. Savannah gave a gasp when she heard it, and yes, dammit, she risked a peek from behind her counter. Her windows were cracking and…

The building across the street is on fire.

Where was Jett? Where the hell was Jett? She started to surge after him—

Baby, I know I told you to keep that sweet ass behind the counter.

She immediately sank low.

Maddox is coming for you. Heading to the back door. He'll take you out that way. Get you to safety.

The sound of her breathing was far too loud and labored. *Are you okay?* Talking to him this way didn't seem strange. Not awkward. It was oddly natural. Like a link had somehow just snapped in place between them.

A beat of silence followed her question. Then…*Never better.*

For some reason, she didn't believe him. Maybe it was because oh, a giant ball of flames had just ignited across the street.

In the distance, she could hear the wail of sirens.

I'll come to you later.

The voice in her mind—his voice—had become fainter and real fear shook her. *You're not hurt.*

He didn't respond.

You're not hurt! In her mind, she was screaming that to him, but the link between them—it was just empty. Too silent. And she was absolutely terrified.

He'd told her to stay down. But a fire was raging. And he wasn't answering. He—

The door to her back room burst open. Footsteps pounded toward her. Then Maddox was there, reaching out his hand to her. "Come on!"

She surged up, grabbed his hand, and they flew through the back of her store, past the boxes, the storage space, and out the rear door. An SUV was waiting there, Savannah saw a quick flash of a dark-haired woman at the wheel. Then she was basically being thrown into the back of the vehicle by Maddox. "Go!" he yelled as he surged back and slammed the door. Instead of getting in with them, he raced away.

The woman immediately had the SUV surging forward. Savannah nearly fell off the back seat. "Where's Jett?" She grabbed for the seat in front of her.

The woman hurtled the SUV down the alley, then came out on the side next to Savannah's store. This was Savannah's first clear sight of the flames. They were huge.

But the driver barely slowed as she shot to the left.

"Where's Jett?" Savannah asked again. She turned around, trying to look behind her —

Maddox had just run into the street. He crouched beside something in the road. Something? Someone? "Jett?" Savannah whispered.

The guy in the road wasn't moving. And his head — his neck seemed to be turned at a funny angle. "Stop the car!" Savannah screamed. "Jett needs help!"

The driver didn't stop the car. She just seemed to speed faster. Screw this. Savannah lunged for the door. Tried to shove it open.

It wouldn't open. And there was no unlock mechanism anywhere in the back seat. Her hands flew over the door, but it was like being stuck in the back of a patrol car. *No way out.* "Stop the car!" Savannah blasted again. "Jett's hurt! I need to get to him!"

"You're the priority," the woman fired back. "Only you."

What? "No, Jett is a priority to me!" She stared behind her. Had Maddox picked him up? It looked as if Maddox had slung Jett's prone body over one shoulder but she couldn't tell for sure because the SUV was already too far away. "He shouldn't be moved, not with a neck injury like that. He shouldn't—"

"Jett is fine," the driver assured her flatly. "He'll meet you at your place, okay?"

She couldn't see him any longer. He...he hadn't looked fine. "Take me back to him."

"Sorry, but it's a big old negative on that one. Jett gave orders for me to keep you safe, and that's what I'll do." Another turn. A sharp one. "Buckle up. I don't want you flying through the windshield."

She was numb. "His neck..."

"He's *fine*." The woman sounded absolutely certain. "Trust me on this, it takes more than a few bumps and bruises to stop Jett."

Savannah had to swallow four times before she could speak. "It looked like more than bumps and bruises." It had looked like death. She hooked the seat belt.

The woman stopped the vehicle. Glanced back at Savannah. Her pretty features softened as she said, "He's going to come back to you."

"I-I don't know you." Was she just supposed to believe this woman who—

"I'm Luna." She gave Savannah a broad smile. "And I'm not lying to you. I know things are crazy, but Jett will be coming back to you. So, do me a favor, okay? Just hold it all together for a while longer." She turned back to the road. "Don't freak out on me."

Savannah was about five seconds away from a serious freak out. "He looked dead."

Luna was already driving again. "Appearances can be deceiving. Maddox had him. Your guy is fine."

He wasn't…her guy.

Was he?

He was just security. The man who was supposed to watch her. But it felt as if someone had driven a fist into her chest. Breathing was hard, her heart wouldn't stop racing, and she was so afraid this Luna woman was lying to her.

Tears pricked her lashes. She kept seeing him on the road, not moving. *Jett?* She tried to reach him, crying out in her mind.

But there was no response. There was nothing at all.

CHAPTER SEVEN

Midnight.

The stars glittered over the water, seeming to stretch forever. Savannah was back in her beach house. Luna sat on her couch, flipping through a magazine, and Savannah knew other guards were out there—somewhere in the darkness.

"You've been pacing for the last hour," Luna murmured. "You sure you don't want to go to bed?"

"*You* said Jett would come to the house." But too many hours had passed. He hadn't come. She whirled to glare at the other woman. "What aren't you telling me?"

"One hell of a lot." Luna gave her a quick smile. "You don't have clearance for all that stuff."

Savannah growled.

"Easy!" Luna immediately threw up her hands. The magazine dropped to her lap. "Look, Jett will be here, okay? Until then, you've got me." Luna was dark-haired, small, and deceptively delicate. She'd stayed by Savannah's side ever since their mad exit from the shop. She had a quick smile and a soft laugh. She also had an intense gaze that would sweep the perimeter every now and then. As soon as they'd arrived, she'd immediately checked all of the security at Savannah's home.

And she'd been adamant that Savannah couldn't leave the house.

"Did someone catch the shooter?" Savannah asked her now, twisting her hands in front of her body.

"No." A quick shake of Luna's head. "He'd left the scene. From what I've been able to gather, it was a trap."

She twisted her hands a bit harder. An old habit. When she'd been a teen, she'd twisted her hands every time she'd gotten nervous. Her father used to chide her about the habit. "A trap?"

"When Jett rushed into the room where the shooter had been, he found the place ready to blow." A shrug from Luna. "At least, that's what Maddox told me."

Maddox had called and spoken with Luna a few times. When Luna talked with him, her voice had softened. So had her expression.

Something Savannah filed away for later.

"He got out," Luna added carefully.

Savannah nodded and made herself stop twisting her hands. She turned away from Luna.

"You care about him." Luna's contemplative voice followed her.

"Yes." She did. How crazy was that? They'd only known each other a few days. "I told Jett I didn't want him getting hurt for me. I don't want *anyone* getting hurt."

"Well, some people can take *hurt* better than others."

What was that supposed to mean?

Before she could question Luna further, there was a sharp knock at the front door. Savannah spun back to see Luna jump from the couch. The other woman hurried toward the door, utterly confident. A quick glance at the security monitor Jett had installed showed —

Jett. Jett is at the door. So is Maddox.

She rushed for the door just as Luna opened it. Jett stood in the doorway, the faint lines near his mouth a little deeper. His eyes appeared grim, his body —

Savannah tackle-hugged him. She threw her body against his and held on as tightly as she could. His arms came around her. He pulled her against him, holding her in a grip that was fierce. She could feel his muscles against her. Those hard-as-stone muscles. His heart raced, so did hers, and she was so incredibly happy that he was there. All she wanted to do was stand there and hug him for the next hour or so.

"Savannah, we need to get back inside."

His voice was deep, rumbling, and she looked up, staring into his eyes.

For a moment, she couldn't move at all.

He moved her. Picked her up easily. Carried her inside.

"Uh, yeah." Luna cleared her throat. "I'm guessing you're in charge of night duty, Jett, so Maddox and I will leave you to it. You and Savannah catch up. We can debrief later. After you've both rested." The front door shut with a soft click.

Slowly, he lowered Savannah until her bare toes touched the floor. She'd changed into an old pair of faded jeans and a t-shirt while she'd waited to get news on him. As she stood before him, Savannah just couldn't take her gaze off Jett. Her hands were shaking a little as her fingers slid over his neck. There was nothing wrong there. No break. No sign of any injury. Luna had been right. He looked fine. A little tired, his hair a little mussed — sexily mussed — but he was fine.

She wanted to hug him again.

Instead, after he locked the door and reset the security system, she found herself confessing, "You scared me."

His hand curved under her jaw. "Why?"

"Because I thought you were dead."

His shoulders seemed to stiffen.

"I looked back as Luna drove away, and you were on the pavement. You weren't moving, and

I could have sworn—" No, the image in her head was wrong. Absolutely wrong. He was fine. Her tongue slid over her dry lips, and then she said, "Don't die on me, okay? Can you promise that you won't die on me?"

He didn't answer. Instead, Jett leaned toward her. His lips brushed over hers. Soft. Gentle. At first.

At first, his lips were soft and gentle on hers. At first, he was carefully caressing her with his mouth. But then he moved his body even closer to hers. His hand slid from her chin to her arm. Down, down...until he clasped her waist. And her hands had moved to his broad shoulders. She held him, gripping too tightly even as she opened her mouth more for him.

She'd been terrified. She'd been lost. She'd been desperate. All for him. All because of him. The man she'd met so recently. The man who made her feel so much.

"I want you," he growled those ragged words against her mouth. Deep and rough, and they seemed to sink right through her entire body.

He wanted her. She wanted him. Sure, there were a thousand reasons why they shouldn't do this. So many reasons why she should step away...

They'd just met.

She was probably riding some insane adrenaline rush or fear high at that moment.

When the case ended, her mystery man would fade into the shadows.

He'd *almost* died that night.

Actually, that last reason—that was why she held him even tighter and said, "I want you, too." Because they didn't have forever. The kidnapping had taught her that truth. No one had forever. People weren't promised a certain amount of time in this world. Why waste what you had? Why not grab tight to what—or who— you wanted? She wanted him. So badly.

So badly that she was the one to shove up his t-shirt. He tossed it aside, and her fingers slid over his chest. Broad, muscled and—

Bruised?

"Jett?" Her touch feathered over him.

"Nothing. Already fading. Forget it." He swung her into his arms. Carried her into the bedroom.

She didn't want to forget his bruises. He'd been so worried about her when she was injured, couldn't he understand that she worried about him, too?

The bedroom was dark, but light shone in from the starlit sky. Although the balcony doors were locked, she could hear the sound of the waves as they crashed into the beach. He lowered her onto the bed. Then Jett's careful hands stripped off her shirt. He unhooked her jeans and slid down the zipper. Her breath came faster as eagerness fueled her blood. He pulled off the jeans, and she eagerly helped him to ditch the denim. But… "You're hurt."

She wanted to help him —

Yet when she reached out to him, Jett caught her fingers. Brought them to his mouth. Kissed her fingertips, then slid her index finger into his mouth. He licked. Nipped. Made her moan.

"I'm hurting, all right, baby," he agreed in a sexy rumble. "But you can make me feel good. And I'll make you feel fucking fantastic."

Her breath was coming faster. She was clad in her underwear, a white bra and panties. Hardly the sexiest thing ever. And he still wore his jeans and his boots — No, correction. The boots had hit the floor. His socks followed.

He crawled onto the bed, stalking and dangerous and sexy. His mouth pressed to her collarbone, and he kissed his way down, down, moving her bra out of his way. Sliding away the straps and unhooking the clasp in a quick, easy move. When the bra fell away, his mouth captured one breast. He licked. Sucked. Had her arching off the bed and wanting so much more.

She was getting wet for him. Already. His hips were between her spread legs, and when Savannah arched up against him, she felt the long, heavy length of his erection shoving through his jeans.

Those jeans needed to go.

Her nails raked down his back, then she remembered his bruises. "Jett—"

He took her other breast into his mouth. Sucked and she shuddered. A long, delicious shudder of need and want and lust.

Things had become very, very basic. Primal. She wanted him. He wanted her.

Her panties and his jeans were in the way. Flesh to flesh. That was how she wanted to be with him. She couldn't remember hungering this way. Couldn't remember needing anyone this way.

And she was scared—not scared of the way she felt. But scared the feeling would go away.

His hand pressed between their bodies. His fingers slid under the silk of her panties. Rubbed against her clit. Had her gasping because it felt so good.

Then he pushed a finger into her. "Baby, you are so tight. Wet…"

She was riding his hand. Pushing herself down against his fingers, trying to get *more.*

He pulled back. Took his hand away. She could have screamed in frustration. But then he positioned his body again. He'd moved down her body. His shoulders were between her spread legs. His mouth—that wicked mouth was over the entrance to her body. She still had on the damn panties!

He kissed her through the panties. Blew a warm breath of air over her. Then caught her clit — sucked. All through the silk.

Her toes were curling.

She was nearly coming.

Savannah was also pretty sure she was chanting his name. Again and again and again. His fingers slid under the edge of her panties. He shoved the silk to the side, and then his tongue licked over her sex.

She came right then as a scream broke from her lips.

The climax ripped through her whole body, sending waves of pleasure surging through her. Her eyes squeezed shut, and her muscles tightened. It was so good, so, so good.

"I don't have a fucking condom."

Her eyes opened. Jett was above her. His face was locked into hard, tense lines. His arms were braced on either side of her body.

"Baby, I'm clean. I swear it. They run constant tests on us at the base."

She could barely catch her breath.

"And I-I can't have kids. You don't have to worry about that risk."

Her hand rose to press to his cheek. "I'm clean, too." She wanted this. Wanted him.

His right hand lifted. She heard the rasp of his zipper. And then the wide head of his cock pushed at the entrance to her body. Savannah sucked in a sharp breath as she arched toward him, and then he was inside, filling her completely. Every single inch.

For a moment, he just stared at her. She stared at him. She'd never felt closer to a lover.

Then he withdrew. Thrust. Withdrew.

Drove deep.

The bed began to squeak beneath them.

Her legs locked around his hips. Need spiraled through her. She'd just climaxed. She should have been sated. She wasn't.

He kissed her. Dipped his tongue into her mouth, and she *loved* the way he tasted. His body angled down so that every withdraw and every thrust had the long length of his cock brushing over her clit. Making her wilder. Making her desperate.

"I want to feel it when you come. I want to feel your pleasure."

He was sure about to feel it. The climax was building, building and —

It hit her. Slammed into her and for a moment, everything went dark — probably because she was squeezing her eyes shut so hard. The pleasure was the most intense that she'd ever felt in her entire life. Toe-curling, body-shaking, mind-numbing pleasure.

And he was right there with her. Driving into her. Growling her name. She felt the hot jet of his release inside of her, and then he was kissing her. Soft, tender kisses.

She heard frantic drumming and realized it was her heart.

Her breath came in hard heaves.

He slid from her body. Pulled her into his side. Held her.

There were things she should say. Things she should do.

But she just curled closer to him. She put her hand over Jett's heart. Felt the frantic beat.

And her eyes closed.

He was alive. He was safe. He was with her. That was all that mattered.

***

"Can you promise that you won't die on me?" Savannah's soft question drifted through Jett's mind as he lay in bed, holding her. She'd fallen asleep next to him. In sleep, she looked so innocent and beautiful.

When she'd asked him for the promise, he hadn't given her those words. Because he *couldn't* give Savannah that promise. Truth be fucking told, he'd died that day. He hadn't survived the force of that explosion throwing him from the second story of that building and careening into the pavement below.

But he'd come back.

As he'd done before. As he'd do again.

Because he was a freak of nature now. A true killing machine who worked for Uncle Sam. His life wasn't his own. His *lives* weren't his own.

So, no, he couldn't promise that he wouldn't die. But he could promise that he'd come back. Over and over again.

For her, he would.

His head turned as he gazed down at her.

He should have kept his hands off her. Should have guarded her and nothing more. But when her door had opened and she'd run to him, when she'd looked at him like he was everything she'd ever wanted, Jett had realized the truth...

She's mine. I'm hers.

It was like he'd found the other part of his soul. Even when he wasn't supposed to have one. Did the dead have souls?

But his heart beat. He breathed. He needed. He ached. He did everything a normal man could do. When he'd died the first time and been brought into the Lazarus program, his body had been injected with a serum that had reanimated him—and given him the added bonuses that made him such a good warrior.

It was those bonuses that would help him to hunt down the bastard after Savannah.

And it was those same things that would force him to leave her.

He lived at the base. He wasn't allowed to stay away unless he was on a mission. His handler said he was too dangerous...

His fingers slid over her arm.

In her sleep, she smiled and murmured his name.

His chest got tight.

Then she rolled away from him. His gaze drifted over her naked back. The gorgeous dip of her spine and her —

Tattoos.

A small, black dragon waited near the curve of her back. The beast's long, serpentine tail slid toward her second tattoo. A dark red rose. When she'd been in the hospital gown, he'd been too distracted by her sexy ass. He hadn't even noticed a hint of the tats.

He found himself smiling. And leaning forward to kiss the rose. His lips pressed over the slightly raised skin —

She gave a little gasp and immediately spun back over, almost hitting him, but he moved quickly. He had fast reflexes, after all.

"Jett?" Her eyes were wide. "Oh, God, did I fall asleep? Right after? That is so embarrassing!"

He had to laugh. She just made him feel good. "You needed a rest, before the second round." He brushed his lips over hers. "By the way, I love the tats." He pulled her up and on top of him, so that she straddled his hips and her knees pressed into the bed.

He made sure that when he positioned her, his cock slid against her sensitive core. Not going inside, not yet.

"I was...ah...." She rocked her hips along his length.

Sexy as fuck.

"I was born...in the...um, the year of the dragon..." She gave him a quick smile. "Always had a...a thing for dragons."

She was driving him crazy. "And the rose?"

Her eyelids flickered. She laughed. He loved that sound. Loved it.

And I could love her.

Jett immediately shut down the thought. This was a mission. This was —

"I figure if you're lucky enough to be that close to my ass, you deserve a rose."

He laughed.

Her hands splayed over his chest. She moved her hips, slid her sex down, and took his cock into her.

She moaned.

He stopped laughing.

His hands locked on her hips.

"Slow?" Savannah whispered. "Or fast?"

He couldn't look away from her. "How about...both?"

She rose slowly, taking her time as she pushed up onto her knees. Sliding that hot heaven of her sex up the length of his cock, then, one small move at a time...going back down until he was balls deep in her.

Once...

Twice...

Three times. Four. So slow...

So—

He flipped her, tumbling her back so that he was on top. "Fast. Fucking *fast.*"

And he drove into her, pistoning his hips even as his fingers stroked over the center of her need. He stroked, rubbed, and didn't let go. Didn't ease up on the tempo of his frantic thrusts, not until she came for him. Not until she choked out his name.

Then he let go. He poured into her.

The pleasure nearly gutted him. His heart was a sledge hammer in his chest, pounding and pounding, and his breath sawed from his lungs. He'd braced his body on his forearms so he could look down and stare at her. She was fucking beautiful.

And she smiled at him. Smiled at him and flashed those cute dimples like he was the best thing she'd ever seen.

She had no clue.

Not for the first time, he hated the fact that he'd been lying to her. But he still leaned down. He still tasted her sweet lips.

Then he eased out of her. Pulled her close. Held her.

What would it be like, if she was really his? If they were lovers with no secrets? Lovers with some kind of hope for a future?

A dream that he couldn't ever have. One that would never come true for him.

"It's...not usually like that for me." Her voice was soft, husky. So sexy. "Is it like that for you?"

To be honest, he had no clue. Sex before her? He didn't remember sex before Lazarus, and she was the only one who'd tempted him since he'd woken in that cold lab. But in his gut, he knew... "No, baby, it's not like that." So intense the pleasure swept away everything else? So consuming, he already wanted to sink into her again? And again? That he wanted to say screw it to everything else, and just be with her?

You didn't need to remember other times, other lovers, to know that something was special. You could feel it.

She was special.

Her hand was over his heart. A soft hand.

"Tell me about you." She snuggled closer. "I don't know much about you at all. I only know that you were a SEAL, and you can kick ass really well."

He was stroking her hair. When had he started doing that?

"Why did you become a SEAL?"

He didn't know.

"I bet your family is proud of you."

His heart rate kicked up, and he knew she had to feel the acceleration beneath her hand. Were they proud? His dad, ex-crime boss? His mom? The woman who'd raised him on her own after his father had been shot down? Who knew?

"You...aren't talking."

No, he wasn't. And he could hear the whisper of pain in her voice. She thought he was just holding back on her. Savannah didn't get it — he didn't have those memories. He couldn't share with her. But he couldn't tell her that truth, either. So, Jett cleared his throat. "There are...things I can't say."

She rolled her body, peering up at him.

"The job means that certain parts of my life have to stay confidential."

"I...see."

No, she didn't. If he tried the full truth with her...*Savannah, baby, I'm a dead man. The guy who was just feasting on your body? He died, got taken out by a hail of bullets on a mission. But because I'd signed some paperwork and done a video providing my consent to participate in Project Lazarus before those bullets came at me...well, I was brought back from the dead. Lucky me, right?*

Oh, sure. She'd be totally cool with that. Never.

"You can tell me other things." Her voice was low.

He was still stroking her. His fingers had moved to her back. He just liked touching her.

"Non-confidential things," Savannah added. "And I can tell you things about me, too. Because I want to know you. I want you to know me."

Fuck, he was going to hurt her. "When the mission ends, I have to leave." He would not be given a choice.

Silence. The kind that made his muscles clench. The kind that—

"I still want to know you."

His breath released. When had he started holding it?

"Though for future reference, don't tell a woman you're going to leave when you're still in bed with her."

He kissed her. Caught her chin and tipped her head back and kissed her with all of the need and the desperate craving that he felt for her.

Because I don't want to leave. He could already feel it. Inside, he wanted her. Wanted to grab tight. Wanted to stay with her. Wanted to say fuck it to the world. Take her, vanish with her. Would it be possible? He had the skills. He could disappear with her. He could—

"My life is here," Savannah continued in her careful voice, and his wild, desperate plans stopped. "My family is here. My job is here. My friends are here."

Of course. She wouldn't want to vanish with a dead man. With a killer. *And I'm both.*

"I get that your world is somewhere else."

In a lab. On the battlefield. Wherever the hell Uncle Sam sent him.

"But I still want to know you because I don't have random lovers. *You* aren't random. You matter to me, and I want to know more about you."

He kissed her once more and knew that he'd always long for her taste. No one else would ever do for him again. "What do you want to know?" He'd tell her what he could.

Not much. It couldn't be anything about Lazarus. About his life before —

"What's your favorite kind of ice cream?"

The question surprised a laugh out of him. "What?"

"Your favorite kind of ice cream. What is it?"

He had no clue.

"Come on, surely you can tell me that."

Jett had to clear his throat again. "I'm not sure." She'd think he was lying to her. He wasn't. Ice cream wasn't exactly on the menu at the base. And when he'd been on missions, well, a lot of those hell-holes didn't have ice cream shops on the corners. Even when he'd been handling domestic cases, stopping by an ice cream shop hadn't been something he'd even thought of doing.

"That is an absolute shame," she told him, voice quite serious. "We'll find out tomorrow. I promise."

He pulled the bedding up to cover her.

"I like chocolate. I'm traditional—just give me chocolate, and I'm in heaven." A little yawn. "What's your favorite color?"

He thought of her eyes. "Hazel."

She gave a sleepy laugh. "That's different. Didn't expect it." A pause. "I like red. And my favorite place to go in the world? It's a beach. I love beaches. Love the sound of the water hitting the sand. Love to watch the sunset or to just stay on a beach at night and see a million stars over me."

Made sense. Certainly explained why she lived right on the beach. If he could live anywhere, where would he go? Jett hadn't considered the question before.

"Where's your favorite place?" Savannah asked him.

And the answer that rolled straight through his mind was…

With you.

She stiffened. "I heard that," she whispered. "And it was so sweet." A sleepy laugh. "Though probably not true."

Actually, it was.

"How did you become...like me?" The question was halting. "Were you in an accident, too?"

Now he was making extra sure to guard his thoughts. "Something like that."

"I don't think anyone has ever been able to hear my thoughts before. Not like you can. That makes us special, doesn't it?"

She was special. He was a freak produced by a lab.

"I-I don't pick up from everyone." Another yawn from her. "I learned to shut down. I put up a guard, and it blocks most people. I try not to let that guard down."

"Why?"

"Because people don't always think good thoughts. Sometimes, the things you can see..." Her voice was drifting away with sleep. "The things you see, they can scare you." A pause. "But you get past my guard. Sometimes, your thoughts just slip right into my mind."

"Savannah..."

"And I like it when you're in my mind. Because you don't scare me."

If she knew the full truth about him, she'd be terrified.

Her breathing evened out. She didn't speak again. Just curled against him.

He replayed her words in his head. Savannah was right. People projected images to the world. Showed you only what they wanted. The true part of people — no, that part wasn't always pretty.

If she'd used her powers, though, would she have seen the truth about Patrick before he took her? Would she have known her lover was a monster?

If I weren't blocking my deepest thoughts, wouldn't she know I'm a monster, too?

Fuck.

***

The phone rang, jarring Savannah from crazy, terrifying dreams. Dreams in which Jett stared at her with his dark turbulent eyes…and died.

Died, only to come back. To rise with blood on his chest and come toward her.

Even as more bullets blasted.

The phone rang again.

She jerked upright and saw that the replacement phone Jett had gotten for her was ringing on the night stand.

"Answer it," Jett directed quietly.

He'd told her his team would monitor her calls, just in case Patrick tried to contact her. Just in case...

The new phone had been programmed to receive calls from her old number. Patrick had that number. He'd called her dozens of times before the bastard had shown his true colors—

The phone rang again, vibrating against the wood of the night stand. Her hand flew out. Caught the phone. Her fingers swiped over the screen, and Savannah made sure to turn on the speaker option so that Jett could hear the call. "Hello?"

A quick rush of breath. Then... "I didn't want it to be this way." Patrick's voice. She'd know his voice anywhere.

"You mean you didn't want me to escape? You wanted me dead? Like those other poor women?"

"They didn't matter. You were different. I wasn't going to kill you, Savannah. That wasn't part of the plan."

Like she would believe him.

"There's more happening here than you can understand," Patrick continued as static crackled along the line. "You're in danger."

Uh, yeah. "From you!"

"Savannah—"

"You tried to shoot me today!" She was supposed to keep him talking. Jett had told her that before. If he called, she had to keep the guy on the line. The longer they talked, the better chance Jett's team had to triangulate the location of Patrick's cell. The better chance they had to find him.

Jett had climbed from the bed. Dressed silently.

"It wasn't me," Patrick told her doggedly.

She gave a bitter laugh. "I think I know you. You were the one trying to cut off my finger, remember?"

"I wasn't going to kill you, though! I was going to take you away! To keep you!"

Shivers slid over her body.

"You can't trust him," Patrick told her. "You can't trust any of them."

What?

"He's not who you think. Not *what* you think. It's all a game, and you're a pawn."

Her heart was beating too fast. She dragged the sheets up to cover her naked body.

"I'm your only hope," Patrick insisted. "Baby, I love you. I can get you out of here! I can take you so far away that no one will ever be able to use you again."

This didn't make any sense to her. "You...you killed those other women."

"I was hired for a job. I did my job."

Was he saying he'd been paid to kill those women?

"Things aren't what they appear to be," Patrick added. A car horn sounded behind him. No, not a car horn. A boat horn? "You're in danger."

From the man who'd abducted her and tried to use his knife on her.

"Your hero is a dead man," Patrick's voice deepened as he spoke those words.

Immediately, her gaze flew to Jett. And instead of feeling fear, rage burned inside of her. "You won't hurt him!" Her voice was fierce and hard. "You won't—"

"Fucking hell. He's right there."

Right there. In her bedroom. He'd been in her bed.

"Savannah…you made a mistake."

The line went dead. She was left just holding the phone in her left hand, clutching the sheet in her right, and feeling a dark rage burn inside of her. *He can't hurt Jett.* Jett was good. Decent. Jett was—

Jett's phone rang. When had he even grabbed it? But it was in his hand right then. He put it to his ear. Listened a moment. Then looked at her. "We've got him. We know the bastard's location."

CHAPTER EIGHT

"Everything...okay?" Maddox eyed Jett with an air of caution. "You seem extra tense."

No, things were not fucking okay. But he couldn't damn well say that. "We got the bastard's location." He checked his gun, then shoved it into his shoulder holster. They'd just arrived at the dock, and it was time to take down Patrick Zane. "In five minutes, this will be over. Savannah will be safe." He took a step forward.

Maddox grabbed his arm. "You slept with her."

"This isn't the time for any jackshit talk about—"

"I need to make sure your head is clear. I don't know what we'll find in there." *There.* The small building that waited on the edge of the dock, shuttered in darkness. "Can I count on you?"

"He tried to hurt Savannah. You can count on me to end him." Was that fair enough?

"It's not just about revenge. It's about your team." Maddox kept his voice flat. "Luna is working back-up. I need to make sure you aren't going to pull some cowboy bullshit and risk her."

Ah. Of course. Maddox didn't like to admit it, but the guy had *always* been soft on Luna. Soft, obsessed, same thing. "Don't worry." Jett gave him a thin smile. "I've never been the cowboy type." Did he look like a cowboy? Screw that shit. He went in first, keeping low and moving fast, and Maddox was on his six.

They didn't make a sound as they approached the shack. The water bobbed nearby, and he could hear the waves pounding against the dock. When they reached the door, Maddox motioned with his hand.

Hell, yes. Time to end this. Jett kicked the door open while Maddox covered him. They rushed inside, guns out now, ready to take out —

Patrick was on the floor, a pool of blood spreading near his neck. A gun was just inches from his right hand.

Another man lay beside him, stiff, unmoving. The guy's hand still clutched a knife. A bloody knife.

"What in the hell?" Jett crouched next to Patrick Zane. Touched his neck. Felt for a pulse.

"This guy's dead. Took a bullet to the heart," Maddox muttered as he knelt next to the other man. "Didn't hear a damn thing when we arrived. Bastards must have turned on each other before we got here."

That was what it looked like. The two men had taken each other out. The redhead near Maddox had sliced Patrick's throat, and Patrick had fired his gun before he fell to the floor and —

Patrick's pulse gave a jerk beneath Jett's hand. "He's still alive!"

With all that blood loss, he wouldn't stay alive for long.

Shit.

"Patrick? Patrick Zane!" Jett snarled. "Look at me!" He needed to make sure there weren't any other bastards out there who were working for this prick. Other jerks who might come after Savannah.

Patrick's lips parted. No sound emerged, but his mouth formed, "*Savannah…*"

"You're never going to touch her again," Jett promised him. "You're dying, you get that? You're bleeding out. Do something useful with your last moments. Is there anyone else from your team of assholes who is a threat to her? Anyone who will hurt her?"

"He can't talk," Maddox muttered. "Look at that freaking damage to his throat."

But Patrick — he was trying to talk. His lips were moving. Jett tried to reach him on a psychic link, but Savannah was the only non-Lazarus person he'd ever been able to communicate with that way. So, when he sent his psychic message thundering at Patrick…

Will anyone else hurt Savannah? Is this over?

There was only darkness in response.

Darkness in Jett's mind, but Patrick's lips trembled. *Pro...tect...*

Protect? That was exactly what Jett was trying to do. Protect Savannah. Eliminate all of the threats to her. Save her.

A low wheeze came from Patrick. And then there was only stillness. Silence.

Death.

Jett looked up. His gaze darted around the small building, scanning over the interior. A computer. Old furniture. A broken phone near Patrick.

The cell phone he'd used to call Savannah?

Maddox stalked toward the computer. The screen was lit up, showing— "Bank accounts...in the Cayman Islands." A low whistle. "Looks like all the cash he took from the other kidnappings."

Just left up there for them to find on the screen? Too convenient.

"Guess that's what they were fighting about." Maddox glanced at the dead man on the floor. "Maybe the other guy wanted a bigger cut." Then Maddox sent out a fast, psychic message. *Scene is secure inside, Luna. All clear.*

Jett leaned forward. Patted down Patrick's body. Found the guy's wallet in his back pocket. He opened it, thumbing through the contents and—

A picture of Savannah. Smiling. Standing on the beach.

No other pictures. A dozen credit cards. Over a thousand bucks in cash.

Jett frowned at the picture.

"Killers keep tokens," Maddox murmured as he pulled out his phone. "To remind them of their victims." He turned away and spoke into the phone, barking instructions back to the base so the clean-up team would move in.

Jett slid the picture of Savannah into his pocket.

"Tech team will come for the computer. When they do their scan, they'll make sure we're not missing anything."

He looked over to see Maddox had already put away his phone.

"It looks like the case is over," Maddox announced with a grim nod.

It looked too damn *tidy* to Jett. The scene felt off.

"Probably realized we were closing in — you said the fellow put two and two together, figured out that you were with Savannah." Maddox shrugged. "Guy must have suspected we'd tracked the call and were rushing over. He and his goon fought — maybe about money, maybe about Patrick being dumb enough to call Savannah and give away their location — and in the end, they killed each other."

That was the way it looked. But…

"She's safe now." Maddox slapped a hand on Jett's shoulder. "Isn't that what matters?"

Yes, Savannah's safety was what mattered most.

So why did Jett feel like she was still in danger?

***

When she heard the key in the front door, Savanah immediately lunged forward. She'd been watching on the security monitor that Jett had installed—she'd seen him approaching her home. So when he unlocked the door and stepped inside—

She hugged him. Wrapped him up tightly in her arms because she was so glad he was safe and sound.

At first, Jett stiffened. Then his arms rose. Closed around her. "I like the way you greet me," he murmured, voice a bit gruff. "Like I matter."

What? She pulled back. "You do matter."

His gaze was intense as it slid over her face. Then he was kicking the door shut. Re-setting the lock and security. He was—

Lifting her up. Holding her easily. Turning and caging her between the door and his body. His mouth crashed onto hers. He kissed her with a wild desperation, and she kissed him back the exact same way. She was so happy to see him, so glad he was safe. Savannah couldn't get close enough to him. Her hands locked around his neck as she arched up against him.

Her legs circled his waist, and she felt the long, heavy length of his erection pressing against her. She rubbed against him, hating her jeans, hating his pants, wanting nothing between them. She'd just gone straight from worry to insane need.

He pulled his mouth from hers. Bit off a curse, and then he was carrying her to the bedroom. Acting as if she weighed nothing. His hands were on her ass. His cock shoved against her, and she just wanted him.

He lowered her onto the bed. Stripped while he stared at her.

At first, she just gawked at him. Would she ever get used to the sight of his body? Those muscles? That strength? That awesome—

All of his bruises are gone. They'd faded completely. Talk about some insane healing rate. What was the guy—magic?

"Savannah."

Her eyes jerked up.

"Strip."

She did. She shoved off her jeans and her panties and—

"Good enough." He caught her ankles. Pulled her to the side of the bed. "Can't wait any longer."

Neither could she. She'd been so afraid something would happen to him. So worried that he wouldn't come back to her. She'd needed him. Desperately needed *him*.

He drove into her. She arched off the bed.

His eyes were on hers. Locked. Seeming to see straight *into* her. Jett withdrew. Then he plunged into her, even deeper than before. He stretched her, filled her completely, and when he leaned close, her nails raked over his back.

This wasn't the type of lover she normally was. She wasn't the nails scraping, wild moaning, fuck-me-now type. That wasn't her. She usually turned off the lights. Pulled up the sheets. She—

His fingers pressed to her clit. Rubbed. Stroked.

His cock moved in and out. In and out. In and—

She came, gasping out his name. But he wasn't done. He kept thrusting, and the surge of his thrusts made her orgasm last and last. The pleasure pulsed through every cell of her body. It filled her, just as he did and then, he kissed her. He kissed her, and he came, and she could almost taste his pleasure.

Her heartbeat thundered. When he lifted his head, his gaze was still full of so much need. He looked at her as if she was the only thing on earth that he wanted.

No one had ever looked at her like that.

Carefully, slowly, he withdrew from her body. Without a word, he headed into the bathroom.

She still had on her shirt. She was still hanging off the side of the bed. Awkward.

Savannah stripped off the shirt. Dove for the covers and—

He was back. He moved the covers out of his way, exposing her body to him. Jett slid a warm washcloth between her legs. Used such gentle care. And the expression in his eyes was still the same.

As if I'm the person who matters most to him.

He took the cloth back to the bathroom. When he returned, Jett sat on the side of the bed. She realized that he'd pulled on his pants. He raked a hand over his face and glanced away from her.

Savannah licked her lips. Then she finally asked, "What happened?"

"He's dead. Patrick Zane was killed by one of his men. Probably the guy who escaped with him the night of your rescue." A rough sigh. "They killed each other. When we arrived, Patrick was in a pool of his own blood. The fellow who'd knifed him was dead, too."

Her heart seemed to jerk in her chest.

"Got a team checking Patrick's computer. Preliminary signs are that Patrick was the mastermind of the kidnapping ring. With his death, it's over."

Over.

His hand lifted. Touched her cheek. "You're safe, Savannah. He won't ever hurt you again."

Her shoulders sagged a little as relief hit her. Safe. She didn't have to look over her shoulder any longer. Didn't have to fear an attack and wonder when Patrick would come for her.

Over.

But pain was there, too. A hard slice to her heart because if the case was over, then Jett would be leaving. Going on to another mission.

He'd told her that before. Told her this wasn't forever. And she wasn't looking for any kind of forever promise. It was just that...

You understand me.

She pushed that thought at him. Because he did. After years of feeling like a freak, she'd finally found someone who could do the same thing she could. Someone who could talk without words to her. Someone who *got* her.

"I do." He gave her a tender smile.

Her lips wanted to tremble. "Maybe...maybe I can see you when you're on leave. That's what it's called, right? When you have breaks from other missions." She knew so little about him. So very little. "Um, we can try all of the ice creams and see which one is your favorite."

A mask seemed to slip over his face.

"Savannah…"

His closed expression said it all. Hot sex. Mind-numbing pleasure. But when the mission ended, so did they.

And the mission was over. "So it's done."

He turned off the lamp. Climbed into the bed with her. Pulled her against him. Held her close, like she mattered.

Just sex. You knew this going in. Just sex.

He hadn't lied to her. One thing about Jett — *he never lied.* Considering what her last lover had turned out to be, Savannah valued Jett's truth more than she could say. Even if it hurt.

"Not quite. It's not quite done." His voice rumbled. She could feel the deep vibration because they were so close. "The team wants to make sure there aren't any loose ends out there. That Patrick didn't have a silent partner waiting in the wings. The mission isn't over until we're sure you'll be safe."

So, he wasn't leaving. Not yet. Though she'd thought they were having awesome good-bye sex. Savannah cleared her throat. "How will you be sure there isn't a partner?"

"We've got a great tech team. They're following the money now. Money always shows the guilty party. People can be damn greedy."

Yes. And they could be cold and cruel. She'd learned all of that.

"The team is also sweeping the scene for any additional prints. Any sign that will point to someone else being involved." His voice had changed. Gone a little flatter.

She couldn't see his face, not clearly in the darkness. But something was off. "Jett? What is it?"

"The scene was too tidy for me. Both of them dead? Right before we arrived?"

Okay, now she was getting worried. "You think it was a setup?"

He didn't answer. Wait, was that an answer?

"Jett?" she prompted.

"Nothing at the scene pointed to anyone else being involved. It's just me, being cautious." He pressed a kiss to her temple. "Don't worry. Like I said, the team is checking things."

He seemed to have total confidence in his team. "You're really close to them, aren't you?" It wasn't just business.

"Maddox and Luna have been with me since I entered Lazarus. I'd trust them both with my life."

"Lazarus?"

A slight pause, then he said, "That's my team."

Why did she feel like he was holding back on her? Deliberately, she pushed, asking, "And the other guy...Andreas?"

"Don't know him as well. The Greek isn't easy to get to know."

"Ah. He has secrets."

His lips feathered over her cheek. "We all do, baby. They go with the job." Another soft kiss. "Andreas has already gone back to base. He won't be working your case any longer."

She didn't think Jett would be working it any longer, either. And that made her heart ache. When he left, she'd miss him. More than she'd expected. The pain was already there, waiting. But for now, they were together. "I'm glad I met you." She cuddled closer to him. "Whatever else happens, remember that, okay?" He'd literally saved her life. How could she ever regret him? Or anything that had happened with him?

"I'm glad I met you." Low words. Nice words. But was he just repeating what she'd said? Playing the polite lover game?

Tears pricked her lashes as Savannah closed her eyes. She concentrated on making her breathing nice and even. She'd known he would walk away. She just hadn't known it would hurt so much.

Soon, sleep pulled at her. The adrenaline high had crashed, and she wanted to escape everything for a little bit. She let go and as she drifted to sleep—

"I just wish I'd met you before I became a monster."

***

Time to go, Jett.

He hadn't been sleeping. Jett had just been lying in bed, holding Savannah. The lights were still off, but he saw her perfectly.

Got extraction orders. Maddox's voice floated through his mind once more. *We're supposed to leave right now.*

He didn't reply. He'd told Maddox that Savannah could pick up on his thoughts, warned the guy not to send any psychic messages his way. But since they were leaving, maybe Maddox figured it didn't matter any longer.

It did.

Jett brushed a lock of hair from her cheek. She was still sleeping. Maybe he should wake her up. Tell her good-bye. Fuck. *Fuck.* He didn't know how to handle this scene, and the worst thing was—

I don't want to leave her.

He was afraid that if he tried to communicate back with Maddox, he might just tell the guy...tell his *friend...Fuck off. Screw Lazarus. I'm done. I only want her.*

He wanted a chance with Savannah. Wanted to see what a normal life could be like. Maybe they'd be happy together. Perhaps they could make it work. He wanted her like hell on fire, but more than that…he *liked* her. He loved her smile. Those damn dimples got him every time. He loved her laugh. And whenever she saw him, she lit up. He'd never forget the way she ran to him when her door opened. Like she was so happy to see him.

And when she hugged him, Jett felt like he was home. Finally, home. She was his home.

No, dammit, no. Lazarus was home. For the time being. Hell, for the foreseeable future. Uncle Sam was the puppeteer pulling the strings. He was the government's weapon. An unstable weapon. An unstoppable weapon. If Savannah ever learned the truth about him, she'd be terrified.

She wouldn't want a life with him. She *shouldn't* have a life with him. She should be with a normal man. A man who had no secrets. A man who gave her the world.

A man who isn't a freak.

She wasn't meant for him. And he couldn't bring her into the darkness that was his life. He wanted to kiss her good-bye, but if she woke…

We've got one more job to do before we leave town. Maddox's voice was different now. Harder. *Then the mission is over.*

One more job? He knew exactly what
Maddox meant. A personal job that Jett would
see to himself. Jett's muscles tightened as
determination filled him. He didn't want to risk
waking her, so he sent out a surge of his psychic
power. Shadows swept around him. He *became*
little more than shadow as he eased from the bed.
His steps didn't make a sound as he crossed the
room. At the bedroom door, he glanced back at
her, helpless not to get that final look.

She was still sleeping. Still perfect. The dream
that would haunt him.

He eased from the room. Crept from her
home without making a sound. Just a shadow.
Just a shadow...

He met Maddox and Luna outside, and they
prepared for the last job.

Good-bye, Savannah.

CHAPTER NINE

A phone was ringing. Pealing, over and over again. Savannah opened one eye, squinting, and for a moment—that first, semi-awake moment— she didn't even know where she was.

The phone rang again.

Awareness flooded back.

Jett. She sat up in a flash because he wasn't there. The bed was empty beside her.

The phone stopped ringing.

Her hand reached out for Jett's pillow. None of his warmth remained. And as her gaze slid around the room, she found no sign of him. Fumbling, she turned on the lamp so that she could see better. No discarded clothing. Nothing. "Jett?"

The phone started to ring again.

She grabbed it, and on the illuminated screen, she saw Sam's face. It was close to three a.m. Why was Sam calling her at this hour? Her finger swiped over the screen before she put the phone to her ear. "Sam? What is it?"

"Are you alone?"

What kind of question was that?

"Tell me he isn't there. Tell me you're safe."

What? "Yes, yes, I'm safe." With her left hand, she pulled the covers closer.

"Is Jett there?"

He wasn't in her bed. Maybe he'd just gone into the kitchen. Or the den. Or —

"If he's there, you have to get the hell away from him." Sam's panting breath carried over the line. "I've got cops on the way to you. Barricade yourself in the bathroom until they get there. Just stay the hell *away* from him."

Her heart was racing. And her hand had become a fist around the sheets. "What is happening?"

"The real Jett Bianchi is dead. He died on a covert mission and was buried a while back. This guy — this guy and his whole team — they aren't who they claimed to be. Their papers were BS. They weren't sent by any government agency. That was all a lie."

In the distance, she could hear the scream of a siren. The cops that Sam had promised?

"He found out too late." What sounded like pain roughened his voice. "Dammit, too late! There wasn't anything I could do. I-I found him this way…"

"Found who?" She slipped from the bed. Kept the sheet wrapped around her naked body as she crept toward her bedroom door. Sam was wrong. Confused. He had to be. Jett had saved her. Protected her. She cracked open the bedroom door, looking for him.

But he wasn't in the den.

He wasn't in the kitchen.

"Jett's not here," she whispered.

"Thank Christ! I was afraid that after he finished here, he'd gone back for you—"

Finished there? "You aren't making sense." And Sam hadn't answered her question. "Who did you find?"

The sirens were louder. When she looked out her window, she could see the flash of blue lights coming closer.

"God, Savannah, I'm so sorry. I should have been here, but I...*I'm so sorry.*"

Why was he saying that? "You're scaring me." The cops were coming. She needed to dress. Needed to find out why they were at her house. *Sam was wrong.*

"He's dead."

She shook her head.

"Your father is dead, Savannah. Those bastards killed him. Jett and his team *killed* him."

***

Cops were everywhere. Men and women in uniforms, talking in low voices. Yellow police tape was outside of the mansion, to secure the scene. She stood there, shaking, dressed in jeans and a t-shirt, wearing her old sneakers. Rain had started to fall, and the drops slid over her cheeks.

The cops had wanted to take her to the station. She'd refused. She'd demanded that she be brought here. To the house that had never really felt like home.

"They're going to bring the body out soon," the cop on her right said softly. Jennifer something. Adams? She'd introduced herself back at Savannah's home, but Savannah had been so shocked then that she'd barely heard the other woman. Everything had felt distorted. It still felt that way. "You don't have to watch this. We can go to the station. After the body has been cleared, you can head to the morgue to — "

The morgue. This was real. All of it. Her head turned, and she stared at Jennifer. "My father is dead?" A last, desperate question. So many lights illuminated the scene, pushing back against the darkness.

"Yes." Jennifer held an umbrella in her hand, and the rain tapped against the top of it.

"But — "

"He didn't suffer," Jennifer added quickly. Her dark eyes showed her sympathy even as she said, "A single gunshot wound to the head. A professional hit."

No. Savannah shook her head. *No.*

But when she glanced back at the front of the sprawling house, a gurney was being wheeled out. And on top of that gurney, she could see a long, black bag. A body bag. Her father was in that bag?

"*Savannah!*"

Sam was shouting her name. He ran toward her and pulled her into his arms. But she barely felt him. She was too numb.

"God, I was so afraid they'd kill you, too."

They? He couldn't mean Jett. Not Jett or Maddox or Luna.

He eased his hold so that he could peer down at her. "I saw them on the security feed. They came into the house. Jett and his buddy Maddox. They came into the house, and then the feed ended. They cut the security." Rain drops slid down his cheeks. "They killed him. We fucking let them into our lives. We trusted them. And all along, they were just planning to take him out."

No, no, that didn't make sense. "Jett…saved me."

"I don't think so. I think he was working with Patrick all along. At least, that's what the detectives are saying." He looked back toward the house. "Because the gun used to kill your father? It belonged to Patrick Zane. Jett and Maddox brought it here. They used it on Phillip." His breath came faster. "They killed him, and now they've vanished."

She couldn't feel the raindrops hitting her. "I want to see him." She stepped toward the black bag. Her dad wasn't in there. He couldn't be in there.

But Jennifer moved into her path. "Not right now. I'm sorry. But his body...evidence has to be collected. We can't allow any contamination."

Her temples were throbbing. "Jett wasn't here. He didn't do this." Sam was wrong. "He was with me." In bed...with her.

"He wasn't there when I called." Sam swiped away the water from his eyes. "When did he leave? What time?"

"I—" She had no idea.

"He snuck out, you didn't know, and he killed your father."

"Why?" It wasn't making sense. But the fear inside of her was changing. The cold ball was becoming something else, and nausea rolled through her. *Jett made love to me. He protected me.*

He...he hadn't killed her father.

Then a man in a suit approached her. A man with dark hair, slicked back from his head by the rain. A guy with an implacable expression, and cold, glittering blue eyes. He flashed some sort of badge her way. Not one of the badges that the Biloxi PD used, but something different. Something she couldn't quite recognize.

"Ms. Jacobs? I'm Special Agent Bennett McNeely, and I need to speak with you."

He was speaking with her. Savannah's teeth started to chatter. The body bag was being loaded into the back of a van.

The agent prompted, "Ms. Jacobs?"

She couldn't take her eyes off the black bag. Was her father in that bag? Cold? Dead?

"I need to know about the people who were posing as government agents," McNeely pushed her. "I need to know where they are now. Can you help me?"

"They're gone." Jett had disappeared, not leaving so much as a trace behind in her home. Jett…Jett had been lying? *No.* "I want to see the footage." She yanked her gaze away from the body bag and focused on the agent. "I want to see that security feed. I want to see everything you've got—right up until the feed ends."

"Ms.—"

"I'm not telling you a thing about Jett or the others until I see with my own eyes what happened here." She trusted Jett. He'd saved her from the worst nightmare of her life. She wouldn't just turn on him. "Show me the footage." Her voice snapped like a whip. "Show me *now*."

***

Jett and Maddox stalked into her father's study. Jett's face was tight with anger. Maddox didn't show any expression at all.

Jett charged right for her father. "You sonofabitch," Jett snarled as his hands fisted on her father's shirt. "Did you think we wouldn't come for you?"

Savannah couldn't seem to pull in a deep breath. Her chest ached as she stared at the monitor. She was in the police station. The special agent was behind her. The female cop, Jennifer, she was close by. And Sam was there, holding her hand. Looking all grim.

The special agent had said he could only show her the footage at a secure location, so now she stood in the overcrowded, too-loud police station, and Savannah felt her world falling apart around her.

Her father shoved at Jett.

Jett let him go. "This ends." He yanked a gun from the holster hidden beneath his coat. "It ends."

Oh, God.

The screen went black.

There was nothing else. There was no more.

Just her father, lying in a body bag.

Just Jett — gone.

"We investigated the Cayman accounts that were found on Patrick Zane's computer," the special agent announced. "The accounts were cleared out, and no trace of the money can be found." A pause. "We believe that the man posing as Jett Bianchi—he and his associates took the money before they vanished. It was a very carefully executed plan."

She pulled her hand from Sam. "Why?"

McNeely shrugged. "They were working with Patrick. Maybe he was working for them, we haven't figured that part out yet. But your father didn't play by their rules. And it cost him his life."

No, no. She rubbed her temples. "Jett was protecting me. He was—"

McNeely tossed a manila folder onto the table in front of her. "This is the paperwork for the *real* Jett Bianchi. Even his death certificate."

With shaking fingers, she reached for the file. Read everything in some kind of blur. Saw all of the official looking signatures. The death certificate. The coroner's notes…

"He was given the Medal of Honor for his sacrifice." McNeely's voice held no emotion. "From all accounts, the real Bianchi was one hell of a guy."

Navy SEAL Jett Bianchi killed in action. The words blurred more before her, and Savannah had to blink a few times so that she could read the notes. *Saved the lives of six men…*

"I want to see his picture." There was no picture of Jett Bianchi in the file. "Show me his picture."

Sighing, the agent opened his brief case. Then he slid a black and white photo toward her. A photo of a man lying on what appeared to be a coroner's table.

A dead man.

Bullet holes were in his chest.

And his face... *"That's Jett."* Not someone who looked like Jett. That. Was. Jett. Same nose. Same chin. Same cheekbones. Even the same faint scar along his upper right cheek. "No." This wasn't possible. Nothing made sense. Her entire world had gone crazy.

"We think the man we are after may have gotten some cosmetic surgery to make himself better resemble the real Jett Bianchi."

What? That was insane. "Why—"

"We're not talking about some amateurs here, Ms. Jacobs. We're talking about a team that orchestrated a kidnapping and murder ring in Biloxi that brought in millions of dollars. My intel says this group may have been operating similar rings in different parts of the world." He waited for her gaze to rise to his face, then added, "My job is to stop them. By any means necessary."

The panting sound of her breath filled the small room. Jennifer stepped closer to Savannah, frowning. "Are you all right?"

No, she wasn't all right. She'd had sex with Jett. She'd trusted him.

Jett. That isn't even his real name.

She'd trusted him. He'd betrayed her. Just like Patrick.

Fool me once…shame on you.

Fool me twice…

Her whole body shuddered.

Jett hadn't just fooled her. If the special agent was right, Jett had killed her father.

The first tear slid down her cheek and hit the table.

PART TWO

"Things aren't always as they appear...
sometimes, they are one hell of a lot worse."

—Jett Bianchi

CHAPTER TEN

Three months later...

He was going to have to beg.

He'd have to grovel.

He'd have to do *anything* she wanted, if it convinced Savannah to let him back in her life.

Jett slowly walked down the beach. The tourist season had come and gone in Biloxi. Three months had passed since he'd last seen Savannah. Three of the longest months of his life. He'd thought about her every single day. Fantasized about her.

He'd gone from one hell-hole assignment to another. Then he'd had his whole fucking world ripped apart when he'd learned that he'd been betrayed by those in power at Lazarus.

Three months. So damn much could change in that time.

But one thing *hadn't* changed. He still wanted Savannah. And this time, he wouldn't be walking away.

His shoes sank into the white, sandy beach. The waves roared as they hit the shore, sending foam sliding onto the beach. The sun was getting ready to set. It was a ball of red that would soon dip beneath those rushing waves.

A few more steps...and he saw her.

Her arms were wrapped around her stomach as she stood at the edge of the beach. The waves were rushing up to wet her toes. Her gaze was directed straight ahead. Straight on the churning Gulf.

For a moment, Jett absolutely couldn't move. Most things in this world didn't scare him, but having to go to Savannah, having to tell her the truth about him and about what he'd done...hell, yes, he was terrified.

He didn't want her to hate him.

Hate was the last thing he wanted from Savannah Jacobs.

Slowly, he advanced on her. One foot. Another.

And then her head turned, as if she'd heard him over the roar of the waves. Her eyes locked on him. The wind caught her hair, blowing it away from her face. And her expression—he saw her shock.

She hadn't expected him to come back. Because he'd been a fucking asshole who left her in the middle of the night.

An asshole who left right before her world went spiraling.

He swallowed. Clenched his hands into fists because his fingers were shaking. *Don't fuck this up. Don't fuck this up.* That had been his mantra the whole time he'd traveled desperately across the US in order to get back to her. *Don't fuck this up.*

He took a step toward her.

Don't —

The shock vanished from her expression. And something else — fear — took its place. She stared at him with absolute terror plain to see on her face. Then she turned and ran.

What in the hell? "Savannah!"

She ran faster. The sand kicked up behind her as she took off running down the beach, going *away* from her cottage. Seeming to run blindly. Because she was that afraid.

That terrified — of him.

No one else was on the beach. Just the two of them. So he let some of his powers out. He used his enhanced speed to overtake her. To come up in front of her, to catch her arms and stop her —

She screamed. High-pitched. Desperate.

He let her go. "Baby, you don't need to be afraid of me."

But she lurched back. Put at least five feet between them, and spun to run again.

Once more, he used his enhanced speed to catch her. To stop her. But this time, he didn't put his hands on her. He just used his body to block her from fleeing.

"How are you doing this?" Savannah yelled. "How are you moving so fast?"

How? Lazarus. But they'd get to all of that, soon enough.

She wasn't running. Not right then. Her breath heaved in and out of her chest. The billowing shirt she wore blew in the breeze, and her jeans hugged her legs. No shoes. Her cute, red toenails were dotted with sand.

His gaze traveled from her toes all the way back up to her gorgeous face. And the fear was still there. She was staring at him in absolute, horrified fear.

Why? *Oh, right. I just did an insane super speed maneuver on her.* Of course, that would make anyone freak out. He should reassure her. Say something soothing. Jett opened his mouth. "I've missed you." The words burst out. All desperate sounding. Only fair, he was desperate.

She shook her head. And her gaze jerked to the left, to the right, as if she was looking for someone else.

But no one was there.

"I know you're angry," Jett began carefully. He'd rehearsed a speech in his mind during the long trip down to Biloxi. Rehearsed it a thousand times. But suddenly, he couldn't remember a single word of his speech.

Shit. Shit.

The last three months had passed in a blur. He'd left her, been sent immediately on another mission—this one out of the country. Then another, and another...The missions had merged together until everything had exploded. Literally, Project Lazarus had gone down in flames. He'd been trapped in a cell, wanting only to escape and get back to Savannah. When the fire had finally died away—

All of Lazarus's dirty little secrets had come spilling out.

He needed to tell her about that time. About Lazarus. But, shit, he also needed to touch her. To hold her.

He advanced toward her, reaching out his hand.

She knocked it away. "Get back! Don't touch me!" That loathing, that horror—it was real.

And Jett realized she might already know about Lazarus. She might know all about the secrets he'd tried to keep before. He swallowed. "Savannah..."

"You belong in a cell. You should be locked up!"

Hell. She *did* know about Lazarus. She thought he was little more than a rabid animal. "I won't hurt you." He would never hurt you. He would—

"You've hurt me plenty." Tears glittered in her eyes. "But you will never do it again." Once more, her gaze jerked along the beach, as if she was looking for someone.

His shoulders stiffened. "Savannah…"

"How could you do it?" She circled around him.

He moved, keeping her within touching distance. But he didn't touch. She'd told him not to touch. "I had to leave." Did she think he'd *wanted* to walk away from her? She was the only thing in this world he did want. And he had to talk, had to explain—

"You killed him."

He'd killed a lot of people. That was what he was, after all. A killing machine. The perfect weapon. *No, not anymore.* Lazarus was done. Falling apart. Ashes. And he was starting over. Trying to start over, anyway. But there were things he had to—

"I saw the security footage."

He flinched.

She saw the move and sucked in a sharp breath. Her hand rose to her mouth. "I think I'm going to be sick."

Shit, shit, shit. "I should have called you."

Her eyes turned to the size of saucers. Behind her hand, she gasped out, "Called? After what you *did*?"

"I was ordered back in. The area was secure. According to the handler, the mission was done. You were safe."

She dropped her hand. She'd gone too pale, and he didn't like that. Savannah swallowed twice, and then voice low and ice cold, she snarled, "Safe? Is that what you'd call it?"

Tension settled between his shoulders. The fears he'd had were right. Danger was around her. She must have sensed it, too. Jett lifted his chin. "I'm here now. I won't let anything happen to you."

And then he heard the sirens. Blasting in the distance.

Her breath eased out. Her shoulders sagged.

His head turned. Those sirens couldn't be coming toward them...*could they?*

Why the hell would they be coming?

She lifted her right hand, and he saw that she was clutching her phone. "I texted Agent McNeely. We had a signal. If I ever saw you again, all I had to do was send him a text with the letter X. He'd track my phone, find me, and *get* you."

Jett blinked. Then he held up his hand. "First, who the hell is Agent McNeely?"

"You sonofabitch." Her lower lip trembled. "After what you did to me, you think you can come back like this? Did you really think you wouldn't pay for your crime?"

Those sirens were getting louder.

"You killed him," Savannah whispered. "And I hope they throw you in a cell and *never* let you out."

Okay. Multiple things were becoming absolutely, horribly clear. One, she wasn't happy to see him. Obviously. But he'd expected some anger. Some rage. He hadn't expected the hate and fear. And next...well, she thought he'd killed someone in particular, someone who seemed to matter to her.

He'd read the newspaper accounts. He'd been fucking obsessed with her over the last few months, so, of *course,* he'd wanted to check up on her. And he knew that her father had died. The guy had been killed by a thief right after —

"You killed my dad. And I hope you rot in jail."

The sirens were way too loud now. That meant the cops were far too close.

He reached out and locked his fingers around Savannah's wrist.

"Let me go!"

"I didn't kill your father, sweetheart. If that's what you think, there's some mistake here." He tried to keep his voice devoid of emotion. "The guy was alive and well when I left town."

A tear leaked down her cheek.

"And I don't know who this Agent McNeely is, but I read in the newspaper — I read that your father was killed by a burglar who broke into his house. That's why your cousin Sam is launching that whole tough-on-crime initiative." Because Sam had taken her father's senate seat.

"Bullshit story. That was just a cover so that you wouldn't know what was happening." Her breath heaved out. "McNeely set it up. He set up *everything*. And he said you'd be back. We just had to wait."

Of course, I'm back. Like I could stay away from you. It was impossible to stay away from the woman who haunted his dreams.

"I waited." She swallowed. "Get your hand off me."

His hold tightened on her. "I didn't kill your father. I wouldn't. But don't think I wasn't fucking tempted."

She gave a quick gasp.

Fuck me. Wrong thing to say.

"I wouldn't hurt him because hurting him would hurt *you*." There. That was true. "And I came back because I know you're in danger. I'm here to protect you."

When he'd learned of her father's death — shit, it had been long after the guy had been buried. Jett had still wanted to immediately run to Savannah, but he'd stayed away. *Because I didn't want to bring danger to her.*

Too late, he'd learned the danger had always been there.

Surprisingly, she stepped closer to him. So close that their bodies brushed. She tipped back her head, and then Savannah whispered, "Liar, Liar."

"Savannah…"

"You used me. You were behind the kidnapping. McNeely gave me all the details. His team uncovered so much."

The McNeely joker was going to be a problem.

"Patrick was a hitman. An assassin. He sold his services to the highest bidder."

Do what?

"The women he took? He'd been paid to kill them. But Patrick decided to double his earnings by pretending that he'd give his victims back to their families. He didn't, of course. But he kept both the ransom money *and* the money he'd earned for the contract kills."

"That's…" Okay, he didn't know what to say.

"You didn't save me. You're the whole reason I was taken."

"No—"

"You were working with Patrick. All along. McNeely *told* me."

He was going to kick that guy's lying ass.

"You wormed your way into my life. My father's life. You destroyed us both." She smiled at him. "It's your turn to be destroyed."

Okay, this was going *way* differently than it had in his mental rehearsals. "You're wrong. There were things I was keeping from you, things I couldn't tell you back then—"

The sirens screamed.

The cops would be there any moment. He couldn't let them arrest him. What in the hell would happen if they ran a fingerprint check on him? *Hello, dead man standing in front of you.* Because of his military history, his records would be in the system.

Of course, there was also the added problem of this Agent Dickface guy—someone who was going to be a serious problem. *I think I'll have to kill him.*

But one thing at a time. First, hell, first he had to leave her—again. "I'm going to tell you everything this time."

"You're going to—"

"I'm not going to rot in jail." He smiled at her. She would probably hate that he thought she was sexy when she was angry. So he didn't mention that. He did say, "Baby, there's no cell that can ever hold me." Not one outside of Lazarus. Normal humans just didn't have the tech savvy to keep him caged. The cops in Biloxi

would not know what they were dealing with—
not when he started breaking the cell bars with
his bare hands. "I'm going to leave now, but I'll
find you again. And the next time I see you,
we're talking about *everything*."

She shook her head.

"I'm going to explain who I am."

A bitter laugh. "That would be helpful
because I know you're not Jett Bianchi. He died a
while back." Her lips pressed together. Then… "I
saw his grave. I took *flowers* to his grave."

Aw, man, that was…thoughtful. Kind. And it
made him feel like extra shit. "Thank you."

"What?"

The sirens were too close. "Don't trust
anyone. You understand? You're being fed lies.
And you are in serious danger." God, he had to
do it—

Jett kissed her.

She kneed him in the groin.

He let her go, and Savannah stumbled back.
More sand went flying as she turned and ran
toward her home—and toward the approaching
police cars.

He started to follow her—

The damn cops. No, if he followed her, he'd
fight with the cops. He'd wind up hurting the
cops. And if Savannah saw him hurting the folks
in blue, she wouldn't exactly feel like he was the
hero of the story.

Instead of chasing her, he turned and headed toward the motorcycle that waited on the main road. He'd stashed the bike close by when he'd first sought her out. He rushed toward it, moving fast, so fast. But he glanced back because he had to see her.

His Savannah. The woman who'd gotten into a killer's heart.

She'd turned back, too. Stopped running. For a moment, they just stared at each other.

Then, testing, he sent a message to her...*I will be back for you.*

She stared straight at him. And he heard her voice in his head.

You come near me again, and I'll kill you.

Well, if that was the case, it was probably a very good thing that he could rise from the dead.

CHAPTER ELEVEN

"He got away." Jennifer Adams stood just inside of Savannah's home, shifting nervously from foot to foot. Her holster rested near her hip. "We found motorcycle tracks near the beach, and we've got an APB out with the guy's description. Don't worry, we are going to catch him."

Savannah wrapped her fingers around the mug she held. "He's pretty hard to catch. Isn't that the whole reason for this set-up?" The set-up. Her, playing her magic X texting game with Agent McNeely. Cops regularly patrolled on her street, keeping an eye out for the man using Jett's name. They were always watching, always hunting. Always being vigilant.

And then their prey had just casually walked down the beach.

I've missed you.

She turned away from Jennifer and hurried back into the kitchen. She put the mug on the counter-top.

"A team is going to stay outside," Jennifer assured her. "Eyes will be on your home all night long."

Jennifer wasn't offering to move her to a safe house. Keeping her hidden wasn't the objective. No, Agent McNeely and the cops wanted to use her as bait. All along, McNeely had thought Jett would come back for her.

She still didn't quite understand *why* Agent McNeely had been so certain of that fact. But, well, he'd been right.

Meanwhile, Savannah had been wrong, about so many things.

"If he makes a move on the house, we've got him."

Savannah turned toward Jennifer. The two women had become friends over the last few months. When she'd buried her father, Jennifer had been there. Tall, curved, with beautiful ebony skin, Jennifer was one fierce cop. She'd told Savannah stories about taking down men twice her size. Jennifer always told those stories with a certain amount of relish.

But…

I don't think she can take down Jett. And the last thing she wanted was for Jennifer to get hurt. She didn't want anyone hurt.

"Do you have the gun I gave you?" Jennifer demanded when the silence stretched a little too long.

"Yes." But she didn't like it. Every time that Savannah looked at the gun, she saw her father.

Or rather, her father's head. The same way she'd seen him when she'd finally been taken to view the body. Now she knew exactly why the cops had called it a professional hit.

Bam. One to the head.

Nausea rose within her. She grabbed for her crackers. Crackers and chocolate milk. The dinner of champions.

"We went to the shooting range. You learned how to use that gun. You're a good shot." Jennifer's voice turned harder as she added, "But the gun won't do you any good if you don't take it out of the drawer when you're threatened."

Savannah forced herself to choke down a cracker. "I don't think I can shoot him."

Jennifer patted her hand. "It shouldn't come to that. Like I said, cops are going to be watching. *I'll* be on the first shift with my partner. If anything goes so much as *bump* in here, I'll be at your door."

Savannah knew she was supposed to smile or nod or do something.

"But you have to be ready to protect yourself." Jennifer's face showed her concern. "Just in case. Always remember that your life is more important than anything else, and a woman should never be afraid to fight for herself. You matter. You fight, got it?"

God, she loved Jennifer. "Thanks. And, yes, I got it."

"Good." Her radio crackled. "I have to get back downstairs, but if you need me, I'm right outside. The bastard is in town. We've got every cop in the area searching for him. He will not be escaping again." Jennifer gave a very hard nod. "I'll make him pay for what he did to you and your family."

Jennifer had lost her father, too. Years ago, in a robbery gone wrong. Her father had run a restaurant on the water. He'd been the only one closing up one night when two teenage boys came in, demanding money. He'd given them everything he had, but one of the boys had still fired his gun before running out.

Jennifer's father had died on the way to the hospital.

Jennifer had finished her last year at Tulane before she'd come home. And entered the police academy.

Jennifer gave her a hug, and Savannah walked her out. She triple-checked her locks. Made sure her alarm was set. And then Savannah turned to face the house that felt far too empty. Empty and cold. Rubbing her arms, she headed for her bedroom. When Jett had first left, she'd felt him in the bedroom. Smelled him. He'd seemed to surround her. And she'd nearly broken apart.

She *had* gotten rid of that bed. Gotten new sheets and covers, too. She'd wanted no memories of him.

She pushed open her bedroom door. Darkness waited inside, the only illumination coming from the moonlight that spilled in through her glass balcony doors. The doors were shut, locked, but the curtains didn't cover them, and the faint glow from the moon drifted into her bedroom. A slow sigh escaped Savannah as she stepped into the room. Her gaze slid around her. Everything was just as she'd left it. Everything—

A hand closed around her mouth. She was grabbed from behind, pulled up against a hard, muscled body. Fear built, surging through her, and Savannah reacted instinctively. Her elbow drove back into her attacker's stomach. Her right foot slammed down on his.

Not again. Not again. She couldn't be taken by someone again. Couldn't become someone's prisoner.

Her hand flew up as she went to grab her assailant's pinky. She'd snap it. That was what her women's self-defense coach had taught her—

"I'm not going to hurt you," Jett's voice whispered in her ear.

Like she was going to believe his lies again? Damn him, *damn him.*

But…he let her go.

She spun to face him. He stood there, the shadows seeming to somehow be extra thick around him. Had he been in her home the whole time that the cops had been searching the beach for him? Had he been in her bedroom while Jennifer had just been steps away?

Jett held up his hands. "I came here to talk with you. You're in danger. Serious danger."

Was there any other kind? "I'm looking at the danger." She took three quick steps away from him. He was between her and the bedroom door. But if she ran out onto her balcony —

"I came to protect you. Not to hurt you. Hurting you has never been part of my agenda."

Bull. "You killed my father. You —"

"I didn't."

"You were working with Patrick all along!"

A furrow appeared between his brows. "Hell, no. I saved you from him!"

"Agent McNeely said —"

His hands dropped. "I don't know who this Agent Asshole is, but he's feeding you lies." A rough exhale. "Probably because he's either in bed with Project Lazarus or he's working for someone who wants the secrets that the group holds. Either way, he can't be trusted."

Savannah risked another step away from him. Lazarus. Hadn't he once said that was the name of his team?

"I need to tell you some things about myself." He exhaled again on a long sigh. Seemed to gather his thoughts. "It's going to sound crazy, but there are things you *have* to know —"

"Like your name?" Savannah cut in.

He blinked. "You know my name."

Okay, it took all of her strength not to launch herself at him. *You can't do that. You have other priorities. Like escaping.* "Thought we covered this already. The real Jett Bianchi is dead. Agent McNeely told me that. He showed me the death certificate. Showed me photos…" She swallowed. "And, yeah, like I said before, I visited his grave. I put flowers there. I don't know who you are. I don't know why you stole his identity, but you belong in jail."

And it *hurt*. So much pain. Because she'd wanted him to be different. She'd needed him to be different. He'd seemed like a hero before.

Not the villain.

"I am Jett." His hands flexed at his sides. "And, yes, Jett Bianchi *is* dead."

Oh, sweet baby Jesus. He was insane. Something she hadn't factored into the equation. Her hand rose to press over her stomach.

"I was involved in a secret government testing unit called Project Lazarus. Certain individuals — most with military backgrounds — were brought into the program because Uncle

Sam wanted to create perfect weapons. When we died, we were given the Lazarus formula."

He was talking *crazy.* And she knew crazy. After all, she'd once spent months locked in a mental ward.

"The formula brought us back from death."

She laughed. A high-pitched, desperate sound. *How can I attract the attention of the cops?* Her phone was in the kitchen. Dammit.

"It's not a joke, baby. Not even a bad one. It's the truth. It's my life." Once more, his fingers flexed. "I was shot on my final mission with my SEAL team, and when I woke up, I was in a lab. Other Lazarus subjects were there, too—Maddox and Luna."

Like she could forget those two.

"I've been with them since the beginning."

She bumped into her nightstand. Could she use the lamp as a weapon?

No, not the lamp. The gun Jennifer had given her was in the nightstand drawer. The gun she hadn't wanted to use. But this was her life. *More than just my life.* And she had to do anything to protect what mattered most. Her hands slid behind her back as she positioned her body in front of the drawer. She didn't want him to notice what she was doing.

"I'm not like a normal man. That's how I can communicate psychically with you. I wasn't in a car accident. Wasn't born with any sort of special powers. When I was pulled into the Lazarus group, they injected me with a serum that changed me. I can communicate psychically with all of the members of my team. And with you."

The gun wasn't loaded. He wouldn't know that. The bullets were in the drawer, though. Should she try to load the weapon? Or just bluff her way through and hope she scared him away with an empty gun?

"I have other powers."

Her racing heartbeat seemed to shake her chest.

"I'm faster than a normal man. That's how I kept getting in front of you on the beach."

She bit her lower lip.

"I'm stronger. Far stronger. My reflexes are faster. And there are other…bonuses."

"Like what?" Her fingers fumbled with the drawer. She was trying to distract him so that he wouldn't see —

Shadows swept around him. One minute, he was in front of her bedroom door, and the next, he'd just seemed to vanish. Her gaze slid to the left, to the right, but he wasn't there. She grabbed the gun and rushed forward. This was her chance to get away.

His hands closed around her shoulders, stopping her.

The shadows vanished. The moonlight returned in full force.

"Powers like that," he whispered. "I can bend darkness. Use it for concealment. I'm also an amplifier, but that power works best with other Lazarus members. I can make their powers stronger. I can—"

He looked down.

She'd pressed the gun to his chest. "Let me go."

His hands immediately fell away from her.

"I'm not going to listen to your lies."

"Don't listen. Watch. Because I don't think you saw it all before." And the shadows deepened around him. She was staring straight at him, but the shadows just *appeared.* Darkness covered him, and he vanished again. Her head whipped to the right and the left. He wasn't there. She only saw the dark. The moonlight had dimmed. There was nothing. No sign of him.

"I'll take that." His breath blew over her cheek. His hands reached around her and, in a lightning fast move, he took the gun from her hand. He'd somehow gotten behind her, moved without making a sound.

Now she spun toward him.

The light had returned.

He smiled at her. "It's not loaded, but you can bluff like a pro. I'll remember that."

"Just because you can do some parlor tricks, it doesn't mean you aren't a killer!"

He tucked the gun into the waistband of his jeans. "I am a killer. I killed as a SEAL, and I've killed while working for Project Lazarus. But I didn't kill your father. I swear it to you. And I wasn't working with Patrick Zane. I was sent to help you. That was why I appeared in the house when you were tied to the chair. I was supposed to get you out. I was supposed to stay with you." His lips tightened. "Though I didn't find out the full truth about *why* until recently."

She could only shake her head.

"Lazarus is real. The things the government did to us — everything is real. They brought men and women back from the dead. They kept us isolated, kept us at their hidden bases to be monitored. Then they used us. Mission after mission, they used us." He rolled back his shoulders. "And they lied to us."

There was a crash from her den. It sounded as if her front door had been smashed in. Eyes widening, she whirled. This was her chance. She lunged for the bedroom door —

Jett locked an arm around her waist. "You're in danger," Jett gritted as he jerked her behind him. "You don't understand the threat. Don't understand how valuable you may be to them — "

"Let her go!" A man's voice blasted. The overhead light in her bedroom flashed on.

She glanced around Jett's body. Agent McNeely was there. She hadn't even realized he was back in the city. When she'd texted earlier, Savannah had figured McNeely had just contacted the local authorities.

McNeely had his gun up, aimed at Jett, and he—

Fired. Once, twice. The bullets slammed into Jett's body as Savannah screamed.

Then Jett was falling. His body hit hers, and they both tumbled to the floor.

"He had a gun!" McNeely yelled.

Cops were rushing in behind the agent.

"I had to take the shots," McNeely added, voice gruff.

But she wasn't looking at him. Jett was on the floor, she was on the floor, and there was so much blood. She put her hands on his chest, trying to stop all of that terrible blood flow. "Jett?"

His head turned. He stared at her with pain-filled eyes.

"Jett?" She could feel tears on her cheeks. For a moment, she forgot everything else. She remembered the lover she'd known. The man who'd held her tenderly. The man who'd come to her in the darkness and saved her when she'd been terrified.

Don't worry, baby. I'll come back.

His words drifted though her mind. She could have sworn that he even tried to smile at her. Smile…right before his eyes changed.

Right before the life left his dark gaze.

Then hard hands were yanking her back. She was being pushed aside as the cops closed in, surrounding Jett.

"Someone get an EMT!" Jennifer yelled.

An EMT wasn't going to do any good. Savannah stumbled back. She looked at the blood on her hands. Jett's blood. Nausea spun through her. Dizziness had her swaying.

He was dead. She'd *seen* him die. This wasn't what she wanted. Jett shouldn't have died. No, no, *no.*

Tears were tumbling down her cheeks. Her body was shaking.

"You need to leave." Jennifer was in front of her. Concern clear on her face. "Come on." Jennifer took her arm, pulling her from the bedroom. But Savannah didn't want to leave. She wanted to stay right there.

I'll come back.

"It was my gun," Savannah whispered. "It wasn't even loaded." And it had been tucked in his waistband. Jett hadn't even been pointing it at— "How did the special agent even get here? I thought he was in New Orleans."

"I don't know." Jennifer's voice was low as she steered Savannah outside and onto the balcony. "Take some breaths. Some deep breaths. You look like you're about to faint."

Jett. Dead. Her arms wrapped around her stomach as she rocked back and forth. This couldn't be happening. Could not be. She *hurt.*

"The special agent just roared onto the scene," Jennifer's voice was for her ears alone. "Raced past me and my partner and into your house before we could stop him. I don't know how the guy even knew that Jett was inside."

He shouldn't have known that Jett was inside.

She tried to think past the pain and the rage and…

Is Jett a monster? Is everything true? Everything that McNeely said?

McNeely…the man who'd shot Jett without hesitating. She glanced back toward the bedroom.

"Get the body loaded. Right the fuck now!" McNeely stood over Jett's form, glowering. "Move it, move it!"

Wait, that wasn't normal. You didn't move a body that fast. She knew…because of her own father's crime scene. She grabbed Jennifer. "What is happening?"

Jennifer had turned to stare suspiciously at the scene, too. The cops had been pushed back. Men and women in dark suits had taken over. Someone was even already loading Jett into a body bag.

Savannah lunged forward as she rushed from the balcony and back into her bedroom. "Stop it!"

McNeely turned toward her. "This is a crime scene." He motioned to a blond-haired agent with glasses. "Agent Lane, take her downstairs and secure her in your SUV."

What?

Jennifer stepped to Savannah's side. "It *is* a damn crime scene, and that is why procedures have to be followed. You don't move the body. Not until the techs get here. We need to photograph everything. Mark evidence. We need to—"

McNeely stalked toward Jennifer and Savannah. "You need to stand down, Officer Adams. This isn't your case any longer." His gaze darted to Savannah. "You'll be coming with us. We have questions that need answering."

Again, dizziness rose within her. Her hand went to her stomach, and McNeely followed the movement. She was pretty sure he tensed.

This is wrong. Everything was wrong. Jett had been shot. *Shot.* Her fingers were shaking, her knees felt funny, and—

"She's going to faint," Jennifer said.

No, she wasn't. *Maybe.*

"*I'm* taking her to get checked by the EMTs, right the hell now." Jennifer glared at McNeely. "Because she's my friend, and you can fuck off."

Then they were brushing past the agents. The body bag was being carried away by a few men. *Carried away?* This was all so wrong. They were just lugging the bag like it was filled with dirty laundry. A sharp cry rose to her lips.

"Yeah, something is very wrong here." Jennifer had a fierce grip on her. "I'm calling the chief. Not my case? The hell it isn't." Then they were outside.

Only...Agent Lane was there, too.

He was following them.

Jennifer motioned to an EMT. He hurried toward Savannah.

"I'm fine." *Lie, lie, lie.*

Her gaze darted to the black bag. It had been tossed into the back of a white van. That van...

"*Jett.*" Savannah whispered his name and *hurt.*

The van practically raced from the scene. The tires shrieked as they hit the road. The engine was growling.

"What in the ever-loving name of God..." Jennifer began.

Savannah couldn't take her gaze off the van. It was hurtling down the road.

"Driving like they stole something," Jennifer snapped. "Doesn't make a bit of sense. That's not even the coroner's van. It doesn't — "

The van flew off the road.

Savannah screamed.

The accident happened so fast. One moment, the van was hurtling away. Insanity. The next — it was rolling, tumbling over and over before it slammed into a power pole.

Jennifer ran toward the scene. Agent Lane rushed ahead of her, pulling out his phone and barking orders.

Savannah didn't move. A dull ringing filled her ears. Jett had told her about a group called Lazarus. He'd told her that he was a dead man who'd come back from the grave. He'd vanished and reappeared right before her eyes.

What if it's all true?

If it was true, if everything he'd said was true…

I'll come back.

His final message replayed in her mind.

He'd been telling her that she was in danger. Now Agent McNeely wanted to take her away.

This was all…*wrong.*

She turned from the sight of the wreck, swiping away the tears on her cheeks. There was one thing she had to do. One person she had to protect. The one who needed her the most. She marched toward her parked car. Her keys were upstairs, but, back in her teenage days, she'd picked up a few tips from her friends at the psychiatric hospital. One friend in particular — a girl who'd been a bit of klepto — had spent hours telling Savannah how to hot-wire cars. Maybe Savannah had practiced what she'd been taught…a time or twenty.

She was almost at her car when…

His arms wrapped around her. "Please, don't scream."

Jett's voice. Jett's hand over her mouth. Jett's other arm cradled protectively over her stomach. The man she'd seen die was holding her.

The dizziness got worse.

And so did…so did the darkness that seemed to surround them.

"I swear, I'm not the bad guy. I'm here to help you."

The shadows were so thick. Like a fog around her.

Agent McNeely ran right by them. Seemed to glance right *through* them.

"I can get us both out of here without being seen." Jett's breath blew over her cheek. He was speaking in a low, rasping whisper. "But if you scream, they'll hear it. So I can keep my hand over your mouth…"

She could fight him. Absolutely could. Only she didn't.

I saw him die. And now he's making us invisible. That was exactly what he was doing.

All of his stories hadn't been lies. And if they hadn't been…maybe, just maybe…

What about my father?

"Option two is that I can move my hand. I can trust you. And that's what I'm going to do, baby." His hand slid away from her mouth. "You scream, and they will come running. I can use the shadows to hide us from their sight, but I can't control sound."

She tried to breathe. It was hard to suck in air.

"The choice is yours, but I hope you don't scream. I hope you don't, baby. Now that you know what I can do, now that you've seen for yourself that Lazarus is no lie, give me a chance to explain everything."

He was using a psychic power to camouflage them. If she hadn't seen it with her own eyes, Savannah wouldn't have believed it was possible. But agent after agent, cop after cop — they were all just running right by them.

"I swear, I didn't kill your father. I told the asshole what I thought of him before I left. I threatened him, but he was still breathing when I exited the mansion. I promise, he was."

She turned toward him. The shadows were thick around them. But she could see him. See his face. His glinting eyes.

"You are in danger. And you're in danger because of me. Because I wanted you too much and because others know about my need." A muscle flexed in his jaw. "We have to leave this scene. Let me get you someplace safe, and I'll explain everything to you." And he pushed a gun into her hand. "It's loaded. You keep it. I stole it from one of the idiots in the van when I shoved out of the body bag."

Hold it together, Savannah.

"If you feel threatened, you shoot me."

But he came back from the dead.

He lifted the gun. Pointed it right at his head. "A shot to the brain will keep me permanently dead. Just consider me your own personal zombie."

She yanked the gun away from his head. "I will absolutely *not*." Her voice was just as low as his. Barely a breath.

"Keep the gun. It will make you feel safer. It will show you that you *can* trust me."

The gun was heavy in her hand.

"We have to get out of here. If I can keep touching you, then my shadows will cover you. We stay close, and we get out of here."

Jennifer had just run toward Savannah's car. The cop glanced around, frantic, then she shouted, "Savannah! Where are you?"

Jett tensed. Savannah knew he thought she'd shout back at her friend. But...

She didn't.

His breath released on a long exhale. *Let's go. It's not safe here.*

His words in her mind were like a familiar touch. And they...they warmed her, as crazy as that sounded.

I can carry you and we can cover one hell of a lot of ground, faster.

She squared her shoulders. *Carry me.*

He scooped her into his arms. Held her carefully. And she kept the gun clutched in her hand. He moved so fast, impossibly, crazily, stomach-churningly fast. She actually felt the wind whipping around them. The dizziness returned. She squeezed her eyes shut because everything was spinning and then—

He stopped. She cracked open her eyes. The fog around them vanished.

They were far from her home. She didn't even recognize the street, but a motorcycle was right beside them. He handed her a helmet, and then he climbed on.

"Just take the damn gun, okay? Put it somewhere safe." She wasn't holding the thing while they were riding on a motorcycle!

He took the gun. Tucked it in the saddlebags on the motorcycle. She climbed on behind him.

"Hold on tight," Jett told her.

Was there any other way to hold on?

She wrapped her arms around him and wondered if he understood. If he fully got just what she was doing…

She was choosing him, despite everything. And Savannah prayed that she was making the right choice.

***

"Savannah Jacobs is *gone*," Jennifer Adams said, her hands on her hips and her tight expression giving away her fear. "She was here one moment and gone the next. Her car is still here. Her purse. Her keys. But she's vanished."

And that just pissed off Bennett McNeely. "I've got a near army of special agents and cops here…and you all lose the woman? The one woman we need?"

They didn't speak. Most didn't even meet his stare.

Jennifer did, though. She glared at him. "You were holding back intel. Keeping the Biloxi PD in the dark."

Yeah, he had held back. He was still holding back. "You don't have the clearance for this case." None of those cops did. That's why he was only giving them the barest of details. And why he was fucking making up the rest.

The van was burning in the distance. That tricky sonofabitch Jett. He'd come back to life far faster than Bennett had anticipated. Next time, they'd restrain the bastard after they killed him.

"I want to start a search for her," Jennifer declared. "We need to take her picture to the media, we need to alert all family and friends—"

"She won't go to any family. And from what I've been told, *you* have become her closest friend." Something he would definitely be using to his advantage. "But, no, we are sure as hell *not* going to the media. This case is top secret. My team will handle it from here on out. The Biloxi PD needs to step off our turf."

There were more glares from the local cops. What did he care? They were in his way now. And he couldn't very well let them see the things that were going to happen with Jett Bianchi.

But Jennifer didn't back down. In fact, she stepped toward him. Her voice lowered and she snapped, "He was dead."

Bennett gave her a patronizing smile. He'd perfected that smile over the years. The one that told junior agents and local officers they had no freaking clue. Unfortunately, they often *did* have a clue—that was why he needed the smile. If you made people *think* they were wrong, most of them would actually start believing your lies. "Of course, he wasn't dead. Dead men don't run away. The guy was injured. The fellows on the scene missed his pulse."

"Missed it? You mean because you were hauling ass and breaking every crime scene protocol there is?"

His eyes narrowed. Everyone was listening. They'd all gone quiet. He straightened his shoulders. "Don't you have tickets to write, *officer*?"

She just laughed. "No, I don't have tickets to write. For your information, I got bumped to detective yesterday. What I *do* have is a friend who is missing. I will be finding her, and I don't give a shit about what kind of rank you want to pull."

With that, Jennifer turned on her heel and marched away.

He nodded to Agent Lane. The guy immediately stepped after her. Lane knew what he wanted.

Follow her. Keep the cop in sight.

Because Jennifer might find Savannah before they did. *Might.* But not likely. Not with the ace up his sleeve that Bennett possessed.

He hurried away from the others. Pulled out his phone. The call was answered on the second ring.

"Did you get him?"

"No," Bennett said. "But he got *her.*"

CHAPTER TWELVE

He drove them to a condo building, one of those new, high-rises that was being built right near the Gulf of Mexico. But this place—it wasn't scheduled to open until the spring. There were "No Trespassing" signs posted everywhere.

Jett still trespassed. He revved his motorcycle right into the parking garage. A garage that *should* have been totally closed and locked down. But when he approached, Jett just leaned near a control panel. He typed in a quick code, and the gate lifted.

He drove them up three levels, and he braked the bike next to an elevator. The engine still vibrated, and her legs felt a little tingly. She was also still holding on to him for dear life.

He killed the engine. Glanced back at her. "You're safe."

She didn't feel safe. "How did you know the code?"

His lips thinned. "Let's go inside. We can talk there." He shoved down the kickstand.

She scrambled off the bike. Shoved the helmet at him.

He took it. Stared at it a moment. Then glanced up at her. "You want the gun?"

"I don't like guns, okay? Considering that the image I get any time someone says *gun* to me is the image of my father's bloody head." The words flew out of her mouth. "I'm not planning to shoot *you* in the head. So, I don't think a gun is going to help me much."

He put down the helmet. Took out the gun. "If your life was on the line, I'd want you to shoot. Shoot whoever the fuck is threatening you." And his gaze slid down her body.

Lingered on her stomach.

Oh, no. Oh, *hell,* no. "You are such a liar."

She whirled away from him. But really, where was she going?

He moved with her and pressed the button for the elevator.

"The building isn't even supposed to be open," she huffed. "How is this happening? How'd you get access?"

"Some ex-Lazarus friends of mine know how important you are. We secured this place to help protect you." A pause. "This is just a temporary safe house. A resting point until you can be convinced that you need to leave town with me."

He thought she'd rush away with him? Ha!

The elevator doors opened. She hurried inside. He came at a much slower, stalker-like pace. He pushed a button for the top floor. And the elevator doors slid closed without a sound.

"Leave town?" she managed to ask. "And go where?"

He hesitated.

Crap.

"We may need to leave the country. Depends on just who is after you and how much of Lazarus is left."

"Look, I'm not some super spy or something, all right? I'm just—"

He moved toward her. His hands lifted, and he caged her between his body and the back wall of the elevator. "You are extraordinary. I knew it from the first moment we met."

"When I was tied to the chair?"

"When you were brave as all hell and you never flinched. When you tried to save my ass on the staircase, never even realizing that I could take those bullets and keep going. Or at least..." A faint grin twisted his lips. "I could rise again."

"That's not funny. Death isn't funny."

The elevator dinged. The doors opened.

"No, I don't guess it is." He moved back. Took her hand. His touch seemed to electrify her. Why, *why* was she still so primed to him? Everything about Jett called to her.

Jett.

He led her down a hallway. Then he was opening one of the doors. 2020. Before she entered, Savannah glanced at him. "Is Jett your real name?"

"Yes."

"You promise?"

He nodded.

She crossed the threshold. And realized they were in the lap of luxury. A top of the line penthouse. Floor to ceiling windows. When the sun rose, she was sure the view would be killer.

"You like the ocean, so when I was looking for safe houses, this seemed like a good bet for you. Since it's not listed as being fully constructed, our enemies won't think to search here. At least, that's what I'm hoping. By the time they do close in, you and I will be long gone."

She curled her arms around her stomach.

And, once more, his gaze dropped. "Are you pregnant?"

He'd just flat out asked. "I thought you couldn't have kids, remember?"

"Savannah…"

"That *is* what you told me. That you couldn't have kids. That it was *safe* for us to have sex."

He glanced down at his hands. "That's what I was told."

She waited. Because he'd sure better have one hell of a lot more to say than just *that*.

"The Lazarus subjects came back from the dead. Yes, our hearts still beat, we still breathe, but we *are* different. Some very fucking distinct differences."

Like the ability to come back from the dead.

She had a flash of him lying on her bedroom floor.

The life had left his eyes...

"The doctors there told us — time and fucking time again — that we couldn't have children. That it wasn't a possibility for us." He raked a hand through his hair. "Those bastards *encouraged* us to have sex after our missions. To blow off steam, they said. To get back to a level of *normalcy*. Told us we didn't need condoms. We can't catch infections — we heal too quickly. Let me show you what I mean." Jett yanked off his blood-covered shirt.

Blood had dried on his chest. But...where there *should* have been two bullet wounds, the skin had already closed. It was pink, healing.

Stunned, she stumbled toward him. Her hand lifted, and her fingers touched those red marks. Closed. Totally closed.

His hand rose and curled around hers. *Oh, God, his blood is still on my hand.* "We heal fast," Jett murmured. "A very accelerated rate."

She looked up at him. *Those bastards encouraged us to have sex after our missions.* Those words hurt. He'd basically just told her that she was another in a very long line for him. Dammit. Savannah wrenched her hand back from him. "I guess you have to go find all of your former lovers now and see if they are pregnant. That the routine? That what you are—"

"There are no other lovers. You are the only woman I've been with since I woke up in that Lazarus lab."

Okay, she didn't know how to respond to that. A lie? A truth?

"You are the only one." His head tilted. "I have *never* wanted a woman the way I want you. I should have kept my hands off you. I knew that. You'd been through hell. But I couldn't. I couldn't stop. I wanted you."

"I need to…" *Get away. Think.* "I need to get the blood off me."

He caught her fingers in his. "There's a shower you can use. Hell, I think there are five bathrooms in this place. Take your pick." His thumb was over her wrist, stroking along her pulse. "But you have to tell me first…are you pregnant? Savannah, are you carrying my baby?"

She stared at their joined hands. At the blood. At his strength. "That's why you came back, isn't it?" He hadn't come back because he loved her. Because he'd realized that he just couldn't live without her. Not because of some mad, desperate desire. He'd come back…

"I learned that Lazarus was jerking us around. *They* are the bad guys. Or at least, some of them sure as hell are. When I was told that you could be pregnant, I knew how important you'd be to Lazarus."

Her gaze rose. "Why?"

"Because it's *my* baby. You will be giving birth to the child of a Lazarus soldier. Think about it. What if my enhancements are passed on to him or her? Don't you see what that could mean?"

She pulled in a deep breath. Let it out. Pulled it in. "I need that shower."

His hold tightened, but then he let her go. "Of course. We can talk when—"

She turned on her heel. Headed down the hallway. Stopped after about five steps. Without looking at him, she said, "Yes, I'm pregnant." Anger was growing, building inside of her. Raging. Threatening to shatter her careful control. Glancing over her shoulder, Savannah grimly told him, "And *no one* will ever hurt my baby."

***

The bathroom door slammed behind Savannah. A few moments later, the shower blasted on, the thunder of water reaching Jett easily.

Pregnant.

When he'd first learned that Savannah might be pregnant — *might* be — his world had seemed to absolutely stop. He'd known he had to find her, had to get back to her right away and learn the truth. If she was pregnant, then others would be after her. A Lazarus baby would be a big fucking deal.

But he and Savannah had only been together a few times. Pregnancy hadn't been guaranteed, it had —

It only takes one time.

He looked at his fingers. Were they shaking? Shit. He clenched his fingers into fists. Pregnant. Savannah was pregnant with his baby. He was going to have a child.

A little girl with Savannah's determination.
A boy with her smile.

He didn't recognize the feelings sweeping through him, not right away. His heart was racing, his hands sweating, his breath heaving — and he was *smiling.*

Because he was going to be a father. Savannah was having his baby. He found himself bounding down the hallway, rushing toward her.

The scene had been all wrong. He should have immediately gone to her, wrapped her in his arms, and sworn that he would protect her and the baby. *Always.* Because that was exactly what he would do. No one would ever hurt them.

Not while he lived. And, shit, not while he died, either.

They were his. And he'd do anything to protect what was his.

His hand reached for the bathroom doorknob. No, no, he couldn't just open the door. His hand lifted, got ready to rap against the wood. "Savan—"

No.

His lips clamped together.

Fucking, *no*. Savannah had thought that he'd killed her father. That accusation had burned him straight to his soul. Over the last three months, while he'd been longing for her, she'd been convinced that he'd destroyed her family?

And…during that whole time, she'd thought he was a monster?

His hand pressed to the wood of the door, but he didn't knock. Mostly because he didn't know what to say. He was *happy* that she was pregnant, but Savannah—he'd just brought her fully into the nightmare of his world. He'd volunteered for Lazarus. At least, that was the story he'd been given. Unfortunately, he'd learned some of the Lazarus test subjects had been manipulated. Hell, they'd been *killed* and brought into the program against their will. The paperwork and the volunteer videos for some of the subjects had been faked.

Had that happened to him, too?

He didn't know. There was so much in this world he didn't remember. Life before Lazarus. So many chunks of time were blank.

But one thing he knew with absolute certainty — Jett couldn't let Savannah go. He had to protect her. Had to protect the baby.

Lazarus could never touch her.

The water stopped. There was a faint *drip, drip.*

He should move away from the door.

She's having my baby.

He'd never thought that he would be a father. Never thought he could have a family. But his family — they were on the other side of the door.

No, she never agreed to any of this. I told her there was no risk. I told her —

The door opened. Steam drifted out to wrap around him. And Savannah was there. With her wet hair sliding around her shoulders. With a towel wrapped around her body. She lifted a brow. "Skulking in doorways now?"

"I'm happy." Shit. *Wrong* thing to say.

Now both brows lifted. "Good for you."

Don't fuck this up.

"I think it's too late for that," Savannah murmured, and he knew she'd picked up on his thoughts. "This whole situation seems well and truly fucked."

"I can take care of you and the baby. I can get you away from here. I have friends who want to help you. Help us. We can start over. We can be safe."

Now her brows lowered. "Let me get this straight. You found out that you could father a child. You realized *whoops,* I might have made Savannah pregnant, and then you hauled ass to get down here to me?"

He nodded quickly. "Yes, yes, that's exactly what happened."

"You are such a bastard. Get the hell out of my way." She stormed forward, with red burning in her cheeks.

Jett got the hell out of her way. "Savannah?"

She growled. Snarled. "I need clothes. And I don't want to put back on the blood-stained ones I was wearing."

"I, um, the room to the right. I made sure to get you some clothes, just in case—"

She whipped toward him, jabbed him in the chest with her index finger, and demanded, "In case of what? In case you had to get me to hop on a motorcycle with you and leave *everything* I owned behind?"

Yes, pretty much in case of that very thing. Actually, that had been the plan.

"You didn't come back for me."

"What? Of course, I did. I came back—"

"You came back because of the baby." Her index finger jabbed into him again. "If it weren't for the baby, I never would have seen you again."

"I…" Shit. This was bad. "Savannah, it was *better* for you if I wasn't in your life. Don't you see that? I bring danger." So much freaking danger. "I'm not safe to be around. Hell, the Lazarus subjects were basically kept in prison cells because we needed to be monitored." He still hadn't told her everything. Mostly because he didn't want her to run from him. Run *to* him, hell, yes, that was his dream. He wanted her to look at him the way she used to. He wanted her to see him and run to throw herself in his arms.

Fantasy much?

But a guy had to have his dreams. What good was a world without dreams?

"*Why* did you need to be monitored?" Her hand dropped.

"You know what?" He smiled at her. Tried to charm and distract. "Why don't you go and get in fresh clothes?" Because she was way too tempting in that towel. "Then I can make you a late-night snack. You and the baby might be hungry. I have some chocolate ice cream in the fridge—"

"*Why* did you need to be monitored?"

He raked a hand over his face. "You're not going to like this."

"Jett, there is very little that I like about this situation."

Check. "Some of the test subjects…some didn't respond so well to the experimental procedure."

Her eyes narrowed on him. "Define that whole 'didn't respond so well' part for me. And, please, go into detail."

"Some of the test subjects…they exhibited too much rage."

She backed up a quick step. "Come again?"

"We lose all of our memories when we wake up as Lazarus subjects." *Wake up, return from the dead. Same thing.* His gaze dipped to her towel. Lingered.

"Jett…"

He dragged his gaze back up. "This would be easier with more clothes."

She gave that little growl again.

He swallowed. Probably the wrong time to tell her the growl was sexy. Unfortunately, he found *everything* about her to be sexy.

"We lose our memories. Our lives before Lazarus are totally wiped away when we are given the Lazarus serum. I woke up in a lab. Strapped to an exam table. Ice cold, and, honestly, scared as fuck. I didn't know where I was or what had happened to me. There were these men and women in white coats, and they stared at me like I was some kind of lab rat."

Which was exactly what he'd been to them. "They told me that my name was Jett and that I'd volunteered to serve my country. I was eventually shown some paperwork with what they said was my signature and a video—in the video, I clearly said that I volunteered for Lazarus."

A furrow appeared between her brows. "You don't…you don't remember your life?"

"When you and I met, I only had memories that started *when* I woke up in that lab." He gave a bitter laugh. "Remember when you asked me what type of ice cream I liked? I didn't know. Had no clue because I couldn't remember the taste of ice cream."

She glanced away from him.

"Cookies and cream."

Her stare shot back to him. And she blinked quickly. Wait, had those been tears in her eyes? Stiffening, he said, "Savannah?"

"It's nothing." She swiped her fingers over her cheek. "Side effect of pregnancy. I cry at *everything.* Trust me, you don't want to see me when any kind of Hallmark commercial comes on. It's an ugly crying fest."

His lips twitched. "I tried twelve flavors of ice cream before I realized cookies and cream was exactly what I wanted." He wanted to touch her, wanted it so badly, but he forced his hands to remain at his sides. "Once you know what you want, nothing else will ever do."

Her chin notched up. "Tell me more. Get back to the whole rage part, if you please."

He'd hoped to get her off that topic. Shit. There'd be no sparing her this. "We all come back with different paranormal powers. I can control shadows. Use them for concealment. And I'm an amplifier. When I work with a team, like Maddox and Luna, I can amplify the powers they have." It was because of Luna that he was there right then. Another story that he'd have to share soon enough.

Savannah just kept watching him.

"Some of the subjects can control fire. Some can control minds."

"That's scary."

She had no idea. "We feel emotions more than normal humans. The darker emotions are the ones that are the most dangerous to us because those emotions — they come more naturally now. Rage. Jealousy. Hate. They can burn in us, and for some test subjects, those emotions push them right over the edge. We've, ah, we've had to put down some of our own."

"Put them down? You've *killed* them?"

"You don't seem to get how dangerous an out-of-control Lazarus subject can be. Humans can't fight someone like that. And the things I've seen…" He expelled a slow breath. "The program itself is fucking dangerous. And now that the bases are burning to the ground, it's a whole new nightmare."

She held up her hand. "I'll take that ice cream." She headed down the hallway.

"Savannah?"

"And I'm getting dressed. Clothing first, ice cream second. The rest of your scary story third."

"I know it's a lot to take in…"

She paused near the bedroom doorway. Savannah glanced back at him. "I just learned the father of my child died and came back with super powers. I also learned that he could have gone insane from the whole process but, um, you didn't, right?"

"I'm quite sane." Except when it came to her. When it came to Savannah and any threats to her, he could let loose the monster inside of him in an instant.

"Good to know." Her hand rose and her fingers curled around the door frame. "You didn't kill my father."

"No."

"Do you know who did?"

Jett shook his head.

Her lower lip trembled. "But you can help me figure it out, can't you? With all of those super bonuses that you have?"

"I'll help you do anything you want."

"I want to catch his killer. I want to make that person *pay*." A shuddering breath. "This is all so hard. I am really, really trying to hold my shit together."

He wanted to hold *her*. Jett bounded forward.

"Stop." One quiet word. "I need a break. A time-out or just some freaking ice cream so I can breathe and *think*."

He froze in place.

"I'm about two seconds from breaking down into some uncontrollable sobs. Maybe it's the pregnancy or maybe it's the fact that you just unloaded a whole world of crazy on me." She pulled in a deep breath. "I've lost my home, special agents are probably searching for me right now, and you—you told me that you didn't come back for me. You only came back for the baby. So, on top of everything else, I'm hurt."

No, no she *couldn't* hurt. He wanted to make sure she never suffered a moment of pain in her life. That was why he was back. To protect her. To—

"Couldn't you have just come back because you wanted me?" Sadly, Savannah shook her head. Then she walked into the bedroom. Shut the door.

The click seemed so damn final.

And he knew that he'd completely screwed his world to hell and back.

CHAPTER THIRTEEN

Walk away. He should do that. He should give her the space that she needed. Absolutely.

But…

Jett strode closer to the bedroom door. He leaned forward, and his forehead pressed to the wood. But he didn't open the door. He just needed her to know… "I thought about you every single day. And every single night."

Silence.

"When I left you, I didn't have memories of my life before Lazarus. *You* had become my life. I would think about you, I would remember your smile with your gorgeous damn dimples or your sweet laugh, and, baby, you got me through some dark days." There were some things that he wouldn't tell her. Some stories she was better off not knowing. She didn't need to know about all of the experiments that had been performed on him. About how he'd been killed and brought back, over and over. About how he'd been used as nothing more than a weapon. How he'd been locked away. Left to burn…

No, don't go back there. Stay with Savannah. Stay with her.

"I'd think about you during the day. Imagine you walking on the beach. Being beneath the sun. And at night, I'd fantasize about you. Imagine you in my bed." His eyes squeezed shut. "Know how I said cookies and cream was it for me? That once you have the thing you want, nothing else will do? Well, you are the only woman I want. No one else will do for me. You got beneath my skin. I think you got into my very soul, and no, I didn't come back. I thought about it. I thought about it a million times."

She didn't say anything, but he could *feel* her on the other side of that door.

"You were better off without me. I'm not normal. I'll never be normal. You deserved *normal*. You deserved a chance to live a regular life. And with me, you weren't ever going to have that." His head lifted. His eyes opened. "If I hadn't found out about the baby, I would have stayed away." Total truth. "And it would have kept tearing me apart. But here's the thing, I had to do what was best for *you*."

The door flew open. She stood there, her eyes gleaming with tears. Her cheeks stained with spots of red. Stood there, looking so beautiful she made him *ache*. And she was glaring with a fantastic fury. "*I* decide what is best for me. Not you. *Me.* I do that. And you want to know how I felt without you?"

He wanted to take her into his arms and never let go. Never. He wanted to hold her so—

"I felt lost. Abandoned. And betrayed. Because all of the evidence I was given—it all showed me that you had *killed* my father. There's a video of you going into his house. Of you calling him a sonofabitch and telling him that something was ending. Then the footage stopped. My father was shot. Execution style. You vanished, and I was left to pick up the pieces." Her voice had gone ragged, and it tore him apart. "I buried him. And I thought nothing could hurt more than that."

"Savannah, the handlers sent me to Mexico right after this case. I didn't know about his death, not for a while. When I got back, I—"

"Stayed away. Because it was better for me."

"You don't believe it. But it's true. It's true because you've never been kept in a cage. You've never been—" He stopped. *No, don't tell her those parts.* He made sure the shield he had in his mind was strong. He couldn't let her hear his thoughts, couldn't take that risk. "I'll get the ice cream ready." He turned away from her.

"I found out I was pregnant a few weeks after I buried my father. Pregnant—with the child of the man who supposedly murdered my father. How do you think that made me feel?"

He looked back at her. "I didn't kill him."

Her breath came out a long sigh. "I believe that. Maybe I'm crazy—"

"*No.*"

"But you've shown me things that are impossible. And I know there is far more going on here than meets the eye. So, when you say you didn't kill my father, I believe you."

His shoulders sagged.

"But I also believe that you *owe* me. You owe me because I've been in hell, and I've been there alone."

She was about to rip him apart.

"So, this is what will happen. You're going to use that super speed and super strength and super whatever else you have, and you are going to help me catch his killer."

He'd expected that reaction from her. "I will do whatever you want."

"Because of the baby, right. Got to—"

No. "Because of *you*. Don't you get it? I stayed away to give you a better life. I came back because I need to protect you both. I can't ever let you suffer because of who I am."

Her hand pressed to her stomach, sliding over the towel she still wore. "What if the baby is…like you?"

His gut clenched. "What will you do?"

Her eyes widened. "Me? I'll love him or her just the same. That's what I'll do."

He couldn't breathe.

"Make no mistake, I love this baby. I loved this baby from the moment I knew I was pregnant. Didn't matter what *you* had done. Or what I thought you had done. This baby was different. This baby is *mine*."

Ours.

"I will love this child whether he comes out flying or if she's a normal baby who doesn't pull an invisible woman act with shadows."

Every muscle in his body locked down. But even as his body locked down, he was making sure all of his mental shields were still in place.

"What?" Savannah frowned at him. "Why are you looking at me like that? I mean, what did you expect me to say?"

I'm looking at you this way because I love you. And because that truth had just punched him square in the face.

"I'm not normal," Savannah fired back before he could think of anything to say. "I can hear thoughts sometimes. I was put in a mental ward because of that crap."

No, not because of that...*Another secret. Baby, I am so sorry.* A secret he was guarding.

"I would never let anything like that happen to my child. No one will ever take my baby and lock her or him away. *Never.* Normal, super powers, what-the-hell ever. I'll love the baby no matter what."

She was the most beautiful thing he'd ever seen in his entire life.

But Savannah wasn't done. "This is the deal. You and I? First, we're making sure the person who killed my father pays. We're going to find the bastard. And then we will do whatever it takes to eliminate the threats to this baby."

Fucking beautiful.

"I hope you have a lot of ice cream," Savannah muttered. "The baby is hungry." Then she whirled around. Headed back into the bedroom.

And never seemed to realize she'd just changed his entire life.

Wasn't just lust. Wasn't just a fierce desire.

No, the reason he'd been so hooked on Savannah…It was because he loved her.

And he'd *left* her. Dammit, just how badly could one man screw up?

***

Jennifer Adams pounded at the front door of Sam Cavanaugh's freaking, sprawling two story antebellum house. Not *his* house, not technically. The too-big, old mansion had belonged to Savannah's father. But when the guy died, Savannah hadn't moved in.

Sam had. Sam had taken over Phillip's position in the government, and he'd moved right into the dead man's home.

Old oak trees lined the curving driveway, and heavy moss hung from their ancient branches. She didn't like the place. Not one damn bit. Being there had her glancing over her shoulder, to the left and to the —

The door opened.

Sam stood there, wearing a pair of jeans and a shirt that was half undone. He was tall, more muscled than she'd realized, and his blond hair was disheveled, as if he'd raked his fingers through it again and again.

Jennifer didn't bother with pleasantries. She wasn't feeling particularly pleasant. "Have you heard from her?"

Sam started to button his shirt. His fingers weren't quite steady, something she noticed right away. Jennifer liked to study body language. People lied with words, she'd learned that truth very early on. But their bodies — their unconscious movements could give them away every single time.

"Her?"

Jennifer rolled her eyes. "Don't play dumb. It's unattractive. And don't give me one of those lame ass performances that you dish out to your constituents. I'm not buying that crap." She shouldered her way inside, her arm brushing against him.

"Well, please, come on in, detective."

She glanced back at him.

He shut the door. Smiled at her. "Heard about your promotion. Congratulations."

How had he heard about it?

Sam shrugged. "You're tight with my cousin. Probably her most trusted confidant. It only makes sense that I'd like to be certain the person closest to Savannah can be trusted."

"I'm a cop. Of course, I can be trusted."

But he shook his head. "We both know there is no *of course* to that. You and I have seen plenty of dirty cops."

She didn't like the jab. "Plenty of dirty politicians, too." She could make a list right then and there.

"Agreed." Sam crossed his arms over his chest and leaned back against the door. "But let's get back to the reason for your late-night visit. And I'm sure it's not because you've just discovered some overwhelming desire for me."

"Are you shitting me right now?"

His lips twitched. "See. No overwhelming desire. Check."

She braced her legs. Glared. And tried *not* to go for the gun holstered at her side. "I'm looking for Savannah. Did she come here tonight? Have you heard from her?"

"Why would she come here? Savannah hates this place." He pushed away from the door. Headed toward the room on the left. A room that when she entered it, Jennifer found the furniture covered in white sheets and piles of boxes stacked in the corners.

"You going somewhere?" she asked, suspicious.

"Yeah, out of this place. Really not my style." He flashed her a smile, but the grin never reached his eyes. "Everything here — everything that Savannah doesn't want — will be sold. The money will be donated to charity. As per her father's will, the money can go to any charity of Savannah's choosing."

She knew about the contents of the will. The will had been part of the original investigation into the murder of Phillip Jacobs. *Who stood to gain from his death?* And the only person had been Savannah. "You still haven't told me if you've heard from Savannah."

A shrug.

"*Don't.*" Anger blasted in that one word. "Don't play your games with me. I know that Agent McNeely probably called you the minute I left Savannah's home. The two of you have been thick as thieves in your secret meetings." Meetings that had excluded the Biloxi PD. "He told you Savannah vanished, and yet you still stand there, as cool as can be, when your only living family member could be in the hands of a killer?"

His head cocked to the side.

She waited for him to lie. She wanted to see what he looked like when he lied.

"McNeely called me." Another shrug. "Told me that he suspected Savannah had vanished with Jett Bianchi."

"Jett Bianchi is dead. He's in a cemetery."

"Yeah, well, don't be too sure of that."

What? But she shook her head. "Listen, Savannah wouldn't willingly run away with the man suspected of killing her father."

He rubbed his jaw, his fingers scraping over the faint stubble there. ""Even though the guy is the father of her child?"

He knew about the baby. She hadn't thought that Savannah had told him.

"No, she didn't tell me," he raked a hand through his hair. "But I have other ways of discovering information."

"Agent McNeely —"

"Is a prick, isn't he? And I have to tell you, the guy doesn't really have Savannah's best interests at heart."

"And you do?" *Try telling me another story. One I might buy.*

His lips quirked.

Bastard. "She could be dying right now! This shit isn't funny."

And his face went completely serious. "Jett won't hurt her. She's carrying his baby."

Was the guy insane? "Two weeks ago, I was called to a crime scene on Japonica Boulevard. A forty-two-year-old man had shot his wife and two kids. I see that same shit too often. Men killing the ones they are supposed to love the most." She took an angry step toward him. "So don't you stand there and tell me that Savannah is safe. She's not. This guy is a suspected killer. He's a wanted man, he's—"

"Not who you think." And Sam raked a hand through his hair. "He's Lazarus."

"What the hell are you talking about now?"

"He *is* Jett Bianchi."

"No, the real Jett is in a cemetery." Why was she having to tell him this again? "He's dead and buried."

"Dead, but not buried. You don't have clearance for this, I just got it myself, but…hey, what the hell? Not like people will believe you if you go spreading the story." He rolled back his shoulders. "Jett is part of something called Project Lazarus. He's a former SEAL who was killed in action, and he was brought back from the dead."

"Bullshit." He was going to jerk her around this way? When she was desperate to find Savannah?

"He didn't kill dear old Uncle Phillip, despite what McNeely would like for you to think."

He spoke with such confidence. "Do *you* know who killed Phillip Jacobs?"

Instead of answering that question, he said, "Jett Bianchi is a trained warrior. He's the best protection that Savannah can possibly have right now. He is exactly what she needs. So, the fact that she's with him? Yeah, it doesn't worry me. It makes me feel better."

She stalked closer to him. Only stopped when they were inches apart. "Don't play with me."

"I am absolutely not."

"You expect me to believe some BS story about SEALs coming back from the dead? Do I look like a dumbass to you?"

"No, you look beautiful to me."

"You are so fucked up."

His expression didn't change. "You're in over your head, Detective Adams. And I'm in over my head. When I started going through Phillip's things, I learned stuff I wish I'd never discovered. When I said I had clearance before? Yeah, I lied. I didn't have it. They don't give that to a junior guy like me. But I'm quite good at finding secrets. And I found Phillip's. I found Lazarus."

So he'd lied, and the man hadn't exhibited a single tell. Not good. "Are you going to help me find Savannah?"

Sam gave a slow shake of his head. "No, I'm not. Because it will be better for everyone if my cousin just vanishes from the face of the earth."

CHAPTER FOURTEEN

"There are ten cartons of chocolate ice cream in your freezer." Savannah slowly shut the freezer and turned to face Jett. "Want to explain that?"

He sat at the table, near her empty bowl of ice cream. "You like chocolate."

"Ten cartons."

"I wanted to make sure I had plenty of your favorite on hand."

She rested her shoulders against the nearby wall. She'd dressed, putting on an over-sized sweatshirt, a comfy pair of yoga pants, and a pair of tennis shoes that felt like heaven on her feet. Then she'd had one bowl of ice cream. Bliss. Items one and two on her to-do list were done. Now...

"I want to hear everything," Savannah told him. "Don't hold anything back from me."

He rose from the table. Took her bowl to the sink. Stood there with his back to her. He'd changed, too. Switched to a new pair of jeans and a white t-shirt. His hair was still wet from the shower. He didn't turn to face her, but just froze there a moment, as if lost in thought.

"Jett?" Savannah prompted. He wasn't going to hold back on her. Not happening.

"Something changed."

That was way too ambiguous. "Don't be mysterious." She stalked toward him. "You have info to share. Share it. No smoke and mirrors." She reached out and touched his arm. "If this is going to work, we need total truth between us."

His head turned. He gazed at her fingers. "Total truth? Okay. When you touch me, I want to fuck you."

Her fingers jerked, but didn't pull away. She kept touching him.

"Actually, when I just see you, I want to fuck you." Now he was staring straight at her. "It's pretty much a constant situation for me, whenever you're around. Figured you should know that."

She focused on breathing. Nice, easy breathing.

"But I get that you don't want me the same way. When you're not confused as all hell by what's happening, you probably hate me."

"Don't." The word snapped from her.

His brows rose.

"Don't tell me how I feel. You don't know how I feel." And hate was the last thing she felt. Did he think he was alone in the crazy fog of lust and desire? No, she felt the same wild need, too. Whenever he was near, she wanted. She ached. But she wasn't giving in to that need. Would not. Because she had to hear the truth—about everything. Her hold tightened on his arm. "Start by telling me what happened the night my father died."

He blew out a breath. "Maybe you should sit down."

"Maybe you should just *tell* me." But she let him go. Marched away from him. Didn't go for a chair but instead headed toward the balcony. She opened the sliding door, aware of him following her. The starlight shone down on them, the scent of the salt water teased her nose, and she could hear the waves hitting the shore far below. The sound soothed her. The ocean soothed her. It prepared her for what she knew would be very, very bad news.

He was silent for a moment, as if gathering his thoughts, then Jett said, "Your father lied to you."

She wasn't going to act surprised. Her father had been a politician. He lied about a lot of things. "About what?"

"About why you were in that mental institution."

Okay, now shock rolled through her. Of everything that she'd expected him to say—*those* words had not been the ones she'd thought to hear. "What?"

"I did some digging." And he was pacing. "It pissed me off that he'd had you locked up."

She could only stare at him in shock.

"No one should fucking lock you up. It enraged me. Maybe because I was spending so much time locked up, too. I don't know. But I hated it, and I got Maddox and Luna to help me investigate." He swung toward her. "Baby, I don't think you started hearing thoughts *after* the accident."

"Yes, yes, I did. I—"

"I think you always heard them. I think your dad was trying to cover up something else entirely when he put you in that hospital."

The wind blew her hair.

"I...shit. I got the files from your shrink. Dr. Anthony Rowe. Or rather, got access to them. There were notes from your freaking grade school teachers in those documents. An elementary school counselor told a story about how you were playing a game one day on the playground. You were surrounded by a circle of your friends. One at a time, you'd go around the group and you'd say what they were thinking. The counselor got spooked because you looked right up at her, and you said *exactly* what she was thinking."

"I don't remember that." Not a bit of it. "And I can't just pick up all of those thoughts. There's no way I could simply look at people and pluck thoughts straight from their heads. That's not how it works for me. It's random. Not some easy thing for me to just—"

"It's not easy any longer. Because of your father. Because of the shrink he had you seeing. They wanted to stop your power. Not strengthen it."

"They wanted me to be normal." For an instant, she could see Dr. Rowe in her mind. He'd been fresh out of school when he'd begun to treat her. Young, but with cold eyes. Icy blue eyes that had stared at her from behind the frames of his glasses as he'd studied her like a bug under a microscope. He'd always made her uncomfortable. Always made goosebumps rise on her arms.

Jett laughed. "Fuck normal."

"Jett—"

"He was covering up the accident, Savannah. Your father put you in that place because he needed to make you forget what you'd seen. And when he got you under the care of that prick doctor, they went a step farther. Why not change you? Why not try to get the perfect daughter?"

"I'm not perfect." Never had been. Never claimed to be.

"You went to hypnosis sessions. One after the other. Dr. Rowe played with your memories. Played with your mind."

"No, my father wouldn't do that." And even the crash of the waves couldn't soothe her. She stormed past Jett, heading into the penthouse again. "I asked for the truth," she snapped without looking back. "But you give me this crap? Are you just trying to jerk me around? To make me angry at my father?"

He followed her inside. Shut the door. "You were always angry with him. Because deep down, I think you *do* remember some things. Despite what they did, the drugs they gave you while you were in that facility, the hypnosis, all of the so-called therapy that I read about and hated...I think the truth is still there."

Focus on me, Savannah. Only me. Dr. Rowe's voice floated through her mind. He'd used those same words at the start of every therapy season.

His image flashed in her mind. The faint smile on his lips.

Goosebumps rose onto her arms. No. No!

She whirled toward Jett. "What truth?"

"The truth about the accident. The truth...that your mother wasn't driving the car. That your father was. That he caused the accident that killed your mother and your twin brother. That it was all him."

"No."

"It was a cover-up. Straight and simple. I saw the photos from the accident scene. The front seat was pushed back too far for your mom's five-foot-two frame. Your dad was obviously driving, I could tell that shit right away. But he *moved* her. He put her in the driver's seat because I'm betting the bastard had been drinking that night."

Her temples were throbbing. "Stop."

"You wanted the truth. I'm giving it to you. Luna discovered his drinking problem. He joined AA the month after you got out of the mental hospital. Maybe he wanted to really change his life or maybe he just got fucking tired of looking at a monster when he glanced in the mirror, but he stopped drinking." Jett's hands were fisted at his sides. "You had to wonder, why would a man like your father let Patrick Zane into your life?"

"He didn't know what Patrick was. My dad didn't know, Sam didn't—"

"Bullshit. Patrick Zane was dirty, but your father *and* Sam—they were cleaning up his image. They even introduced the bastard to you. Vouched for him. And you know why?"

"You obviously do." She had chill bumps on her arms.

"Maddox and I found the evidence at the shack on the dock. The night Patrick was killed, it was all there on the computer."

Her throat had gone dry.

"Patrick had pieced together everything, just like I had. He knew your father was driving when the wreck happened. Patrick knew Phillip had been drinking. Patrick found a witness, you see. A fucking first responder on the scene. A uniformed cop who should have been there to help you all, but instead, he protected your father."

Her temples were pounding. Her breath heaving.

"Your father was driving, *not* your mother. But the cop helped your dad to put your mother's dead body behind the wheel. He helped your dad to stage the whole scene. Your dad paid the bastard because the great Phillip Jacobs didn't want to lose his senate seat. His position mattered more to him than anything else. His family was dying around him, but he was covering his own ass." Rage beat in Jett's words. "Your father is the one who crashed the car. Patrick had dirt on him, and in exchange for keeping quiet, in exchange for making that witness go away, Patrick wanted inside of Phillip Jacobs' world." A stark pause. "And he wanted you."

If all of this was true…*Dear God.* The cop wouldn't be a witness. An accessory? "Where is the cop now?"

"Dead. I suspect by Patrick's hand."

Oh, God.

"The cop's daughter was the first victim of Patrick's kidnap scheme. You see, the cop came into a great deal of money right after the crash that killed your mother and your brother. The guy's whole life changed. And then when Patrick took his daughter, it changed again."

She tried to calm her racing heartbeat.

"Think about the crash, Savannah. Go back there. *Look at it again.*"

An image of the crash flew through her mind. The scream of metal. The pain when she hit the seat in front of her. Steven's yell that was cut off so quickly, too quickly. "He wasn't wearing his seatbelt." Her eyes squeezed shut. "Why didn't Steven have on his seatbelt? We were taking Driver's Ed. We'd just watched all those videos about how important it was to buckle your seatbelt." All of those videos with the crashes and the blood on the highway.

She felt Jett's fingers brush over her arm. Her eyes opened.

"Your brother was thrown from the car."

Yes, he'd died at the scene.

"Your mother and father weren't. But your mom—she didn't survive her injuries."

No, she hadn't. "When I opened my eyes, my dad was there. Telling me…"

But she couldn't say it.

I'm so sorry, Savannah. I'm so sorry. Tears had streamed down his face.

"What did he tell you?" Again, Jett's fingers stroked over her arm. A soothing caress.

"He said he was sorry." Because it had been…his fault?

She wanted to double up because the pain hit her so hard. A blow right to the heart.

"The night I left you, I went to see Phillip Jacobs. While I had been with you, I had been working with my team to get all of this information. When we protect, we do it fully. There was no aspect of your life that we weren't going to examine. Nothing that could be a risk. We uncovered the truth, and there was no way I was vanishing without making sure no one would hurt you again. No one, including your father."

If this was a dream, she'd like to wake up now, please.

"I told that bastard that he would never hurt you again. No more lies. No more tricks. I told him that he had to tell you the truth, and if he didn't, I would be back for him." He gave a rough laugh as his fingers slid away from her. "He'd just been fully briefed on Lazarus by this point. I'm not sure what he knew before that — maybe just some PR bullshit that skirted over the truth about what the test subjects really were. He was terrified, knew that he was staring straight at a monster."

"You're not a monster." The words came automatically.

But he gave her a level look. "I am, baby. You shouldn't forget that. When it comes to you and to the baby you carry, I will do whatever it takes in order to protect you both. If that means I have to become the devil himself to everyone who threatens you, if that means I have to hurt and kill, I will do it."

She believed him.

Her dad…her dad…

He'd caused the accident? Killed her mother? Her brother? And lied for years? What would those lies do to a man? What would he become?

"When I left him, Phillip Jacobs was alive. He was sitting at his desk."

She shivered. "That's where…where he was killed. Shot in the back of the head." The crime scene photos would haunt her. "The blood sprayed over his desk."

"Savannah…"

Even if all of this was true…"You'll still help me find out who killed him?" Because she wanted to know. Needed to know. Even if he'd —

She had to blink away tears. *My mother, Steven…*Her heart *ached.*

"I'll do my fucking best."

She sucked in several deep breaths. Just *felt* the pain for a few moments and, God, it was terrible. All of those years…and it had been her father?

"There's something else you need to know, baby." His voice was gentle.

She tried to square her shoulders. *I'm scared to hear anything else.* But she couldn't hide. Couldn't bury her head in the sand.

"I don't believe Agent McNeely is FBI."

Her jaw dropped. "What?"

"I suspect he works for a far more covert division in the government. A division that has a tendency to silence those who get in their way."

She shivered and tried to understand exactly what he was hinting at. *I hate hints. Just say it.* "You think he killed my father?"

"I think your father was asking too many questions about Lazarus. And I think that got him in trouble."

Another shiver. Why was it so cold in there? "If you knew this, *why* didn't you come back and tell me? McNeely has been around me so long—"

"Because I didn't know, not at first. Shit, baby, I didn't even realize your father was dead. My handlers sent me to Mexico. Then to another mission. And another. I went off-grid. Didn't have any outside contact with the world for weeks. Then when I came back, let's just say that things went to hell damn fast. Lazarus burned. And I freaking mean that literally. We had traitors in our midst. People looking to destroy us from the inside. Turns out Project Lazarus was never about protecting our country. It was about creating unstoppable killers. Having ultimate power." He heaved out a breath. "I made mistakes. *I* trusted the wrong people, and I wound up as a prisoner in a building that was an inferno."

This time, she was the one to reach for him.

"Maddox got me out." He looked at her hand on his arm. "Maddox dragged my ass out even though he should have left me behind. Because those people I betrayed? Maddox was one of them. I should have trusted him, but I didn't, and I almost got him *and* Luna killed."

"Where are they now?"

"Safe." His fingers curled around hers. "Actually, they'll probably be arriving soon. They want to help you. There are a whole lot of people very interested in you."

Not her. The baby.

"Luna has a gift. Something that is a game changer for everyone in Lazarus." His lashes flickered. "Remember how I said everyone had different, uh, bonuses when they came back from death the first time? Luna is a healer. She can use her power to heal those who get injured — I've seen her save a dying kid in the middle of a war zone. The things she can do — they are absolutely incredible." He pulled in a deep breath. "But it turns out, the longer we have our powers, the more they evolve. And when she heals now, she can heal Lazarus subjects completely."

She was trying to follow along, but…"I don't understand what that means."

"Our minds weren't the same after we were given the serum. Our memories were erased. She can give them back to us."

Now she felt her eyes widen. "You remembered your life? Before Lazarus?"

"I haven't been around her long enough to remember everything. I just got a taste." A low exhale. "Before Luna tried to help me, I couldn't even remember my own mother. A handler at Lazarus—the guy must have felt sorry for me because he gave me access to my files one day. I saw a picture of my mother. Read her bio." He swallowed. "From my files, I learned she was in the Cantonese Opera. I read everything I could in those files. That's how I knew about her falling for my Italian father. It's also how I learned that I was with each of them when they died. I knew that stuff because I'd read it. Not because I remembered it."

What would it be like…to remember nothing of your early life? For it to be so completely erased?

But, wait, he'd said he thought someone had played with her memories, too. That wasn't possible, was it? Wouldn't she know?

"After I left you, in those hellish months, Luna gave me a flash of my mother." His voice turned ragged. "My mother was in a hospital bed. Hooked up to a dozen machines. I was holding her hand, and she was telling me…saying that she was *proud* of me."

There was grief in his voice. Pain. And Savannah wanted to hug him. If there wasn't a chasm between them, if there wasn't—

Screw it.

She threw her arms around him and held tight.

"What are you doing?" he rasped.

"What does it feel like? I'm hugging you."

"Savannah…"

"You need a hug, don't you? Because I do. This asshole jerk who left me—who got me pregnant and pretty much turned my world upside down—just told me that my dad killed my brother and my mother in a car accident." When she sucked in a breath, it seemed to chill her lungs. "So, you know what? I could use a hug." *And so could you, Jett. I feel your pain, and I hate it.*

Despite everything that had happened between them, she didn't want him to suffer. If she could, she'd take away all of his pain.

And I would take away yours. His voice drifted through her mind. *I would go back and change our ending. We wouldn't end. I wouldn't walk away. I'd*

*stay with you. You'd wake up in my arms, and
everything would be different.*

Her head lifted. She stared into his eyes. So
dark. So deep. No one else had ever looked at her
quite the way Jett did. She didn't think that
anyone else ever would. "What happened to your
mother?" she whispered.

"Cancer. She…didn't get better."

"I'm so sorry."

She saw his Adam's apple bob. "I am, too.
But I want to be the man she was proud of,
Savannah. I want to be a man that you can be
proud of. That our child can be proud of." His
hold tightened on her. "I will never let you down
again. I will never give you cause to doubt me
again. When you need me, I swear, I will be right
there." Then he pulled her closer. Put his head
next to hers. "And I'm sorry about your father. I
wish I'd been at the cemetery with you. I wish I
could have stopped his death."

She blinked quickly, held him tighter. She
held him so tight, and Savannah realized that she
didn't want to let him go.

But then a low beep filled the penthouse. Jett
swore and pulled back.

Savannah missed him immediately.

"They got here sooner than I thought."

Unease slithered through her. "They?"

He caught her hand. Threaded his fingers
with hers and led her down a hallway. He

opened the door to what she'd assumed was another bedroom, but when they stepped inside, she saw the left wall was full of monitors. Each monitor showed a different part of the building. He pointed to the monitor on the lower left. She could see his motorcycle. The elevator. And...two people. A man with dark hair and a fierce, hard face. The guy glanced over his shoulder, his gaze sweeping the area even as his arm stayed curled around the waist of the woman at his side. Her hair was pulled back, twisted at the nape of her neck.

"That's Sawyer Cage and Dr. Elizabeth Parker."

Deep breath. "Since they're here, I'm guessing they're your allies?"

When he looked at her, his gaze appeared guarded. "Elizabeth is the woman who first created the Lazarus formula."

"And that's a good thing?" Didn't sound like it to her.

"The formula was taken from her, used to do things she never anticipated. She's doing her best to right the wrongs."

Okay. Her gaze darted back to the monitors. "So that's why she's here?" Guilt. Savannah could understand that. "What's his story?"

They'd entered the elevator. Savannah could see them on another monitor.

"Sawyer is her lover. As far as I know, he is the first Lazarus test subject. And there is no way he'd let her out of his sight on a mission like this one."

She turned her head and found Jett staring at her. "What?" Why was he looking at her that way?

"If you don't want them here, I can stop the elevator. Everything that happens from here on out — we do it as a team. We agree. We work together."

But she'd already put the puzzle pieces together. "In case I was pregnant, you asked her to come." *Doctor* Elizabeth Parker. "Can she help me? Help the baby, if there are any problems?"

"If anyone can, it would be her."

"Then we are absolutely letting that woman inside."

***

Bennett McNeely stood in the middle of Savannah Jacobs's house. The balcony doors were open, and he could hear the rush of the waves outside. His agents had torn the place apart. Just in case she had hidden any information about Jett Bianchi and his associates, just in case the woman had fooled Bennett for all of these months, he'd wanted to be sure.

But they'd found nothing. Nothing but the listening devices he'd had his team install. Those devices had been the reason he'd rushed in her home, with his gun at the ready. He'd been two blocks away, hunkered down in a black van, and then he'd heard Jett speak.

I've got you.

And he'd even shot Jett, but the bastard had gotten away.

The APB had turned up nothing. As far as he knew, Jett and Savannah weren't even in the city any longer. They could be on their way to Mexico. They could be heading fast for the Caribbean. They could be any damn place.

And that meant he was screwed.

He pulled out his phone. Called the guy who'd been the mastermind behind the whole operation. Bennett had wanted to take Savannah in weeks ago. As soon as they'd found out she was pregnant. Why waste time? Why not secure the asset? But *his* boss had other plans. He hadn't just wanted Savannah. He'd wanted a real Lazarus soldier, too.

The phone rang once, twice. On the third ring…

"Let me guess…Jett appeared. Took Savannah Jacobs. And now you've got jackshit." The voice was smug. Too knowing.

The guy was such a prick. "I shot him, but he came back fast."

"How fast?" Real curiosity was there.

"A matter of minutes. He took out my guards. Then vanished with her. No freaking trace of them has been found anywhere. For all I know, they've left the country."

"Relax. They're still here."

"How the hell do you know that?"

The guy laughed. "She's my most valuable asset. Did you honestly think I wouldn't have a way of locating her, twenty-four seven?"

"You know where she is." He stared at the wreckage around him. "And you didn't tell me?" Bennett had wasted all of that time?

"Well, you *just* called, didn't you?"

He hated the sonofabitch.

"But, yes, I know where she is. I can always track her. It's very handy tech, actually. In fact, the jerks at Lazarus stole the tracking technology from *me*. Used it for their own gains. Then they shut me out." Frustration hummed in his voice. "I'll show them, though. My plans for the Lazarus evolution were perfect. They should have recognized that fact."

Okay. Sometimes, the fellow seemed straight-up crazy. But he had to follow orders. "Where is she?"

The guy rattled off an address instantly. Then said, "Looks like the building is supposed to be closed, but I assure you, Savannah *is* there. And if she's there, Jett will be there, too. Go in prepared. Armed. Very heavily armed."

Like he had to be told. "Jett won't get away again."

"He'd better not."

Teeth clenched, Bennett gritted, "Just how the hell do you know where she is?"

"Because I lojacked her, of course." Laughter. "Did it ages ago. Wasn't about to lose someone as special as she is."

Bennett frowned. "How long ago?" Just how long had the fellow been watching Savannah Jacobs? Not for the first time, unease slid through him. The boss had been adamant that the Lazarus soldiers were monsters, that they had to be stopped. But now, shit —

Now we're dealing with a pregnant civilian. And I don't like this mess.

"Savannah was sixteen the first time we met. I knew back then that she'd be able to change the world."

Bennett glanced around at the wreckage in Savannah's home. He stepped forward, and his foot brushed over a blanket.

A baby blanket. A tiny, yellow baby blanket that Savannah had purchased for her child. He pulled in a breath. Slowly released it. "What are you going to do with her and the baby?"

"It's really not your concern. You're a special agent for the United States government. Your job is to protect this wonderful country of ours. Go out and capture Jett Bianchi. Secure him. And secure her. But remember, Savannah won't rise from the dead like Jett. Order your men to treat her with care."

The line went dead.

Bennett shoved the phone into his pocket. He bent down and scooped up that little, yellow blanket. It was soft. Delicate.

Fucking hell.

Once more, his gaze swept around the home. He'd ordered the place searched. He'd ordered the wreckage.

His hand closed around the blanket. Was he really about to order his men to hunt Savannah down and bring her in…in for who the fuck knew what?

Lojacked. Those words whispered through his mind. He shoved the blanket into his pocket even as he pulled out his phone again. He dialed quickly and didn't identify himself when the caller answered. He simply said, "Tell her we're closing in. She's *lojacked.* Tell her that, exactly."

He ended the call. Then he marched outside. The men and women there immediately sprang to attention. They looked to him for leadership. They looked to him in order to do what was right.

The problem was that he wasn't sure what was right any longer. What was right. What was wrong.

He'd seen a dead man *rise*.

There were some things that, when you saw them, they could change your whole world.

What would an army of men like Jett Bianchi do? How would they be stopped? His gaze swept the team. They were waiting. He had orders to give. "I have a location. It's time to move out."

CHAPTER FIFTEEN

"I know this is all pretty overwhelming." Elizabeth gave Savannah a tentative smile.

"Overwhelming is probably an understatement. Twelve hours ago, I didn't even know that Lazarus existed. And now..." Her gaze darted to Jett. He and Sawyer stood near the balcony. With all of their super senses, she had no doubt those guys could overhear every word they spoke. *Super vision, super hearing, super speed.* Yes, she'd learned all about that. Her head was still spinning.

"Now you found out your lover is a real-life super soldier."

Savannah's attention flew back to Elizabeth. "Did he tell you...about us?" Her voice was halting.

Elizabeth shook her head. "Our time together was pretty brief. The guy basically found out that you *could* be pregnant, and he was off like a rocket. The only thing he wanted was to get close to you." She bit her lower lip. "You know he truly believed that he couldn't have kids. When he found out that his handlers had been lying to him…that you could be in jeopardy, he could not get to you fast enough."

"But he had no trouble staying away before that."

Elizabeth nodded. Understanding filled her warm gaze. "Yes, I'd be pissed as all hell, too."

Savannah studied the other woman. "Did you really invent Lazarus?"

"I did. And I swear, my intentions were good. Or at least, I thought they were." She twisted her hands in front of her body. "But then the formula was taken. Even though I knew there were problems with it. Increased aggression being the scariest. Back then, I didn't even know about the memory loss. We're talking about tests that had only been performed on lab rats. This formula was *never* supposed to be given to humans at that point. Because the testing process was still in the early stages, I didn't realize that the rats were only maintaining procedural memories—"

"Okay, wait, just back up. What do you mean, procedural memories?"

"How to walk. How to tie your shoes. How to drive a car. The things that you do over and over again." She pointed toward the two men. "For them, for men who'd been trained for most of their adult lives in combat situations, some of their procedural memories were a little more...intense."

Killing.

"Until recently, the test subjects would just get a few random flashes of their pasts. Flashes that seemed to be triggered by emotional connections to others or by high stress events." Elizabeth's gaze slid to Sawyer. Softened on her lover. "He didn't volunteer for the program. Sawyer was *killed* and put in Lazarus. By the time I got to him, he didn't remember me." There was pain in her voice and on her face.

Sawyer immediately turned toward Elizabeth. Then he crossed the room. Kissed her. A kiss of tenderness and absolute love. Savannah averted her eyes because the display seemed so personal—

"I remember you now," Sawyer told Elizabeth tenderly. "You are my world."

And Savannah's eyes darted to Jett. He was staring back at her. Staring at her as if—

Get the hell out of that place, right now!

The voice blasted in Savannah's mind. Hard and dominating, and she shook her head. That...that wasn't Jett. The voice felt different. Familiar, but—

The agents are coming. You've been lojacked. Get out!

The voice was so clear. So insistent.

And then...just gone.

She put her fingers to her suddenly throbbing temple.

"Savannah?" Jett was by her side, reaching for her. "You went pale. What happened?" His gaze dropped to her stomach. "Everything okay?"

"The baby is fine." She bit her lip. "Lojacked?" That made no sense. She wasn't a damn car. "Someone was just in my head." She grabbed Jett's hand. "Did you hear him?"

Elizabeth and Sawyer exchanged confused glances.

Jett just looked straight at Savannah. "No, baby, I didn't hear a thing." His eyes were blazing. "Who the fuck was it?"

"I—" The voice had seemed familiar, but the thunder of words had been so quick. "He said we have to leave. The agents are coming." Then… "That I was lojacked?"

Sawyer put his hand on Jett's shoulder. "Want to tell us what's happening?"

"I can hear thoughts," Savannah answered. For once, she didn't believe revealing her secret would make others think she was the freak in the room. Super soldiers could hardly judge, could they? "And someone was just in my mind. Someone told me that the agents were coming here. That—"

"You'd been lojacked," Elizabeth finished. Her gaze turned accessing. "You're psychic."

Savannah nodded.

"OhmyGod." Elizabeth's eyes squeezed shut. "Jett, you didn't mention this before."

"Because her secrets aren't mine to share," he threw back. "Besides, it doesn't matter. It — "

Elizabeth's eyes flew open. "It matters a whole lot. You think I was the only one doing experimental research for Uncle Sam? The government has wanted to tap into psychic powers for years. If they found someone who has some sort of genetic — "

"It's not genetic," Savannah spoke quickly. "It's from a car accident when I was sixteen. It's — "

Jett shook his head. "No."

Her heart pounded hard in her chest.

"You *always* had it. I told you that before."

"This is going to change things. This…" Elizabeth bit her lip, then added, "This means you weren't random. You were picked, specifically *for* Jett because those pulling the strings didn't just want any Lazarus baby. They wanted a baby from a Lazarus soldier and someone like you."

Someone like you. "No one could have known that Jett and I would wind up in bed together." No way. "That's crazy."

Elizabeth shook her head. "It is possible to analyze genetics and to see which individuals have characteristics that would make them good mates for others."

Even Sawyer frowned at her.

"Not my area of expertise," she muttered. "But others have done it. And maybe there are some who have even gone a step beyond that. I mean, the dead have been brought back to life. You all don't think it's possible that someone else figured out a way to determine which would-be lovers would react the strongest to each other?"

"Adrenaline does some crazy shit," Sawyer added as he seemed to consider her words. "You throw two people together in dangerous circumstances, you keep them in close quarters, together twenty-four seven, and what the hell outcome do you think will happen?"

Savannah's cheeks were burning. She wasn't even going to touch this stuff. Not yet. Right then, she had another concern. "How could I be lojacked?"

Jett and Sawyer shared a long look. A look she didn't like.

Then Jett said, "Impossible. She isn't part of Lazarus."

"If they were planning to use her, planning to pair her with a soldier all along, then there is no way they'd risk losing her."

Oh, Savannah didn't like this. "*She* is right here." She snapped her fingers and all gazes flew to her. "Some jackass was just in my head, telling me to run." And they weren't running. They were all just standing there, talking. As if agents weren't about to storm the building.

"The psychic message she got *could* be the trap. Maybe whoever sent it was bluffing." Sawyer nodded. "Wanting to make her leave her safe hiding spot. Run into the open."

"He didn't sound like he was bluffing." Savannah rubbed her inner wrist. "He sounded...scared."

"Your tracker was cut out, right, Jett?" Sawyer asked abruptly.

Jett nodded.

Elizabeth was biting her lower lip again. Looking worried. "We can't run an X-Ray check on her. Not while she's pregnant."

"Uh, yeah, you're not doing that." But Savannah's gaze was flying around the penthouse. She wanted to run out of there. The voice in her head... "Listen, I get that all of the psychic power stuff is probably totally normal for you all, but I *don't* typically get voices blasting messages at me. That's not the way it works. I can pick up some thoughts here and there, mostly when people are scared or angry, but the only person that I tend to communicate easily with that way—it's Jett."

She could tell by Elizabeth's expression that the woman had just filed that tidbit away for later analysis.

"So, um, what I'm saying is…this shit isn't normal for me. And I think we need to heed that warning and get the hell out of here."

Sawyer moved into her path when Savannah would have hurried for the door.

Jett gave a low, warning growl. "Back up, man. Now."

Sawyer backed up, but his expression remained grim. "If she's got a tracker, there is no safe place for her. Not while it's in her body."

Now Jett stood toe-to-toe with the guy. "No one is cutting her. Do you understand me?"

Wait. Had he said *cutting?*

"There might be a different way. We've been working on this. Trying for a more…sanitized solution." Elizabeth cleared her throat. "But we need to find the tracker first. Make sure it's there."

"*No* X-Rays," Jett snapped. "Not with the baby. And if it's there, you know the tracker is going to be fucking microscopic. I mean, if she isn't aware it's it her, odds are that it's small as hell."

They were talking about a tracking device being inside of her. Savannah laughed — and really wanted to run for the door. They were wasting time. *We need to get out.* "You guys — people aren't lojacked. I mean, I know pets get microchipped. Sure. But not people."

They all just looked at her. Then, Sawyer said, voice flat, "You don't know Lazarus."

Elizabeth nodded decisively. "Jay can help us — he's been working on some experimental tech that should be able to disrupt the tracker's signal without us having to cut blindly into Savannah."

"No one is cutting me." Just so they were all clear.

Jett was at her side. "Hell, no, they're not."

Sawyer's expression hardened. "If she's got a tracker —"

"I think I'd know if someone put a tracker under my skin!" Savannah huffed at him. "Look, first I have Jett telling me that I don't really remember my life before my car accident —"

"When was your car accident?" Elizabeth demanded at once.

"When I was sixteen." They were so off track. "I think we need to —"

"Any other accidents or injuries since then?" Elizabeth immediately asked. "Things that would have required a hospital stay?"

"I, um, had a concussion a few months back but —"

"But I stayed with her every second," Jett interrupted with a shake of his head. "She never left my sight. The tracker wasn't put in her then."

Why weren't they rushing out? Didn't they get that danger was coming? *Unless the guy in my head was trying to trick me. To make me give up my location like Sawyer suggested.* What was real? What wasn't?

Elizabeth gave a low hum. "Then odds are the tracker has been there for a while. Savannah was targeted long before the two of you met, Jett."

Now Sawyer looked worried.

Welcome to the party, buddy.

"If that's true." Sawyer tilted his head as his gaze raked Savannah. "That would mean someone was planning for a very long game with her." He studied her like she was some kind of bug under his microscope. The same way Dr. Rowe used to look at her.

Elizabeth circled her, then touched Savannah's shoulder. "Do you have any scars from the accident?"

Wasting time. "Look, can't we cover this *after* we're at another location? Another place that's safe?"

It was Jett who spoke. Voice gentle, he said, "If they have a tracker in you, baby, there won't be a safe place for you. They'll be able to follow you wherever you go. You'll be in danger as long as it's activated."

"If we're with you, they can track all of us." Sawyer's gaze swept her.

He meant they were all in danger. Because of her. "You should leave." She waved them away.

"All of you. Just go. We can all separate and come up with some sort of plan later. Go get that Jay guy you mentioned. Go get —"

"She has two tattoos on her back," Jett said suddenly. "Fuck me. And the rose is slightly raised."

Savannah became very, very conscious of her lower back. "The rose covers a scar that I got from the wreck. When I was pulled out of the car, some of the glass bit into my skin. I didn't even realize I'd been cut, not until I woke up in the hospital, and the doctor told me that it was a small wound, that I'd been lucky —"

No, I wasn't lucky. I lost my mother and my brother. Not lucky at all.

She'd covered the scar years later with her mother's favorite flower. And the dragon tattoo? She'd been lying when she told Jett about the tats. Just bluffing her way through the conversation because she hadn't wanted to bare her soul to him then. The tats hadn't been for her. The dragon had been for her brother. He'd always loved dragons. He'd been the one to excitedly tell her — when they were just ten years old — that they'd been born in the Chinese Year of the Dragon. He'd been so excited.

It means we're special, Vannie. Only Steven and Sam ever used that nickname for her.

"It could be under the rose." Elizabeth nodded. "May I see the tattoo?"

Savannah just stared at her. Then…
"Whatever. Look at it, then let's get *out* of here."
She turned her back and pulled up her shirt just
enough to expose the tats on her lower back.
Then she felt Elizabeth's fingers slide across the
skin.

"It could be a tracker."

"And we could be screwed." Sawyer had
started to pace. He rather looked like a caged
tiger. "I'm getting Jay on the line. We'll need his
jammer, if that shit is really working now."

Savannah yanked down her shirt. "Look, I
get that I fell down some rabbit hole, but just
because I have a scar on my back, it doesn't mean
I've been microchipped like a lost pet!"

But everyone gazed at her with solemn
expressions.

"Is a team coming here? Are the special
agents coming and we are really just sitting here,
doing *nothing*?" Savannah demanded. She had
her priorities—and priority one was getting out
so that nothing would happen to her baby. If they
weren't leaving, she was. She was running—

"It's okay," Sawyer said with a nod. He'd
stopped his pacing. "The chopper should be here
soon."

Her jaw dropped. "Excuse me?"

Jett glanced at his watch. "We should start
making our way to the roof."

"But — what — chopper?" Okay, she wasn't even speaking in full sentences now. That was how crazy they were all making her. "I thought the folks following us would be able to find me because of the tracker." Great. Now she was on the tracker party bus. "We need to separate." She squeezed Jett's hand. "You need to go. Get away from me. We can meet up later."

A muscle jerked along his clenched jaw. "Baby," he gritted out, "I won't ever be leaving you again."

"But if you're in danger…" Didn't he get it? "I was the bait, Jett. McNeely had eyes at my place because he thought you'd come back for me. I didn't believe it. I knew you weren't coming for me." In the end, she'd been right. He hadn't returned for her. He'd come for the baby. "But I can't be bait again. I can't be the reason you get caught." Her stare darted to Sawyer and Elizabeth. Sawyer was texting someone. Not even glancing at her and Jett. "I can't put you all in danger."

Jett's gaze didn't waver. "And I won't leave you unprotected."

"But the tracker —"

"Good news. Jay has the jammer on his chopper. Says it should work to destroy any signal from a tracker." Sawyer glanced up from his phone. "His ETA is less than three minutes. We need to be on that roof."

"See?" Jett smiled at her. "We can take care of the tracker if one's inside you. There's no need to separate." He pulled closer and whispered in her ear, "Though I wouldn't have left you even if it meant I had to fight a dozen fucking agents. I will never leave you again, no matter what."

Then everything happened really fast. They all rushed to the elevator. A few moments later, they were on the roof. Savannah could see the lights from the chopper in the distance. Jett's arms were around her shoulders.

"Who is this guy?" Savannah asked. "And can we trust him?"

"Jay is a man I've known for years. We can trust him," Elizabeth quickly responded. "Like the rest of us, he has a personal stake in this."

"Personal?" The wind whipped at Savannah. Jett pulled her closer.

"His wife is Lazarus," Elizabeth explained. "And he will do anything for Willow."

Savannah shivered. She'd fallen so far down the rabbit hole. So very far…

"They're here," Sawyer announced.

No, the chopper wasn't there yet.

But she saw Jett turn his wrist. A light was flashing on the watch he wore.

Sawyer had on a similar watch. And she realized he was staring at the screen of his watch, too.

"Tripped the alarm downstairs," Jett muttered. "Must be coming in with a full force."

They. The agents. They were the ones who'd arrived.

The chopper needed to *hurry.*

"I disabled the elevators. They'll have to break the stairwell doors down, then climb all the way up here to get us." Jett brushed a quick kiss along Savannah's temple. "Don't worry. We'll be out of here by then. Normal humans just aren't that fast."

"And protocol will demand they check the floors as they rise." Sawyer rolled back his shoulders. "We should have plenty of time."

But Jett shook his head. "Not if someone is feeding them tech from her chip. In that case, they'll come straight to the roof."

The chopper's lights were getting closer.

The wind kicked up around them.

"The agents could be coming in with air support, too," Sawyer noted grimly. "We need to be ready for anything."

Her body trembled.

I've got you, Savannah. Jett's voice stroked through her mind. Tender. Warm. *No one will hurt you.*

She turned toward him. Pressed closer. *What about you? They want to hurt you.* Didn't he get that? McNeely had shot him on sight at her home. She feared that, at any moment, armed agents would burst onto the rooftop. A hail of bullets would rock the night, and Jett…

I don't want to watch you die. Seeing him on the bedroom floor, seeing the life leave his eyes — it had torn her apart. That terrible moment had let her know that, despite everything — the rage, the fear, the hate — she'd still cared.

Maybe she always would.

The chopper was above them. Jett curled his body around hers, protecting her from the wind as the swirling blades sent the air pounding at them. And then Jett scooped her into his arms. He ran fast and hard for the chopper. He put her inside first, then Elizabeth jumped in.

"Buckle up!" The woman in the front yelled. "Get secured because we have to *vanish.* We're going to building hop and get the hell out of here as fast as we can."

Building hop? Was that a real thing?

But then Jett and Sawyer were inside. Relief had her breathing harder. Or maybe that was fear. Whatever. Savannah looked back at the building. Saw that the roof door was still shut. They'd made it. They'd —

The roof door burst open. Armed agents stormed out.

They lifted their weapons at the chopper.

But they didn't fire.

***

"*Hold your fire!*" Bennett shouted. His clothes blew back against him even though the chopper was already in the air. He didn't want anyone firing. If a stray bullet caused that chopper to go down, he was sure any Lazarus subjects on the helicopter would be fine.

But what about Savannah and her baby? They were too important to lose.

A chopper at the ready. Smart. Fucking smart. He'd known Jett had connections and resources. He should have expected this. Bennett yanked out his phone and called his prick of a boss. "They're in the air!" He rushed back into the building and ran down the stairs. "Had a fucking chopper that took them from the roof. Going to need to get local air support—"

"Don't worry, I can still track her. I see her on my screen right now. She won't get away."

"Send me the coordinates. When that chopper touches down, *I* want to be there."

The mission was becoming too personal. He'd put in too many months of his life. No, he'd given up his life. He'd see this thing through to the end.

No other option.

***

The chopper was lowering. Heading toward the top of another condo building — they'd barely seemed to be in the air long at all.

Savannah's hands were clenched in her lap. She hadn't said a word since the bird had taken to the sky. Jett knew she was terrified. Fear wasn't good for the baby — and it wasn't good for Savannah. He never wanted Savannah to be afraid. He wanted to take her away from all of this.

From any fear or pain or danger.

*When we touch down...*Sawyer's words reached him although the other Lazarus subject never spoke out loud. *We see if Jay's latest tech works. If he can jam her signal, then you can make her vanish.*

Literally, he could. But...

What if it doesn't work? No one was going to cut her. He wasn't about to let someone take out a knife and dig into the skin near her spine.

We come up with a Plan B.

Savannah grabbed Jett's hand as the chopper touched down. The blades slowed, slowed...

He hurried to jump out, turning to lift her into his arms and hold her securely. Elizabeth and Sawyer followed. So did the blond-haired Jay, pulling a small, black bag with him.

The pilot stayed put. Jett understood why. She needed to be ready for lift-off if things went south. Which they probably would.

"Okay, let's see if this works." Jay pulled out a small, about five-inch-long black wand. Like the kind used by cops to check for weapons at security entrances. Then Jay jerked a laptop out of his bag. He opened it up and when a security screen flashed on, he typed in a quick code. Then one more code on the next screen, and… "She's definitely transmitting."

Jett saw a line of text flashing on the screen. He swore.

"Yeah, it's a bitch. But at least I've found a way for us to destroy the transmission without anyone having to get bloody." Jay glanced up at Savannah. "Jay Maverick, by the way. Pleasure to meet you."

"Jay *Maverick?*" Savannah repeated. There was recognition on her face. "The tech giant?"

"Well, I'm not really a giant." He lifted the wand. "But I do have my uses."

The pilot called, "Hurry the hell up, Jay!"

"That's the love of my life, Willow. And she's right. We do need to hurry the hell up." He lifted his brows as he studied Savannah. "I need to run this device along your body, has to be within five inches of your skin. When it comes near the tracking device, it will send out a…" But he broke off, frowning. "How to explain this?"

"Jamming signal?" Sawyer supplied. "Shit, you're calling the thing a jammer so it's a *jamming* signal. But, hell, don't explain, just *do* it, man."

"It's more of a hack, than a jam. I get the code, and I take over." Jett lifted the wand toward Savannah.

She caught his hand, stopping him. "I'm pregnant. Will this put my child at risk in any way?"

"No. Absolutely not."

She let him go. "Then you should probably begin with my back. That's where the others think the tracker may be." She turned, offering him her back. She lifted up her shirt. "Start with the tats."

"Nice ink," Jay said as he lowered the wand.

A rumbling growl came from Jett. Jealousy rose within him. Fucking crazy because this was *not* any sort of romantic or sexual situation, but it was there. He didn't like the guy being so close to Savannah, didn't like him being near her bare skin. Didn't like—

"Aggressive emotions," Jay muttered. "They are really bitches for you guys, huh?"

"Jay…" Willow's voice held a warning edge. "Don't poke the bear."

Jay glanced at his laptop. "She's definitely tagged. Or rather…" A smug smile. "She was. I hacked the transmission. The code is scrambled, and no one will be following her any longer."

Savannah's hand flew out. Locked with Jett's. He held her tight.

"There could be others," Elizabeth spoke, voice urgent. "You need to scan her whole body, and then we have to get the hell *out* of here."

***

Bennett slammed his hands against the steering wheel. "Her signal stopped transmitting? What does that *mean*?"

"It means her lover probably figured out how we were tracking her, and he cut the device out of Savannah."

Fuck, fuck, *fuck.* "You told me those guys are unstable. How the hell can you possibly expect her to stay safe with him?"

"I've got the last coordinates from her transmitter. You're less than ten minutes away from the location. Air support is coming in. They aren't getting away."

"Easy for you to fucking say. You weren't there at Savannah's place when she and Jett just vanished in freaking plain sight. There one moment, gone the next." This was a nightmare containment situation. "By the time I arrive, they'll be nothing but wind." He'd gotten local back-up on this thing because he needed more cars. Though he had made sure Detective Jennifer Adams wasn't part of that back-up.

"Savannah won't leave. Not yet." The boss was so arrogantly confidant.

"You don't know that shit! You don't know —
"

"I know exactly how to control her. You do, too. You just have to be ready to use the pawns. If you won't make the call, don't worry. I'll do it." A cold laugh. "I'm used to getting my hands dirty."

No, the bastard *wasn't*. He was used to getting Bennett to do the dirty work. Bennett had the blood on *his* hands. And before this case was over, hell, he'd be freaking swimming in blood.

CHAPTER SIXTEEN

The chopper rose into the sky, the pounding of its blades beating against the night.

"Are they going to be okay?" Savannah asked, her voice quiet. Breathless.

He let his shadows deepen around her. The chopper was flying away as a trick, to lure the bastards hunting Savannah into giving pursuit. "You heard them. Willow and Jay already had this plan in motion. They're going to building hop again to throw off those looking for you. They've got their escape from the next building planned."

She turned toward him. "They'll all be okay? Elizabeth and Sawyer, too?"

Because they'd all been in the chopper. Jett's shadows could only stretch far enough for him to cover one person. *Savannah.* And just in case Jay had miscalculated and the enemies on their trail caught up to them, Sawyer had wanted to be at the guy's side. Jay wasn't enhanced, but Sawyer could pack quite a paranormal punch. "They'll be okay." They'd better be. If Sawyer needed him, Jett knew the guy would send him a psychic SOS.

Jett curled his fingers with hers. "We need to get off this roof." Damn fast. They raced into the building. A building that Jay and his tech-crazy-self had cleared for them. As soon as they entered the elevator, Jett pushed the button for the parking garage. Jay had said a ride would be waiting below for them. Jett kept the shadows around them. Video surveillance would pick up nothing but darkness.

When he'd first woken, he hadn't been able to use the shadows. Amplification had been his strength. But the shadows came easier to him now, as if the darkness somehow spread from within him.

"I can't believe that Jay Maverick is working with us. I think he was on the cover of *Time* a few months back. The guy *is* the tech world right now. Stories say there isn't anything he can't do."

He'd heard those same stories. "Then I'm extra glad he's on our team."

She rubbed her back. "It's really shut off? The tracking device?"

It had better be.

"Someone put this *thing* inside of me without my permission. My dad's death…you…us meeting…it's all tied together, isn't it? All of it linked to this stupid chip inside of me?"

It looked that way.

"Jett, if we get the device out of my body, can you learn who put it inside of me? Like, does it have a serial number or something you could trace?"

Not a serial number, no. "Cutting you open isn't high on my list of priorities. And even if we did that, there's no guarantee we can get any sort of intel from the device." *In other words, hell, no, I'm not cutting you open to get that.*

The elevator doors opened. The cavernous parking garage waited. Only one vehicle was there. A silver SUV. He started advancing toward it.

Just as he caught the wail of sirens.

Not coming in quietly, are you?

He and Savannah were almost at the vehicle. Almost there.

But we won't get out of here before the cops arrive.

Jett grabbed Savannah. Pulled her close. Pressed her between him and a stone column. "Baby, it's going to be just like before." The fog around them deepened. "You'll see me, you'll see some fog, and you might see the people hunting us. But they *won't* see you."

Her hands curled around his shoulders.

"Don't scream. Don't give in to any panic. I have you, and I won't let anyone hurt you."

The sirens grew louder. Sure, he and Savannah could jump into the SUV. Rush away.

But they'd be spotted and tailed. The cop cars were too close. They'd gotten to the scene far faster than Jay and Sawyer had anticipated.

Then the agents and cops were there. Patrol cars. Black SUVs. They surged into the parking garage. A glance to the left showed Jett that other cars were stopping in front of the building. There was no security guard at the building right then — mostly because Jett's team had planned things that way. And when the cops and the agents jumped out of their vehicles in order to rush toward the elevator bank —

Savannah sucked in a quick breath.

He knew she'd spotted Agent McNeely. The guy looked pissed as hell as he approached the elevator with his gun drawn. "Secure the fucking scene!" McNeely thundered.

Jett pressed closer to Savannah. He sent his shadows out, sweeping around her even tighter.

McNeely stopped near the elevators and glanced around the garage. "That vehicle." He pointed to the silver SUV. "It doesn't leave, understand?"

Some random cops nodded. The uniforms on scene looked nervous, uncertain, while the men and women in suits — the ones Jett pegged as agents — wore angry, tense expressions.

Didn't like that we gave you the slip, huh? Too bad.

McNeely glanced to the left. For an instant, he seemed to look straight at Jett and Savannah.

Jett tensed. *Baby, he can't see us. Don't make a sound.*

McNeely kept staring. Then the elevator dinged. The doors opened. McNeely turned and stormed inside. "Lock down the freaking building—"

The doors shut.

Two uniformed cops and an agent stayed in the garage. The uniforms headed toward the silver SUV. They tried to open one of the doors.

Not happening, fellows.

After a few failed attempts, they turned away from the vehicle. Started mumbling to each other. Kept looking uncomfortable. Too green for this case.

Savannah trembled. Her sweet scent surrounded him. He loved her light, flowery scent. They were pressed together, bodies flush, and he knew she had to feel his growing arousal. Not something he could help. More a perpetual state around her.

Savannah's fingers bit into his shoulders.

She was afraid. He didn't want her fear. So why the hell not try distracting her?

His lips pressed to hers. He kissed her, a fast, open-mouthed kiss. Just to get Savannah's mind off her fear. Just to try and help her to—

She kissed him back. Her hands pulled him ever closer, and her lips parted for him. Her tongue met his. Desire ignited. Not just a hard-on because he wanted her…a fucking wildfire of need because he was desperate for her. His mouth was rougher on hers, wilder. He couldn't get enough. Couldn't taste enough, couldn't—

Dammit. I need to hold the shadows in place.

He tore his mouth from hers. Sucked in a deep breath. But still *tasted* her. So, yes, kissing her had obviously been a colossal mistake. He'd made her forget fear for a moment, but he'd almost lost control.

A good mental note for next time. Her kisses packed too much punch.

Time to get moving. *Savannah, I'm going to distract them, then we're heading for the garage exit.* They'd go on foot. They'd stay in the shadows until they were clear of danger. He wanted to be long gone by the time McNeely and the others came back downstairs. *Just remember, I need to keep touching you.*

The longer he was with Savannah, the easier communicating psychically with her seemed to be. The more natural it felt.

Savannah gave a small, nearly imperceptible nod.

Jett shoved his left hand into his pocket. Jay had tossed him a set of keys before the chopper had lifted, and Jett pressed the alarm button on those keys now. When he did, the SUV's horn blared, over and over again, even as its headlights flashed.

The two cops and the agent immediately jumped. They whirled and aimed their weapons at the car. The agent even fired.

The bullet flew into the windshield, right on the driver's side.

Then the cops and the agent closed in on the vehicle.

This is our chance. He laced his fingers with Savannah's, and they ran for the sloping exit of the parking garage. As soon as they cleared the exit, he saw the other cops and agents waiting out there. But they never even glanced Jett's way. The night was working to their advantage. He never would have been able to pull up such strong shadows in the day.

They hurried down the sidewalk, not making a sound, and, wanting to cover more ground faster, Jett scooped Savannah into his arms. He took off, never looking back. Leaving the agents and the hapless Biloxi PD in their wake.

He kept going, running, pushing his body to full speed as they covered block after block. He wasn't going to stop, not until Savannah was safe. Not until she was clear of the danger. Not until—

"Jett." Her breathless voice. "I'm getting dizzy."

He slowed down. Went from a blurring run to a walk.

"And I think we're far enough away that you can take a break."

He wasn't sure how many miles they'd covered. Wasn't even sure how much time had passed. But, up ahead, he saw a small motel. One with a flickering *vacancy* sign.

Perfect.

He approached the little motel. No one was out front, and he eased Savannah down to her feet. "The desk clerk won't remember my face."

She gave him a doubting look.

Jett's lips curled. "I promise. I can use the shadows so that every time he looks at me, he sees someone different." It was all about angles. Perceptions. "Just stay right here, and I'll be back."

She gave a nod. Jett hurried inside, the bell above the door ringing to announce his presence. A fast survey showed no security cameras were perched anywhere. The place looked as if it hadn't been updated in about, oh, fifty years.

A bored guy — maybe in his mid-twenties — sat behind the counter, flipping through a magazine. "Fifty." He didn't look up.

Jett tossed a fifty across the counter.

The check-in clerk slid him a key. "Number eighteen. If you're here more than two hours, it's another fifty."

Right. He'd figured it was *that* kind of motel.

Without a word, because speaking would just give the guy a voice to remember, Jett swiped up the key and headed out. Savannah was standing in the same spot, and when she saw him, relief flashed on her face. He curled his arm around her and led her to lucky room number eighteen.

The lock was flimsy as hell and wouldn't keep anyone out, but at least they were off the streets and sheltered, for the moment. He'd wait until some poor fool left a good ride nearby, and then they'd split. Until then... "Why don't you get some rest? You've been up all night."

"Are you kidding?" Savannah stood in the middle of the tiny room, staring at him as if he'd lost his mind.

"No, you have been up all night." He pretty much knew jackshit about pregnant women, but weren't they supposed to need extra sleep? Because their bodies were all busy making a new human and stuff?

Her brows climbed. "There is no way I'm sleeping in that bed. I feel like I can catch something just by being near it."

His lips twitched.

"It's an hourly motel," she added grimly. "I'm not touching the bed."

He closed in on her. Told himself to keep his hands *off* her. But he didn't listen to himself. His hands rose. Curled around her shoulders. "It's not hourly. It's *two* hours at a time."

Her eyes squeezed shut. "Oh, my God."

"Savannah…You can sleep on top of the covers. You have to be exhausted."

Her eyes opened. "I know who it was."

What? "Baby, you should—"

"I know who gave us the warning to leave the penthouse. I know who was in my head. I…I think you were right. I think I was always…" Her words trailed away, but then he heard her finish the sentence, in his mind.

Always like this.

"Savannah…"

"If it's genetic, if there is just something different about me or my brain that lets me hear the thoughts of others and even send out my own thoughts the way I just did to you…then doesn't it stand to reason that someone else in my family could do the same thing?"

Yes, it did. He'd had the same suspicion. But… "It could be another Lazarus subject. That's right in line with our powers. It doesn't have to be—"

"My cousin? Sam? No, it doesn't have to be him, but I told you, the voice seemed familiar. I couldn't place it at first because I was so shocked someone else could get it my head." Her shoulders lifted and fell. "It was him. Sam warned us to get out. He knew that McNeely had found me, he knew that I'd been, um, tagged or lojacked or whatever the hell it is. He knew, and Sam was trying to warn me."

Jett needed to play this scene carefully. "We have some time before I'm supposed to use the burner phone Sawyer gave me. A new location will be set up for us soon. A temporary safe house." But just moving from safe house to safe house wasn't going to work. "I need to get you out of town, Savannah." She'd asked him to find her father's killer. Asked him to give her justice before anything else happened.

And he couldn't do it. He was going to fucking let her down already, but her safety had to come first. "I need to get you away from Biloxi. I need to make you vanish."

Her head tipped back as she stared up at him. "You did that earlier. You made me vanish when a special agent was staring right at me in the parking garage."

"Savannah…" Dammit, he could get lost in the woman's eyes. And the hard-on he'd gotten from their kiss was just getting worse. "I have to protect you first, before anything else. I have to get you settled. I'm going to get you out of here, but I'll stay behind. I'll make sure I figure out who killed your father."

Her head cocked. "You think I'm leaving you?"

"Being around me puts you in danger." He'd done nothing but put her in danger from the very first moment.

"No." She shook her head, sending her hair sliding over her shoulders. Savannah just said the one word and nothing else.

"Uh, Savannah…"

"Don't you get it?" She blew out what seemed to be a very frustrated breath. "I'm safest when I'm with you. You can literally make me disappear. Who else is going to be able to do that with a touch?"

No one else came to mind.

"You send me away, you get your buddy Sawyer or Jay to whisk me out of town, and then what happens? Do you think they'll watch after me the same way that you will?"

"Savannah, they *would* keep you safe."

Then she shocked the hell out of him. She reached for his hand. Brought it to her stomach. Pressed his palm to the small mound there. "You have a vested interest in keeping us alive. We're a part of you."

We. Yes, *they* were. It wasn't just about the baby. For him, it never had been.

"We're kind of a package deal," Savannah noted with a soft smile. "And we both want *you* with us. All the time. So don't go getting any ideas about putting us in a plane and watching us fly away. That's not going down."

His hand stretched, his fingers flexing against her. His child was there. Savannah's baby. "But you wanted justice for your father. I have to find out who killed —"

"Yeah, you know what?" Her lips trembled. "I choose us. I choose the baby. I choose you. I choose all of us getting out of here alive. I said I wanted to find out who killed my father. And I do, despite anything that he may have done, I want to find his killer." She licked her lower lip. "But you weren't lying to me."

Baby, I never want to lie to you again.

"Good, you'd better not." Her fingers were still curled around his wrist as his hand pressed to her stomach. "There was a tracking device in my body. People with very big guns located us at the penthouse. You came back from the dead — everything you said was true, and I can't just pretend it's not." Another deep breath. "You didn't kill my father."

"No, I swear it."

"I believe you."

His heart raced faster.

"I also believe that it is far more important for us all to get out of town than it is for us to catch his killer. Me, the baby, and *you*. Our lives matter. I don't want you getting captured. I don't want you getting locked away. I want you with me, every step of the way, and if that means I have to find out who killed my father later, if that bastard has to wait on his justice, then *that* is the choice I make." She stared into his eyes. "Because the family I have is more important than the family I lost."

Oh, God. "I fucking want to kiss you right now. More than I've ever wanted anything else."

"And I fucking want to kiss you, too. But I am *not* touching that bed, so when we make love—which we are about to do because I have *missed* you—you are going to hold me up the whole time, got it? You're a super soldier." Her voice dropped to a husky whisper. "I think you can handle that."

"Yes, ma'am." He could handle anything. But he really wanted to back up to that part about when they made love…

"Kiss me again," she seemed to breathe the words as Savannah tipped back her head. "Because I've thought about you every single night. Sometimes, I'd cry myself to sleep."

Baby.

"Sometimes I'd pray that the evidence was wrong. I wanted it all to be wrong because I wanted you—the hero I'd known."

Jett shook his head. "I'm not a hero." She shouldn't think that.

"Let me decide *what* you are, to me." She gazed into his eyes. "I want to be with you again, Jett. Before anything else happens. Before any bad guys find us. I want to be with you."

He wanted her. Was absolutely desperate for her. But… "I don't want to hurt the baby."

Her laugh was like sweet music. "Loving me can't ever hurt the baby."

Did she know…did she realize what he felt for her? How deeply? He'd fallen hard and fast, and he hadn't even realized the truth, not until he'd walked away and discovered that he'd left his heart with her. A man without a heart — that was just not really a man at all.

A shell. A shadow.

All that he'd become.

He leaned toward her. His lips pressed to hers. Did she know that he'd longed for her taste? Imagined touching her? Seeing her? Over and over again? That she'd been his sanity when he'd been in hell?

Did she know how much she mattered?

No, because he'd never told her. But maybe he could show her.

He curled his hands around her hips. Lifted her up. Held her easily. Kept kissing her. Her lips parted for him, and his tongue dipped into her mouth. His Savannah. Brave and strong and beautiful. Her tongue slid against his. Her hands curled around his neck. He kissed her slowly, he kissed her deeply. Her legs wrapped around his waist, and he knew she felt the hard shove of his cock against her. But she just gave a moan, one that he greedily swallowed up, as Savannah rocked her hips against him. Rocked her body over and over, and made him ache for her even more.

He turned, caging her between his body and the wall. He eased back, just enough to reach down and tear away her shirt. He tossed it behind him. Her breasts were covered in silky lace, and he lifted her up higher, wanting her nipples in his mouth.

"Be, ah, careful," she whispered. "They're more sensitive."

He'd always be careful with her. *Always.* He licked her nipple through the lace. Sucked the tip. Licked, sucked—

"Oh, God, that's good." Her hips were arching hard against him.

And he was so swollen he hurt.

Jett pulled away the bra, and her beautiful breasts waited for him. Tight, dusky nipples. Were her breasts a little bigger than before? So freaking sexy. He lifted her even higher. Caught one nipple. Licked it. Pulled it into his mouth. Nearly went crazy because she was so sexy.

His hand fell to her waist. He eased his fingers down the front of her yoga pants. The pants were thin, the material soft cotton, but Savannah was so much softer. He stroked her, again and again with his fingers. He held her up with one hand and his other explored everything that he'd missed.

It had been too long since he'd held her. Too long…

"Jett!" His name was a sensual demand. "The clothes have got to go!"

He let her feet touch the floor, but only long enough for him to strip away the yoga pants and her underwear. His fingers feathered over her stomach. Still so small. His baby was inside? His fingers trembled.

"Jett."

He kissed her. Kissed her with all of the need and love that he had. Did she realize he would do anything for her? Absolutely anything. Lie. Steal. Kill. Without hesitation. Over and over again. She owned him that completely.

He would move heaven and hell for her.

"Jett, you still have on clothes!"

He wasn't worried about what he had on. His fingers were between her legs. She was wet and hot, and he was stroking her toward orgasm. He needed to give her pleasure. Needed her to see that he would always put her first. He kissed her, caressed her, then drove his fingers into her. She was so tight. So perfect. His hand pulled back, his thumb going to press against her clit. He remembered what she'd liked. Remembered the way she'd enjoyed his touch. He slid his fingers over her. Moved his mouth to her neck. Kissed her over her pulse. Licked. Sucked.

She came for him. He felt her whole body jolt as Savannah cried out his name. And her pleasure was so perfect. His head lifted so he could see her face and watch the release wash over her.

"Want…more…" Savannah panted. "Want…you."

With one hand, he unhooked the snap of his jeans. Then he eased down his zipper. His cock shoved toward her. She helped to position him, arching up, and then—

"Slowly," Jett cautioned roughly. "I don't want to hurt you. I *never* want to hurt you."

Her gaze held his. She took him inside slowly, inch by careful inch.

He couldn't look away from her eyes, her face. She was so beautiful to him. Did she understand that?

"I'm not glass." Savannah leaned forward. Caught his lower lip between her teeth. Nipped. "I won't break."

No, but the woman could easily break *him*. Jett put a stranglehold on his control. He let her set the pace. Rising up, arching down. He gripped her hips with easy strength but made sure not to hurt her. Never to do that. Again and again, she slid up and down his length. Driving him to the absolute edge of sanity because she was a hot, wet heaven. Gripping him so tight. Fucking. Insane.

His right hand slid between them. His left kept her pinned carefully to the wall. He stroked her clit again because he was hungry for her pleasure. Addicted to it.

She moved faster against him. Harder.

"Savannah—"

He felt the contractions of her release around his cock, and they drove him straight over the edge. His orgasm hit, pounding through Jett's body, and he buried his face in the crook of her neck, shuddering as he came, as he poured into her.

The pleasure seemed to last forever. So much better than the dreams he'd had of her. Reality was always better than the dreams.

Without a word, he carried Savannah to the bed.

He lowered down, on top of the covers, keeping her on top of *him*. She'd seemed to go boneless, and he wanted her to rest. If she didn't want to touch the bed, she could just sleep on him. Problem solved.

Besides, he liked having her that way. Soft and sexy and sprawled on top of him.

He wrapped his arms around her. Thought that she was drifting to sleep…

"Promise me one thing," her sleepy voice asked.

Anything.

"Don't ever leave me without a word. Don't do that to me again." A pause. "Promise?"

"I fucking swear." He wouldn't be leaving her at all. He'd have to be a dead man first.

CHAPTER SEVENTEEN

Someone was knocking at her door. Correction, not knocking, pounding. Jennifer cracked open one eye and glared at her alarm clock.

The pounding came again.

Growling, she threw off her covers and jumped out of bed. She wore jogging shorts and a PD t-shirt as she headed for the door. Jennifer put her eye to the peephole. But when she saw her guest...

Jennifer yanked open the door. "What in the hell are you doing here?"

Sam stood in her doorway, wearing one of his fancy suits. Looking way too fresh and alert for four a.m. "I need your help."

She motioned for him to come inside. As soon as he cleared the threshold, she shut and locked the door behind him. "You've heard from Savannah?"

"Not exactly," he hedged. Sam swiped his hand over the back of his neck. "Have you been in on the investigation? Did you hear what happened during the night?"

No, she hadn't been in on the investigation. She'd been benched, courtesy of McNeely. But… "I wasn't there, but I heard what went down." She'd actually spent the night following her own leads and then checking in with her people to see just what the hell McNeely had been up to. And the news she'd gotten had confused her even more. "How the hell did Savannah get access to a helicopter in order to make her escape?"

He just stared back at her.

"Uh, yeah, you need to speak up at this point, Sam. Because the money goes back to Savannah and *you*. So if someone got a chopper—"

"Savannah never cared about the money. It was a bother to her more than anything else."

Someone could bother her with money any day of the week. "The owner of the helicopter will be tracked down. I mean, that's just basic shit. You don't have a bird in the air that doesn't belong to someone. I actually suspect that McNeely already knows who owns it or he *will* know, probably within the next hour."

"Not if he's dealing with Black Ops. He won't learn anything. Government clearance or not."

Black Ops? "I need coffee." She turned on her heel and headed for the kitchen. "A lot of it."

He was silent while she put the coffee on. She glared at the machine. It was ancient and did a slow drip-drip-drip, but damn, it made some good coffee.

"Jett Bianchi isn't an imposter."

She glanced over at him. "Come again?"

"No one is buried in the grave that Savannah visited. The guy is Black Ops."

Drip-drip-drip. Her temples were throbbing.

"Jett was brought in to save Savannah when she was kidnapped. I think the guy fell for her. He didn't want to let her go."

She grabbed a mug. "But he did let her go. Then the sonofabitch killed her father."

Sam glanced away.

That wasn't good. Sam was hiding secrets from her.

"Life is about secrets. Everyone has them." He exhaled. "I don't think Jett killed Phillip."

"You don't *think*—"

"Fine. I know he didn't. Because…there was more to the security footage." His jaw clenched. "The original footage showed Jett leaving while Phillip was still alive."

"You sonofabitch. You framed a man?" Did he *get* that he was confessing to a serious crime? Admitting his guilt to a police detective?

"Shit, it seemed easier at the time."

Easier than what?

"I mean, Jett was gone. The guy was in the wind, and I knew he'd never be back. I knew that, for all intents and purposes, he was a dead man. So why not let him take the fall?"

"You framed a man for murder?" Just so they were clear.

Sam shook his head. "You don't understand. I was trying to protect Savannah—"

"Sounds like you were covering your own ass." And she was suddenly far too aware of the fact that she didn't have her gun. It was in her nightstand drawer. How many times had she told Savannah that a gun was of no value if you didn't use it? And she'd freaking left it behind.

He flushed but said, "This isn't about me. It's about Savannah. I know she's still close by. We need to get to her."

"We?"

"You're coming with me. You're her friend. She'll trust you."

"And she won't trust her own family?" Her hand reached for the handle of the coffee pot.

His sigh easily reached her. "Don't think about it."

Think about using the coffee pot as a weapon? Jennifer absolutely was thinking about it.

She gave him the side eye and saw that he'd just pulled a gun from beneath his suit coat. Rat bastard. "You just got a whole lot less sexy to me."

The gun didn't waver. "I need your help. I want you to contact McNeely. Tell him that Savannah reached out to you. That she said she was hiding at the family's cabin just outside of town, on Wichitaw Lake. Get him to go there for her."

He wanted her to give McNeely a false trail?

"After that, you're going to come with me to meet Savannah. She won't panic when she sees you."

"Put down the gun."

He didn't.

"I need you," he said again. "And I'm afraid I can't let you go."

***

Jett's hands stroked over Savannah's back. She was on top of him, her body so soft and warm. Her hair trailed over his shoulder. He wanted to stay like that with her, to just hold her for hours.

And if they didn't have a whole team of special agents on their trail, that was exactly what he'd do. Just stay there. Hold her. Try to imagine what a life with her could be like. Her and the baby.

"I'm not asleep," she whispered.

His lips twitched. "You mean you're not asleep…anymore."

Her fingers slid down his arm. "Maybe."

Warmth filled him. She did that. Made the cold places inside of him seem to vanish. "Do you...um, have you felt the baby move?"

"I think it's too early. The doctor said that would come later." Her head angled up so she was staring at him. "But I heard the heartbeat."

His own heart raced faster.

"And I saw an ultrasound." She gave a little laugh. "The baby is *tiny*. The ultrasound pic was basically swirls of black and gray. I won't find out if we're having a boy or a girl until I'm around twenty weeks."

He concentrated on breathing.

"Jett?" Savannah frowned at him. "Are you okay?"

"I wish I'd been there. I wish I'd been with you every moment."

She gave him a slow smile. "You're here now."

His burner phone rang, vibrating from the nearby table.

"Better get that," Savannah whispered.

Yeah, he had.

She climbed off him. Stood there, naked and gorgeous, perfect enough to make a man go insane.

"Jett? The phone?" She scooped it up and tossed it to him.

He caught it and slid his fingers over the screen. Jett turned on the speaker when he answered because he wanted Savannah to hear everything that was said. No more secrets.

"*Are you secure?*" Sawyer's voice.

"We didn't get out in the SUV, so I'm hoping there's no way to trace the ride back to Jay, but yeah, we're good. For the moment."

There was a rumble of voices in the background. "Jay said not to worry. The SUV will never be tied to him." A rough laugh. "But then, the guy fixed it so the chopper couldn't be tied back to him, either. The man is a serious menace when you get a computer near him."

Yes, Jett was getting that.

"We need to rendezvous. Need to get you and your lady out of this town. It's too hot here."

Savannah cleared her throat. "Tell us where and we'll be there."

Because she was ready to leave everything behind.

He would *never* deserve her.

"We're monitoring the local PD's communications right now. Seems that a detective named Jennifer Adams just called in a tip, saying you'd told her that you were at some lake. Wichitaw Lake?"

Tension swept into Savannah's body. "My family has an old cabin up there."

"Yes, well, the cops are about to mobilize with the special agents and head up there. That should cool things down here in town a bit." He gave a rough laugh. "Or maybe not. Either way, we'll be going the *opposite* way. There's a small airport about twenty miles east of Biloxi. Mostly used for crop dusters and private planes. You two meet us there while the cops are distracted."

"I know the place." Savannah was putting on her clothes. A real shame, that. "We'll be there."

"Keep a low profile, Jett," Sawyer warned.

"It's what I do best."

"Got a call from two of your old team members. Luna and Maddox are on the way. They wanted you to know they'd have your back."

Yeah, they always did. He could count on those two. As for Andreas, the Greek wasn't someone he hoped to encounter anytime soon. Another betrayal. A story for another day. "Tell them to stay away. I don't like that so many Lazarus subjects are getting pulled in. It feels like…" His words trailed away as he looked at Savannah. He hated to say it, but everything inside of him was screaming—

It feels like a trap.

Her head whipped up. She stared at him with wide, worried eyes.

But it was the truth. What the hell else would bring so many Lazarus subjects out into the open? What would make them vulnerable?

They would all come to protect one of their own. They would all come to protect their future—a Lazarus child.

"They're not going to stay away." Sawyer's voice was low. "You know that. And we *all* know the risks. But you don't leave anyone behind. That's the code we've always followed."

Yes, it was.

"See you at that airport, Jett," Sawyer said quietly. "I'll be the one covering your six."

"Wait—there's something you need to know." He stared down at the phone. "Savannah thinks her cousin Sam is the one who sent that psychic message to her."

Again, he heard the rumble of voices in the background. Then… "Elizabeth said that makes sense. Whatever power Savannah has could run in her family."

"He was trying to protect me," Savannah added. "He warned us."

Sam had warned them, but Jett wasn't so sure they could fully trust the guy. Mostly because…*shit, the cousin was my chief suspect in Phillip's murder.*

He heard the growl of an engine. "We'll be at the airport. And thanks for the help, man. Thanks to all of you." He ended the call. Jumped up and dressed in a flash. Then he went to stand near the small window beside the room's entrance. He peeked through the curtain and saw a guy climbing out of an older pick-up. The guy made his way to the check-in office with a smiling blonde.

"You can't super speed us through the city in the day time, uh, can you?"

"No need. We're going to be driving through the city in a truck."

The floor creaked as she stepped closer. "We're stealing a truck?"

He glanced at her. "I'm good at hot wiring. Have I ever mentioned that skill?"

She just gave a shrug. "I'm pretty good at it, too."

He almost smiled. "Something else we have in common?"

But she didn't tease him back. Instead, she nibbled her lower lip and asked, "Why would Jennifer lie to the cops?"

He'd turned back to the window. The owner of the truck had stopped for a serious make-out session with the blonde. *Go on, buddy. Take it inside.*

"She's my friend, Jett. She's a cop who has helped to keep me sane over the last few months, and she's also probably the one person in this town I trust the most." She bit her lower lip. "So why is she lying? Why is she telling the cops that I'm at the cabin?"

He didn't know. He didn't like it, either. "We're getting you out of town." That was the priority. Get to the airport. Put this place in the rear-view mirror.

The guy and his lady finally made it into room six. The blonde's shirt was off before she went inside. "Time to go." Jett took Savannah's hand. Opened the door. And headed straight for the truck. An older model like that wouldn't have GPS tracking, and it would be child's play to crank that baby up.

The door was locked, but he just used a little extra strength to break the lock. Jett lifted Savannah up and she scooted across the seat, moving to buckle her seat belt. He slid in after her and immediately got the motor to growling…

"Hey!" An angry shout. "Get the fuck away from my truck!"

Well, shit, that had been *fast.* He'd sure expected the blonde to keep the fellow busier for longer than *that.*

Jett looked up, saw the naked guy stumbling toward him. "Sorry!" Jett shouted as he slammed the driver's side door shut. "I'll try not to damage her."

"You'll try — " The guy ran at Jett.

Too late. Jett already had that truck moving. He shot them out of the parking lot.

"You bastard!"

Savannah glanced back. Cleared her throat. "There's a naked man chasing us."

"Don't worry, he won't catch up."

***

"Sir, sir!"

McNeely spun around as the uniformed cop raced toward him. They should have already been on the road, heading for the lake.

"Just got a call," the out-of-breath cop huffed. "A man says his truck was stolen at the Sunlight Motel here in Biloxi."

"Why the hell are you telling me this?"

The fellow's face flushed an even darker red. "The guy said an Asian male took the truck—and that a woman was with him. He couldn't see much about her, just her long, dark hair. His description sounded like it could be the people you're looking for."

It sure as shit did.

Jennifer is trying to throw us off. She was protecting her friend. He should have expected this. "Find that truck. *Now.* I want teams on the roads near the motel. Get me access to traffic cams. Get me every damn thing that you can!"

***

The truck braked at a red light. Savannah twisted her hands in front of her even as she leaned forward. Was that a camera near the traffic light? It sure looked like—

Savannah. Get to your shop. We have to talk.

Her breath rushed out as she grabbed for Jett's hand.

You can't disappear. Not yet.

Sam. His voice. She recognized it so clearly this time.

There are things happening that you don't understand, he continued. *Get to the shop.*

The light turned green. The truck eased forward, nice and slow. She knew Jett was trying not to look suspicious.

I can't go to the shop. She didn't even know if Sam could hear her. She just tried to think of him in her mind and send out the thoughts to his image. *Cops could be watching it. I can't take that risk.*

I have Jennifer with me. I don't want to hurt her, but I will, if you aren't at the shop in thirty minutes.

What? Shock rolled through her. *Don't! Let Jennifer go!*

I will do what's necessary. Come meet me. The cops won't be here. I sent them to the lake. Park in the alley. Slip in the back. I'm waiting.

The connection ended. Like a phone, hanging up in her head.

For a moment, she couldn't even think.

"Savannah?" Worry was clear in Jett's voice.

"Turn right—up ahead."

"What's happening? You seem—"

"Sam just sent me another message. We have to go to my shop. And we have to get there as fast as possible."

Jett braked at the next light, and he turned his head to stare at her. "That's not a good idea."

"Sam *has* Jennifer! He said he'd hurt her." Since when had her cousin become a monster? "He said I had to come. Jennifer is my best friend! I can't let him hurt her."

No, no, no. None of this made sense.

"It's a trap," Jett said flatly.

Did he think she didn't know that? "Give me the phone. Please."

He tossed the phone to her. The light changed.

She dialed Jennifer's number, praying frantically all the while. Maybe Sam had been bluffing. The phone rang once, twice—

"Hi, Savannah." Jennifer's voice was devoid of all emotion. "Sam said you'd probably call. Don't get how he knew…"

"Jennifer! Where are you?"

"In your shop."

"Where's Sam? What's happening?"

"Sam is standing in front of me. He's holding my phone in one hand and a gun in the other."

Again, her voice was completely flat. "I'm tied to a chair, and I've decided that I hate your cousin."

"Jennifer..."

"Don't come here. I don't care what he said. You stay the hell away, do you understand? Don't you—"

A gunshot blasted.

The line went dead.

"*Fuck,*" Jett snarled.

***

Jennifer didn't make a sound when the gun blasted. She expected to feel pain tearing into her body, but instead, the shot went wild.

Sam stared at her with wide eyes.

Right before he slumped to the store room floor.

When he fell, she saw the person who'd been standing behind him. A person she hadn't even realized was there. Her gaze met the wide-eyed stare of Savannah's assistant, Megan. Megan's short, spiky, blonde hair framed a face that appeared far too pale. Megan dropped the lamp she held. It shattered when it hit the floor.

"Oh, my God, Megan!" She hadn't thought anyone else was at the store. "Get me out of these ropes! Help me!"

Megan headed toward Sam. Biting her lip, she nudged him with her sneaker. "He's not dead. I just knocked him out." She scooped up his gun.

"Megan!" Jennifer twisted in the ropes. "Get me out of here! Call the cops."

Megan frowned. "That was Savannah on the phone?"

"Yes, yes, he was setting a trap for her—"

Megan turned the gun on Jennifer. "No, I think he was trying to protect her. *I'm* the one setting the trap. You would *not* believe how much money that woman is worth right now."

Oh, hell. "You know what, Megan?" Jennifer muttered as the rope cut into her wrists. "I never really liked you."

***

"You're not going in that shop."

They'd braked and were in some alley that she'd never seen before. "Jett, she is my *friend*—"

He pulled her close. Pressed a frantic kiss to her lips. "And you're my fucking world, Savannah. You and the baby are all that matter to me." He leaned his forehead against hers. "You can't go in there, with bullets flying, with a psycho who is willing to hurt your friend in order to get to you. You can't do that."

"I can't let her die—"

"That's why I'm going in. He won't ever see me coming, I promise you that. You'll stay a safe distance back. Hell, you'll stay a few blocks away. If there is any sign of trouble..." His index fingers pressed lightly to her temples. "I'll send you a warning. Then you crank the vehicle, you drive hell fast for that airport, and you never stop, do you understand?"

"Jett..."

"I'll get her. This is kind of my thing, baby. I'll make sure she's okay, and once she's good, you and I are out of this town." He gave her another kiss. "But if there is any sign of trouble, you just drive. Understand? Drive fast and hard for the airport. You contact Sawyer. Just press one on the phone, and it will connect to him."

He turned and started the truck again. She clutched the phone in her hand.

"I'm going to find a safe place for you to hide. You stay there, and you trust me, okay?"

"I do trust you." It was more than just trust. So much more.

He slanted her a fast glance.

"I trust you," she whispered again.

Did he realize she might as well have been saying...*I love you?*

CHAPTER EIGHTEEN

"Someone heard the gunshot," Jennifer snarled. "It's only a matter of time before—"

"Uh, it's not even six a.m. yet. *And* it's a Sunday. No one is in this section of town. No one heard a damn thing." Megan paced and kept the gun in her hand. "I was only here because dumbass Sam over there—"

She'd tied his hands behind his back, tied his ankles together, and left him in an unconscious heap on the store room floor.

"Well, that joker flipped the store's alarm. But don't worry, the alarm only went to my phone. I might have, you know, tampered with things here a bit." She gave Jennifer a wide smile. "The cops don't know that anyone is in the shop. The security firm that watches this store—" She shrugged. "It's not really a firm. It's my employer. He always keeps tabs on Savannah."

"I don't understand what in the hell is happening."

"No, you probably don't. Because you shouldn't be involved. But, that's life." Megan sighed. "Just so you know, I will have to kill you. No loose ends will be left when this deal is done." She headed for the front of the shop. "I need to make sure the front area is set. Thanks to the explosion that happened across the street, all of the front windows are boarded up. No one can see inside. The front door is still just fine, though, and I want Jett to be able to get in easily. If he comes in the front, I'll hear the bell jingle, and I'll know it's show time."

When she vanished, Jennifer struggled with her ropes. If she could just get out—

"Got a big surprise waiting in there." Megan was already back, and she was grinning. "Things are going to get so hot."

"What in the hell does that mean?"

Megan rolled her eyes. "I've got an explosion all set to go. Don't worry, it's going to project out, at first. Destroy the front of the shop."

Was that why she wanted the front door unlocked? So that Jett would have an easier time getting in that way—only so the guy would get blown to hell?

"If Jett comes in the shop's back door..." A little shrug. "I'll just shoot the bastard. *I'll* be ready for him, no matter what."

Jennifer narrowed her eyes on the woman who'd seemed to be a mostly clueless assistant. "Who the hell are you?"

"For the last year, I've been Megan Johansen, Savannah's assistant. I was *supposed* to be her best friend, but I guess we never really clicked. Then you rolled in. Messed up my job. Made things harder. *I* was supposed to be the one going to the doctor visits with Savannah. I was supposed to be the one keeping tabs on the pregnancy. Isn't that what besties do?"

Was this some Single White Female shit?

"This is so beyond your pay grade," Megan muttered. "I feel sorry for you. Feel sorry for Savannah, too. She's about to be locked away in a lab until that baby is born. Then — who knows?"

Jennifer jerked hard on the ropes, and the chair jerked with her. "You aren't hurting Savannah *or* her baby."

"I'm not going to hurt her. That's not my job." Megan looked shocked. "I'm just here to transport her. I mean, my boss is waiting. I'm doing things the *easy* way. You don't want to see what the hard way looks like."

"When I'm out of these ropes, I'm going to show you the hard way."

Megan smiled at her. "I think we would have been friends. Good friends. You and I both have the same killer instinct." Then, keeping one hand on the gun — and keeping that gun aimed at Jennifer — Megan pulled out her phone. Her fingers swiped over the screen before she pressed the phone to her ear. "They're coming," she announced to whoever was on the other end of the line. "If Jett stays true to his profile, he'll be the one to enter the building. He'll think that he can leave Savannah some place safe. You'll want to tell Agent McNeely to start scanning the nearby area."

McNeely? "You're working with *him*?"

Megan put down her phone. "No, he's working with *me*."

***

"Get your team over to Savannah's shop. Start searching the garages and alleys near the place. She'll be hiding in a parked car nearby." The boss's words tumbled out quickly.

Bennett narrowed his eyes as his hand tightened on the phone he held. "She'll be in a fucking truck." Because he was staring at the traffic camera footage that had just been pulled up for him. A late model Ford. Jett was driving. Savannah sat in the passenger seat.

"She'll be waiting for you. She'll be alone," the boss assured him. Then there was a pause. "It should be really hard for you to screw this one up."

Asshole. Go fuck yourself. Bennett swallowed, choking those words down. "And where is Jett?"

"He'll be distracted. Or he may be dead." Careless words. "Good thing he'll rise again."

***

"Are you all right? You feel okay here?" Jett asked again as he paused by the driver's side window. The vehicle was parked near the entrance of an alley. In case things went south, Savannah would be able to slip right onto the street. She'd be able to get away fast, *if* he didn't come back.

She reached for his hand. "I don't like this."

Neither did he. This trap was obvious from a freaking mile away. And that was why he'd taken a few precautions on the way over.

He smiled at her. "I have too much to live for. Nothing will be taken from me."

"Jett—"

I love you.

Her breath caught. "That doesn't count."

His brow furrowed.

"You have to actually *say* the words. You have to tell me—"

He kissed her. Then, against her lips, he whispered, "I love you, Savannah Jacobs. I fell in love with you from the very beginning." Another kiss. "And I will have a life with you. Nothing is going to stop us from being together." He made himself pull back. "I'm going to get your friend. Then I'm eliminating the threat to you." Or maybe he'd reverse the order on that. Kill, then save? Yeah, he could do that.

Save, then kill.

Either worked.

I love you, too.

His heart slammed hard into his chest. "When I get back, you're going to say those words out loud."

"Jett—"

"When I come back." He winked at her. "Gives me something to look forward to."

She smiled at him, showing off her adorable dimples. And he knew he *would* be back. There was nothing that could keep him from Savannah. Nothing.

He backed away from the vehicle. Stayed close to buildings. Made sure to keep himself hidden as much as possible. After a few turns, he saw Savannah's shop up ahead. It waited on the corner, a closed sign hanging in the front door. Boards covered the windows that had been shattered when the building across the street blew. The street appeared deserted.

Appearances could be deceiving.

He slipped into an alley. Edged toward the back of the building. Then he smiled when he saw the control box that connected to the retail spaces there.

Using a little extra strength, he ripped off the lock on the box. Then he cut the power to Savannah's shop—and to all of the shops connected to that box.

***

The store room plunged into darkness. There were no windows back there, and when the lights went out, Jennifer blinked desperately, trying to get her eyes to adjust—

"Clever. But not good enough." Megan's voice was low. "He won't get past—"

The bell over the front door jingled. Megan's footsteps immediately rushed toward the front of the shop.

Jennifer heaved hard, and her chair toppled to the floor. "It's a trap!" Jennifer yelled. "It's Megan! Megan is the threat! She's the one—"

"Good to know," a low, masculine voice whispered in her ear as the ropes were torn away, and she was hauled up—up and thrown over someone's shoulder.

"I can walk!" Jennifer snarled. The last thing she needed was to be carried.

"We're not walking."

She could have sworn wind whipped around her. She opened her mouth, trying to figure out what the hell was happening, but in the next breath, she was outside. Standing on her own. About twenty feet from the back of Savannah's store. And a handsome man with dangerous eyes stood in front of her.

She recognized him from the photos. "Jett."

"Get out of here. When you're far enough away that you feel safe, call in some of your cop buddies."

She looked back at the shop. "Sam is still in there." Sam—good guy, bad guy, she had no clue.

"I'll get him," Jett said, already turning away and then racing back to the store. Moving *far* too fast.

Way faster than a normal human could move.

"Holy shit," Jennifer whispered. "Holy. Shit."

***

They'd found the truck. The Ford sat near the mouth of an alley, its windows up. It wasn't running. But Bennett could see the shadowy figure of *someone* in the driver's seat.

"Are we ready to move in, sir?" A younger agent asked Bennett.

He gave a grim nod. "Do *not* fire on Savannah Jacobs." The truck had been waiting, just like the boss said. Savannah had fallen into the trap. And if she'd fallen...

He glanced down the road, his gaze lingering on the exterior of her shop. He could just see it, about three blocks away. If she'd fallen into the trap, then Jett would be taken down, too.

Two agents reached the truck. They grabbed for the door. Wrenched it open.

And the truck was empty.

An agent yanked out what looked like an empty, bulky jacket. "This was stuck behind the driver's seat!"

Positioned to look like a person from a distance.

Bennett blinked. Shit, Savannah should have been *in* the truck. His boss had planned everything so perfectly. He yanked out his phone. Got the asshole on the line. Frantic, he said, "She has to be with him! The truck is empty! It's — "

The front windows of her shop exploded outward as flames seemed to engulf Savannah's shop.

***

"*Jett!*" The flames shot from the front windows of her shop, and Savannah grabbed for the car door handle, ready to race toward him.

Baby, I'm okay. Stay where you are.

His voice slid through her mind, and she hunched back down in the vehicle. Not the truck. They'd left that ride down the road. She was in a little red sedan, a ride that *she'd* hot-wired.

Jennifer is out of the building. She's okay, so you just breathe, got it? In and out. Stress isn't good for the baby.

Seriously?

I'm getting your cousin, but Megan is trickier than I thought.

Megan? What would she —

Her car door was wrenched open. "Hello, Savannah." A man stood there. Tall, with slightly stooped shoulders. Curly hair. His bright blue eyes were shielded by the lenses of his glasses. She *knew* him. He'd haunted her nightmares for years.

Focus on me, Savannah. Only me. The voice that she still heard whispering to her, late at night. The voice she'd never been able to fully escape.

She blinked, stunned.

"It's been a long time," Dr. Anthony Rowe added softly.

Her gaze fell to the gun in his hand.

"Too long, I think."

She cut the connection to Jett, severing it instantly.

***

Flames crackled around Jett, and smoke burned his eyes. The explosion had come from the front of the shop. He didn't know what kind of game Megan was playing —

"I can see you, Jett."

She stood over Sam's crumpled form, holding a gun.

He cut the connection to Savannah, not wanting her to pick up on anything that might happen. Mostly, he didn't want her connected to him when he killed Megan. *Assistant, my ass.*

Megan didn't have her gun pointed at Jett. Instead, she had it pressed to the side of Sam's head.

"The fire is spreading quickly." She smiled. "That was the plan. When this place is done burning, two bodies are going to be found inside. A man and a woman. They'll eventually be identified as Sam and his dear cousin Savannah. You see, Savannah has to vanish now. It's time. With this being the second explosion to happen on this block, folks will say some crazy pyro is at work. Everyone will be sad that two people died in his latest attack."

Sam coughed, groaned.

Megan's gun remained on Sam, but her eyes were on Jett. "I want you to put down any weapons you have, or I will lodge a bullet into his head. Even a Lazarus soldier couldn't come back from that, and we both know Sam's not exactly Lazarus material, is he?"

"I don't have any weapons on me." Jett kept his hands up, but he started to pull out his shadows. He let the darkness sweep —

"Stop," she snarled. "You pull your vanishing act, and I'm going to fire."

"You're going to fire either way, so it doesn't really matter what I do."

"No? But I bet it matters to Savannah. I bet it matters one hell of a lot to her if you just stand there and let her only remaining family member *die.*"

She was stalling. Obviously trying to buy time for something. "You willing to die in this fire, Megan?"

Her laughter crackled like the flames. "I don't plan on dying at all."

"You're stalling. If you weren't, you would have pulled the trigger on him."

"I'm good at my job. Always have been."

Sprinklers shot on from overhead. Soaked the flames that sputtered around them. *About damn time.* "Your job...watching Savannah?"

A roll of one shoulder.

And he remembered something else. Sonofabitch. "Savannah said you and she shared a tattoo artist."

Megan's smile flashed. "Figured that one out, did you? Yep, I'm the one who put the tracking device in her rose. I mean, not like she could see what was happening behind her back, right?" A wink. "But you were sneaky when you cut it out of her. Got to say, I didn't think you'd use a knife on your girl."

"I didn't." *She's stalling.* Because he was so worried, Jett sent a fast, psychic message to Savannah. *Baby, get out of here. Crank the car. Go. I'll meet you —*

There was nothing. No response.

His hands fisted. "What's happening outside of this building?"

She was keeping him there. Keeping him *away* from Savannah.

Megan continued to hold her gun on Sam. "Once we have her, you'll be easy to control, won't you, Jett?"

Savannah?

Nothing.

"Because you'll do whatever we say. If you can keep your precious Savannah and that baby safe, you'll do *anything.* It's not just a two-for-the-price-of-one deal any longer. We get a three-fer."

She was going to get nothing. "Who are you working for? That special agent bastard?"

"That special agent bastard isn't in charge of *me.*" Her laughter rang again even as streams of water from the sprinkler slid down her face. "The fire will attract all the local cops. I planned that. You're a wanted man. Be careful when you go outside. I'd hate for you to get shot and killed."

No, she wouldn't. She'd planned that, *too.* "So you've been a spy in Savannah's life all along?"

"Someone had to keep watch. You would not believe the secrets in this town," Megan all but purred. "Take her father, for example. I was barely on the case for a few weeks when I realized the guy practically oozed guilt. I got the proof I needed, did a little digging, and realized I could make myself some side cash."

Shit. "You killed Savannah's father." Because he was looking at a trained killer. Cold to the core.

Megan shrugged. "If he'd just paid the hundred grand I wanted to keep quiet, I would have taken the money, and we could have all gone on with our lives. But the jerk started blustering about calling the cops, about clearing *his* conscience, and I couldn't exactly let him call attention to me, now could I? Not when I was supposed to be the one flying under the radar."

So she'd put a bullet in Phillip's brain. The same way she was about to fire a bullet into Sam's head.

Megan glanced at her watch. No, at the *text* that had just come through on her watch. "Time to move along." She offered him a sunny smile. "Can you get to me fast enough?" Megan asked as she tilted her head and looked down at Sam. "Before I pull the trigger?"

She was going to do it. Her stalling was over. Someone had just texted her a kill order.

Jett leapt forward, surging toward her, racing with all of his power even as—

Bam.

Megan blinked, then looked down at her chest. Blood was already spreading to cover her shirt. "You…no weapon…"

"It's not his." Jennifer rushed forward, breath heaving. "It's mine. Sam took *my* car when the guy brought us here, and I always keep a spare weapon locked in my glove box."

Megan sprawled on the floor, the gun falling from her fingers.

Jett kicked it out of the way. Looked over at Jennifer.

"Sorry." Her breathing was ragged, as if she'd been running too fast. "I, uh, had to break the window to get in my car, then had to break the lock on the glove box. That unconscious asshole we just saved—Sam still has my keys."

Jett put his fingers to Megan's throat. Her pulse was weak. And the wound to the chest told him she wasn't going to make it.

"Get your ass moving," Jennifer snapped. "Go find Savannah. I don't get what's happening here, but I'm seeing some trippy shit, and I'm scared for my friend. *Get to her.*"

Without a word, he rushed for the back door. *Fast.*

Jett raced into the alley, circling around the building. But when he headed out, a team was waiting. They lifted their weapons. Started shooting on sight. He leapt to the left, to the right, and felt a bullet slide over his shoulder. Felt it burn along his skin.

Fuck it. Jett ran faster, jumping over garbage cans, pushing himself until he knew he'd be nothing more than a blur to those behind him.

Shouts echoed. He didn't even look back. He turned to the left, rushing between buildings, and then the pathway spit him out right next to the Ford sedan.

Only Savannah wasn't sitting in the car.

Special Agent Bennett McNeely was. The driver's side door was open, and McNeely's fingers were wrapped tightly around the wheel.

Jett didn't slow down. He barreled forward and grabbed the guy by the neck, hauling him out of the car. "*Where is she?*"

A car horn honked. A long, angry blare.

Jett turned his head and watched a dark van hurtle toward them.

The van braked just a few feet away. The side door slid open, and Jett saw Savannah. A man with curly, dark hair sat beside her, glasses perched on his nose, and a gun in his hand. The gun—equipped with a silencer—was pressed to Savannah's stomach.

"You're fucking dead," Jett told the bastard.

The guy smiled. "Let go of McNeely. You're choking the life out of him."

Jett dropped McNeely.

The SOB in glasses smirked. "You'll do anything for her, won't you?"

"*Let her go.*"

"Or is it the baby you care more about? I've been curious about that part."

He cared about them *both*. They were his family.

McNeely was wheezing and gasping for breath. Jett didn't spare the guy a glance.

"If I let you in the van as you are, you'll just try to overpower me. Or if it's dark enough in here, you'll play your shadow games." The prick smiled at him. "You've grown very good at those, haven't you?"

"Who the hell are you? Another Lazarus doc with a god complex?"

"No, I'm Dr. Anthony Rowe, and I'm Savannah's psychiatrist. I've been taking care of her for years."

Fucking hell. The name clicked for him. Dr. Rowe had been the prick in charge of the psychiatric facility that Savannah had stayed in when she was just sixteen years old. He'd been the man who'd "treated" her — the bastard who'd suppressed her psychic powers and changed her memories. "You were on my list, Rowe. You didn't have to come for me. I was going to come for *you*." He'd planned to make anyone who ever hurt Savannah *pay*.

For an instant, fear flashed on the man's face. But it quickly vanished as the doc curled one hand around Savannah's shoulder. "I'm afraid the next step is necessary, Savannah." His gaze flickered down to her.

Savannah just kept staring straight at Jett. There was so much trust in her eyes. Faith. She thought he'd get her out of this. *I will, baby, I will.*

Dr. Rowe sighed. "Believe it or not, Savannah, I'm doing this so the ride will be easier for everyone. But take a deep breath. Maybe close your eyes. We should try to lessen the emotional impact on you. Don't want the baby being stressed."

What?

The doc's gaze lifted. Focused not on Jett but on Agent McNeely. "McNeely, kill him. Fire the gun. Not the head. Be sure not the head—"

Jett whirled for the jerk.

McNeely had his gun out. Face grim, he said, "I'm sorry."

"No!" Savannah screamed.

McNeely fired. The silencer had the bullet coming out with just a gust of wind. The bullet tore into Jett's chest. Missed his heart. Jett lunged for the van.

Bam.

Another bullet tore into his back. Jett immediately felt his legs give way. His eyes were on Savannah as she fought with the bastard in the glasses.

The guy hit her, driving his fist at her face.

"You're...dead," Jett promised as the blood pumped from his body.

Once more, the bastard smirked at him. "No, that would be you."

Darkness closed around Jett. His last thought...*Joke's on you, you sonofabitch. I don't stay dead. You will. I guarantee it.*

CHAPTER NINETEEN

"Get him into the van! Let's get the hell out of here!"

McNeely grabbed Jett's limp body. Tossed him into the van. Jett's head slammed into the bottom of a seat.

Savannah cried out and reached for him, but the doctor grabbed her and jerked her back.

"Savannah, stay here!" He motioned to the driver. Even as McNeely jumped into the van and slid the side door shut, they were hurtling forward.

Dr. Anthony Rowe. She hadn't seen that bastard, not in years. She'd thought that he was just a nightmare from her past.

Some nightmares seemed destined to haunt you.

"I'm sorry I had to hit you. I couldn't have you taking the gun from me."

She was going to do more than take the gun from him. She was going to shoot him. Her gaze stayed locked on Jett.

"Have you seen him die before?"

She had. And it wasn't any freaking easier the second time. Savannah pulled in a deep breath, let it out. "I feel dizzy." She made her breathing come faster. Harder. "You need to stop the van, I'm going to be sick."

He laughed.

She wondered if she could vomit on him. "I'm dizzy, I-I think something is wrong. Stop the van!"

"I'm not going to buy your act, Savannah. You think you can jump out and escape? Run away?" He motioned to McNeely. "Make sure she doesn't move."

McNeely slid toward her. "Savannah?" His voice was low. "Look at me."

She was still staring at Jett. "This is the second time you've killed him." Her lips curved into a cold smile. "He's going to really hate you when he wakes up."

McNeely's fingers feathered over her cheek. "She's already getting a bruise. You said she wouldn't be hurt."

Her hand pressed over her stomach.

"Don't fucking hit her again."

"It's nothing," Dr. Rowe huffed. "Shoot him again. Right in the heart this time. You said he recovers very quickly, and I don't want the guy springing at me before we get to our destination."

"No!" Savannah yelled.

McNeely pulled out his gun. Aimed it at Jett's body.

"Don't!" Savannah shouted as she clawed at his arm, trying to wrench the gun away. "He's already out! Don't —"

Rowe jabbed his gun into her stomach. "Freeze, Savannah. Right now."

"You won't shoot me or the baby," she whispered.

"Can you take that chance?"

No, she couldn't risk her baby, and the bastard knew it. She stilled.

McNeely fired.

Savannah squeezed her eyes shut. "I'm sick. I'm going to be sick. *Stop the van! Stop!*" She slapped her hand over her mouth.

"Blood is already pooling on the floor. Do you think I mind some vomit?" Dr. Rowe asked coldly as he finally moved the gun away from her. "You misjudge me."

Her gaze cut to him. He'd been fresh out of school when she'd first met him, so she figured he had to be in his late thirties now. There were only the faintest of lines on his face. He looked normal. Not like a monster.

Appearances were so deceiving.

"Concentrate on your breathing, Savannah," McNeely told her softly. "In and out. Just breathe. You're not in any danger."

Was he fucking kidding her? He'd been the one to shoot Jett! He wasn't about to —

"Breathe. Focus on me, Savannah. Only me."

Her face throbbed from where Rowe had hit her. But instead of reaching to touch her bruised skin, she slowly lowered her hand. Let it slide down low, back over her stomach, as if she was cradling her baby.

Her fingers pressed over her shirt.

Pressed against the phone that she'd hidden in the pockets of her oversized sweatshirt. She'd had that phone with her when Rowe had grabbed her, and when he'd opened the door of the van, when he'd been yelling at Jett…

I freaking dialed one. Jett had told her that in order to reach Sawyer, all she had to do was push one. *I pushed.*

She hoped like hell that the call had gone through. She hoped that Sawyer and Elizabeth had been able to answer. Could they hear what was happening in the van? Could they trace the phone as long as it was on? She had no idea how all that tech stuff worked. She was just willing to try anything.

Anything.

She breathed slowly. In and out.

Her eyes closed. Then, concentrating as hard as she could, she sent her thoughts blasting out, projecting straight to the image she'd just pulled up in her head. An image of her cousin. *Sam. I don't know if you're the good guy or the bad guy…right now, I'm leaning hard to bad. But I need help. A guy named Dr. Anthony Rowe has me and Jett. I need help. I need* —

"Interesting," Rowe murmured. "Since I haven't worked with you to grow your psychic powers, I didn't think that you'd learned how to communicate with others. I believed that I'd frozen your progress."

How the hell did he know what she was doing? Her eyes flew open, and her head whipped toward him.

His smile stretched. "I heard you, Savannah. Heard you loud and clear."

No, *no*.

"But you should know that your dear cousin has been working with me for quite some time. He's not going to save you."

Had he just heard her one message to Sam? Or could he read *all* of her thoughts? If he could read all of her thoughts, she was screwed. He'd know about the call to Sawyer.

She kept her fingers pressed over her stomach. Over the phone.

But he made no move to take the phone from her hiding spot. He said, "No one is going to come for you. As far as the rest of the world is concerned, you just died in a fire at your shop. No one will look for you, Savannah. Soon, you'll be nothing more than a headstone."

***

The scene was freaking chaos.

A fire truck had just rushed up the road. Squad cars were everywhere. Cops were running to the left and right but…

Where were all the federal agents who'd been working the case?

Jennifer spun around, her gaze scanning the street. She didn't see any of those bozos. And that was *wrong*.

"*Jennifer!*"

Her gaze snapped over at that desperate yell.

A uniformed cop was shoving Sam into the back of a patrol car. Good. Sam needed to be locked away.

"Jennifer, Savannah is in trouble! She needs you!"

Her eyes narrowed.

The guy was resisting arrest. Fighting hard. And he was about to get his ass tased. Fine by her. Sam deserved some pain. He'd *tied* her up.

Now *two* cops in uniform were working to shove him into the patrol car. She sauntered toward them. The fool had kidnapped a detective. What did he *think* was going to happen? But if he wanted to keep talking without a lawyer present, if he wanted to spill his guts to her, she'd let him.

The two uniforms finally succeeded in shoving Sam into the back seat. They slammed the door. And glared.

"Mind if I sit in the car a moment?" Jennifer asked the cops. "Got a few questions." She knew the guys, and she offered them a tired smile.

One hurried to open the driver's door for her. Jennifer slid inside. "Thanks." She waited a moment, waited for the cops to back away...

"My head hurts. I think I have a concussion."

"And why would you think I care?" She turned to glare at Sam through the partition that kept the perps in the back. "Look, there is some trippy shit happening here. But I want to focus on *why* you decided to kidnap me."

"Savannah is in danger!" His eyes were wild. "I fake kidnapped you because I knew Savannah would come for you! She wasn't going to let anything happen to you!"

And Savannah *had* sent Jett racing to the rescue.

"I needed to talk with Savannah. I needed a safe place for us to meet." He leaned toward the partition that separated them. "I'm always watched." His voice dropped. "I sold my soul to the devil, and I had to find a way out. I thought that if I could get her to the shop, where he couldn't hear what I said to her..."

The guy was delusional.

"*He* can hear my thoughts. Stupid fucking experiment. He plugged into my head, and I can't get him out. So, he knows that she just contacted me. He would have heard *her* because he can hear *me.*"

"Okay." Frustrated now, she tapped her fingers against the steering wheel. "Obviously, you're trying to set up an insanity defense, and I just don't have time for —"

"You must have seen what Jett can do! He's a super soldier. A real, honest-to-God, super soldier. And I'm psychic. So is Savannah. I know it sounds crazy. It just…" Sam banged his head against the partition. He was *so* far from the perfect guy he'd seemed to be. "She just sent me a message. Rowe has her. Her and Jett, and if we don't do something soon, she'll vanish. We'll never get her back."

"Rowe?" That was a new name.

"He's the shrink who treated Savannah after her car wreck."

"When was Savannah in a wreck?"

"*When she was sixteen!*"

"Jesus, you need to calm the hell down. I didn't know her back then. Didn't know about the wreck, okay?"

He sucked in several deep breaths. "After the wreck, her dad put Savannah is some weird-ass mental ward, and when I went there…" His voice dropped. "I met Dr. Rowe. He promised he could help me, too."

"Help you? Help you *how?*"

Silence.

Whatever. She started to climb from the car—

"I can hear thoughts. Pick them up so easily. I've always been able to do it. I knew when Savannah had the crash. I could hear her screaming in my head. She screamed for her brother over and over again, but I knew he was dead. I'd felt Steven die."

She whipped around to glare at the guy. "You're bullshitting me."

"Sometimes, I couldn't shut it off. It was driving me crazy. Back then, I thought...hell, maybe I should be in the same place Savannah is. Maybe I should be in the psych ward."

She was sure thinking a psych ward might do the man a world of good.

"I mean, when I saw what the doctor could do, he seemed perfect. And at first, Dr. Rowe *did* seem to help me. My parents died when I was kid, and Phillip didn't really give a rat's ass what I did. So when I said I wanted to see Dr. Rowe, he just wrote checks for me. I went to the shrink for weekly sessions. I learned to channel. To focus my talent on reading specific people. I didn't realize until much later..."

His words trailed away. So, in her head, she finished for him…*That you'd sold your soul to the devil?*

He nodded.

"Prove this shit. Tell me something—"

"Think something very clearly."

I want to kick your ass. You tied me up. You betrayed my trust, you prick. And here I'd always thought you were—

His eyes widened. "You liked me? You thought I was sexy?"

"No, I don't fucking like you. I want you in a cell." But her heart was racing too fast. "Where is Savannah?"

"I…I think I know where they are taking her."

"You gonna take *me* there?"

A quick nod. "But you can't go in with a swarm of cops. They'll clean up their mess at the first sign of trouble. Do you know what clean up means?"

Yes, she knew what it meant.

"They'll kill Savannah. And Dr. Rowe has ties to the government. They'll make me and you vanish. They'll make this all go away."

Without responding, Jennifer reached for the keys that the cops had left in the ignition. Bad mistake on their part. You never leave keys in a patrol vehicle. She cranked the car. Reversed.

"Uh, Jennifer…"

"Just tell me how the hell to get to Savannah and Jett." Because maybe this insanity was actually real.

And if it was, then she was damn well saving her best friend.

***

The van braked. Savannah sucked in a sharp breath. Her gaze was still on Jett. He'd come back much faster the last time he'd died. They'd driven and driven, but his body hadn't moved. He'd been stone cold the whole time.

She had no idea where they were, and Jett— *come back to me. Please.*

"Uh, Dr. Rowe?" McNeely cast a nervous glance at Jett's body. They'd put thick handcuffs around his wrists. "Shouldn't he have woken up?"

"He will." Rowe didn't seem the least bit worried. He shoved open the van's door. Jumped out.

Savannah didn't move.

Rowe turned to smile at her. "I am so happy that you've made it past your first trimester. I was waiting for that, you know. No point grabbing you and making you disappear until I was sure the fetus was viable."

"You aren't touching my baby."

"Your baby is going to be the start of something brand new." An armed guard appeared behind Dr. Rowe. "If the child inherits your genetic anomalies…"

Anomalies?

"*And* if the child exhibits any of the Lazarus traits, then we're looking at the future. A great and powerful future."

Her gaze slanted to McNeely. "You seriously work for this prick?"

Dr. Rowe grunted. He turned to the guard behind him. "Bring Jett. If he twitches, just shoot him again."

"No!" Savannah lunged out of the van, McNeely surging out with her. She put herself in front of the guard with the gun. "What do you jerks know about Lazarus?" She was totally talking out of her ass. "Because *I* know more." No, she didn't. "If they die too many times within a twenty-four hour period, their bodies can't recover." Did that sound good? She hoped it sounded real enough. "Their cells just aren't up to the challenge. If he dies again, that's it. Jett won't come back."

Dr. Rowe frowned.

All during the ride, Savannah had been working to put up a mental shield in her mind, trying to keep her thoughts blocked because she didn't know just what he could do. What were the extent of his psychic powers? Since she didn't know, Savannah just stared at him. Tried to only think…

Lazarus soldiers can't regenerate that quickly. They need more time. They need…

"Don't shoot him," Dr. Rowe announced as his brows furrowed. "Just drag his ass to confinement. Shackle his legs and make sure those restraints are on tight."

Her breath left in a quick exhale.

Dr. Rowe laughed. "It doesn't matter, don't you see? As long as we have you, Savannah, he *is* controlled. Jett will never do anything to jeopardize you. That's what this whole thing was about. Lazarus made a major mistake by cutting me out of the research. They should have used my skills. They should have seen that evolution was necessary. Now, I'll show them."

"Show them what? That you're crazy? That you're a killer?"

But he only shrugged. "I am what I need to be."

More armed guards were running toward them.

"McNeely, escort Savannah to her new home. I want her and Jett put in the cells right next to each other. As long as he sees her, he won't make a move."

The guy was so confident.

He was also a fool.

McNeely moved closer to Savannah's side. She watched with wide eyes as several men pulled a still-not-moving Jett from the van. "He's not breathing," she whispered.

McNeely tensed.

"How did it feel to kill a man who was a US patriot?" She glared up at him. "I know you read Jett's file. He was a decorated SEAL. He saved lives, over and over again, and this is how you repay him for his service?"

McNeely's jaw tensed. "I work for the government. I work for—"

"You work for a sadistic bastard." Her head turned. She watched as Jett was strapped onto a gurney. Wheeled away. She immediately followed, not needing anyone to "escort" her. "I hated Rowe when I was a kid. Couldn't stand him. He locked me away. Drugged me. Half the time, I felt like I was in a fog." And now, she knew Jett had been right. Dr. Rowe had played with her mind. He'd made her forget things from her life.

She didn't even know what all she was missing.

"You didn't pick the right side here," she muttered to McNeely. "And to think, I actually believed you were helping me all of these months."

They headed down a long corridor. The armed men turned to the right. Entered a small room. *A cell.* Jett had told her before that he'd been kept in a cell. And now he would be again. She tried to follow, but McNeely pulled her back.

"Savannah…"

She tried to run into Jett's cell.

Swearing, McNeely lifted her up, held her too fucking easily, and carried her into the next room. Another cell. She twisted and punched at him.

"I don't want to hurt you!"

He let her go, and she whirled to confront him. "You don't? What do you *think* is going to happen to me here? What do you *think* is going to happen to my baby?" Her gaze flew around the room — *cell.* A prison cell. Three of the walls appeared to be made of metal. One of the walls — it was glass. She could see through it. See Jett in the other cell. His hands and feet were now locked in heavy, vice-like restraints. He was on the floor, not moving.

What if he doesn't come back? What if he's dead? He'd told her only a shot to the head would take him out. He'd better have been right. *Dammit, Jett, I need you.*

"I…you will be taken care of here." McNeely was sweating. And sounding uncertain. "Your child will be given the care he or she needs."

Her incredulous stare flew back to him. "Are you shitting me? There is no way you can believe that."

He backed away. And his gaze jerked up, to the video cameras that she hadn't noticed until that moment. "Ordinary doctors will never be able to give your child the proper care—"

"Stop bullshitting!" Savannah yelled at him. "Rowe is going to take my child from me! He's going to use my baby! Then he'll probably kill me!"

McNeely flinched.

"Who is it that you think you're working for? You're not FBI. The FBI doesn't do this crap. Just what government agency do you think would order this?"

He stared back at her.

"And do really want to be this monster?"

He was inside the doorway. Away from the view of the cameras. "I'm sorry." McNeely didn't speak those words, just mouthed them.

Her eyes turned to slits. "You will be sorry. Especially once Jett wakes up. You've killed him what—two, three times now? Yeah, *three*. If you count when you shot him in the van. *When he was already dead!* Payback will be a bitch."

McNeely whirled to leave.

The phone she carried gave a growling vibration.

Oh, shit.

McNeely's shoulders stiffened. She knew he'd heard the sound. He looked back at her. His gaze swept over her body. A faint smile curved his lips. He still stood just beyond the range of the cameras. They were focused on her. Not on the door.

She waited for him to come forward. Waited for him to search her. To take the phone.

But he just walked away. Shut the door behind him.

She lunged forward and immediately tried to open the door, but it wouldn't move at all. She was sealed in. Locked in tight.

And while she was pressed to the door, while the cameras couldn't pick up her movements, she pulled out the phone. Looked at the screen. Read the text.

We're coming.

Hope had her fingers trembling as she hid the phone again. Then she whirled and ran for the glass that separated her from Jett. She banged her hands on the glass. "Jett! Jett!"

He was still out.

"Jett!"

***

Bennett McNeely closed his eyes as he stood just beyond Savannah's cell door. She had a phone. No one had searched her — probably because all of the guards felt bad enough about abducting a pregnant woman.

She was right. He hadn't signed up for this. This twisted sci-fi shit hadn't been on his agenda. He'd been military, too. A Ranger back in the day. Before he'd been approached by the US government. Told that his services were needed.

Now he looked back on his cases, and he tried to figure out...

Had he been the good guy in any of them?

And was it too late to ever be good again? Or had he already sold his soul with no hope of a fucking refund?

CHAPTER TWENTY

Jett let out a groan as awareness flooded through him. His muscles and cells felt as if they were on fire. The burn consumed him, pulsed through him, and then —

His eyes opened. He was on a cold, tiled floor. His hands and feet were bound.

And Savannah wasn't *there.*

A roar came from him. And he *ripped* those metal cuffs apart, freeing his hands, and then he grabbed for the restraints around his ankles. Whoever these bastards were — they weren't used to Lazarus soldiers. It took a whole lot more than this flimsy crap to keep someone like him secured. He ripped the restraints from his ankles. Free, he surged to his feet.

Bang! Bang!

He whirled. His gaze zeroed in on the glass to his right. Savannah was there, tears in her gorgeous eyes, as she pounded her fists into the glass that separated them. She pounded again and again. He bounded to her. "Baby..." His gaze flew over her. "Are you okay?"

In the next moment, she was in his mind. *I was so scared you wouldn't wake up! I was afraid you had left me!*

Jett shook his head. *No, baby, never happening. I told you that.* He gave her what he hoped was a reassuring smile. *Never gonna leave you again.*

It's the shrink who treated me when I was a teen. Dr. Rowe. He's behind all of this. He's —

Are you okay? Is the baby okay?

She nodded. *He wants to use us all. I think we're some kind of experiment.*

Story of Jett's life. *He's not going to use you. We're all getting out of here.*

Her gaze dropped. Seemed to linger on the front of her shirt. One of her hands moved near the oversized pockets. *I still have the phone. The others are coming. They just sent me a message.*

Hell, yes. If the others were coming, this place would go down in flames.

McNeely is working for him. Do you remember seeing —

The bastard had killed Jett. Again. Jett's hands fisted. Yeah, he remembered. *Back away from the glass.*

Jett?

Get as close to the far wall as you can. When the glass breaks, I don't want you getting cut. Because objective one was getting to her. Being there to put himself between Savannah and any threat.

She backed away. *I love you.*

And he'd die for her. Over and over again. *Baby, it still doesn't count when you don't say it out loud,* he chided her. Jett slammed his fists into the glass.

But the glass didn't break.

He hit it again.

It's reinforced, isn't it? Savannah's worry was clear. *They fixed it so that we couldn't get out.*

He hit it again. And again. The glass didn't break. But his rage did grow. *Don't worry, baby. I've got this.* Nothing would stop him from getting to Savannah. *Nothing.*

***

Anthony Rowe smiled as he stared at the monitors. This was his first chance to really see a Lazarus soldier up close, and he wasn't disappointed. The guy had risen from the dead. Absolutely fantastic. And his strength — he'd snapped through those restraints as if they were nothing.

Jett wouldn't get through the glass, though. That was fortified. Built for use on submarines, that glass could withstand pressure up to —

"He's going to get free."

Agent McNeely was behind him. Sounding far too confident.

"Jett's going to get free, and then he's going to come for us both."

Rowe smiled. "No, he won't get out. I knew the restraints wouldn't hold him for long. They were just an experiment."

"Everything is an experiment to you."

McNeely didn't understand. He didn't know what it was like to spend most of your life feeling like you were a freak. Anthony had gone into psychiatry in the first place because — after growing up his whole life hearing voices, trying to pretend to be normal because his father had refused to have an *"insane friggin' son"* — he'd wanted answers. Medication had never made the voices stop. All of the therapy in the world hadn't made them stop. He'd finally just pretended the treatments had helped him so the world would stop seeing him as a freak.

He'd pretended so well that everyone had believed him.

And I got into the best damn college I could find. Graduated with honors. Went on to become a psychiatrist. Then fate had given him the best present possible. While he'd been down in Biloxi, trying to get funding to start up his own clinic…

Savannah Jacobs had walked into his life. Savannah — who shared so many of the same traits he possessed.

Savannah had been his key. Phillip Jacobs had known that his daughter had gifts, and he'd been afraid of those gifts coming to bite him in the ass.

"What if she remembers? What if she hears my thoughts? I know I sound crazy, but she can do it. And I can't stop thinking about the accident. You have to help me. You have to make sure Savannah stops getting into my mind."

He'd stopped Savannah, and he'd found a powerful ally in Phillip Jacobs. The senator had gotten Anthony access to the D.C. movers and shakers. The government had given him clearance to begin psychic testing and evaluations on others. He'd become one of Uncle Sam's pet project leaders. When he'd learned about Lazarus, learned that the Lazarus subjects were waking with psychic enhancements, Anthony had known he should be involved with that program, too. It had seemed to be a perfect fit for him.

Only the powers-that-be at Lazarus had shut Anthony out. Soon after the rejection, he'd gotten word that all of Lazarus was going dark. Something about dangerous results in the test subjects. Unpredictable aggression.

The government wanted Lazarus gone.

But *he* wanted a new chapter. If no more Lazarus subjects were going to be made, then Anthony had figured the subjects would be *born*.

He'd wanted to enhance the child's likelihood of developing psychic powers, so he'd decided the mother needed to have gifts, too. Savannah had been perfect.

But her father hadn't thought so. When he'd realized that Anthony had pulled strings to get one of the last Lazarus teams in Biloxi, when he'd realized that Jett was getting obsessed with Savannah…

Phillip Jacobs tried to stop everything. Megan had taken care of him, though. Oh, sure, Anthony knew about her little blackmail game, but he didn't particularly care. As far as he was concerned, she'd gotten rid of a useless pawn. Phillip hadn't been valuable any longer. But Sam…Sam was definitely someone valuable in the new game.

Because I control him. He'd gotten into Sam's mind years ago, and the man had never been able to get him out.

Anthony's gaze lingered on the security monitors. He ignored McNeely's last comment. Why bother to reply? Yes, everything was an experiment. *Life* was an experiment. He opened his mind, wanting to catch some of McNeely's thoughts…

But there was nothing there. Interesting. "You've gotten better at shielding yourself."

"What happened to all the people my team brought in? All of those *threats* to society?"

"You think I lied to you? Don't be naive. Many of those bastards were more dangerous than you can possibly imagine. The US government backs me. I was given a team of special agents for a reason."

Because I had a senator in my pocket. Because he'd been able to work Phillip Jacobs for years. Until the very end. The senator had only balked when he'd realized Savannah was part of Anthony's plans.

"Savannah Jacobs isn't dangerous."

"Don't be too sure of that." A woman protecting her child could be the most dangerous individual on the planet. "Never let your guard down around her. I think she'd kill you in an instant, Agent McNeely."

Jett pounded harder on the glass. Anthony chuckled as he watched the scene. "He's just not giving up. He's—"

"I think the glass is breaking," McNeely noted quietly. "Better take a closer look."

Anthony stopped laughing. He leaned closer to the monitor. A crack had appeared in the glass. A quiver of what could have been fear slid through Anthony. "He's stronger than I thought."

"We all fucking are."

What?

Anthony whirled around—just as McNeely's fist drove into his jaw.

***

The glass was breaking. Jett snarled as he pounded his fists over and over into the barrier that kept him from Savannah. Blood flowed from his knuckles, but he didn't care. She was what mattered. Always Savannah. Always.

The glass shattered. An alarm blared. He leapt into the other cell, crunching the chunks of glass beneath his feet as he ran for her.

Savannah threw her arms around him, holding him tightly. "Don't die," she whispered, "don't die again. *Don't.*"

He kissed her. Was so desperate for her. His arms were locked around her, and his mouth was wild on hers. His Savannah.

Against her mouth, he muttered, "I'm getting us out of here."

She pulled back and stared at him with her amazing eyes. "The door—I think it will be harder to break than the glass." Her gaze searched his. "And there are guards outside. We need—"

He heard the heavy groan coming from the door. Immediately, Jett shoved Savannah behind him. As soon as he'd gotten through the glass, he'd known guards would rush inside. That was why he hadn't been too worried about getting through the door. That problem had solved itself.

Now, he had to take care of the guards. But before those guys could rush inside—

The cell plunged into darkness. Savannah gave a sharp gasp.

And...

I got your six, buddy. Sawyer's voice drifted through Jett's mind. *Took out the power. Thought it might give you an advantage.*

Hell, yes, it gave him an advantage.

Use the advantage while you can. I'm betting there is a fail-safe that will have the electricity coming back on soon.

Just as he'd done in Savannah's shop, Jett instantly let his shadows sweep out. He could still see perfectly in the darkness, but the two guards who now rushed into the cell — they weren't so lucky.

Both of the guards were armed. Jett didn't give them the chance to fire. He erupted in a flash and took their weapons. As soon as they were disarmed, Jett slammed the men into the nearest wall. When the guards fell to the floor, they were unconscious. They'd be staying that way for a while.

He gripped one of the guns.

Savannah held the other.

They hurried into the hallway. Darkness was everywhere. The only illumination came from the faint, golden glows near the floor. Probably some sort of back-up security lighting. It was no match for the darkness, though. And with the dark, his shadows would win.

Savannah twined her left hand with his.

Let's get the hell out of here, sweetheart.

***

Bennett had his gun aimed on Rowe — and then the lights went out. The alarm that had been blaring fell silent as the control room was plunged into thick darkness. "Shit!" Bennett fired anyway.

But…

"You missed."

The voice came from low and to the left. He fired again.

"I had my doubts about you," Dr. Rowe announced. "Always thought you might be a weak link."

Now the doctor's voice was to the right. Bennett whirled.

But he didn't fire, not this time. Because he was starting to suspect…

"I mean, I think this case changed you. It's the straw that broke the camel's back, so to speak. Let me guess…it's because she's pregnant? And there's just nothing more innocent than a child."

This time, the doctor's voice seemed to be behind him. Bennett held himself perfectly still. *I don't think that voice is coming from the right or the left. I don't think it's behind me at all.* He thought the voice might just be in his head. He'd always wondered exactly what Rowe was capable of doing…

Isn't that why he'd needed an in-person meeting? He hadn't been face-to-face with the bastard since he'd signed on for the team. But he'd known that if he could deliver Savannah and Jett, then Rowe would come out in person to claim that special prize.

He'd just had to wait for the right moment. Wait until the moment when other agents weren't around…

"You're right, McNeely. I am in your head. And I know that you went soft because of the kid. I can't have someone like you working for me any longer. So if you're not with me…"

Bennett knew Rowe was armed. He knew —

A bullet fired. This time, it wasn't from Bennett's gun.

"If you're not with me…"

Bennett fell to the floor.

"Then you're dead."

***

"Turn here!"

Jennifer yanked the steering wheel to the right. The patrol car fish-tailed, then was lunging down a tiny dirt road.

"Savannah is this way, I'm sure of it!"

Sam had better be sure.

"I can feel it. Savannah gives off—shit, it's like a little light, okay? She gives off a little freaking light path for me, and the closer we get, the warmer I feel."

He was just pissing her off more and more. "If you can *feel* her, then when she was abducted by Patrick Zane months ago, why the hell didn't you go and save her?"

Silence. Which meant…she was going to hate his answer.

"Because Dr. Rowe planned her kidnapping. He wanted her thrown together with Lazarus soldiers. He arranged for three of them to find her." Sam's voice was miserable. "And he'd hoped that the longer she was thrown with—"

"Just *stop!*" And she slammed on the brakes. The patrol car bounced. Jennifer whirled toward him. "Tell me how to find Savannah."

He swallowed. Looked grim. "Go straight down this road. She's there. I feel her."

"And this Dr. Rowe jerk—he can feel you, is that the deal? So he'll know that you're coming?"

A miserable nod.

She jumped out of the car. Opened the back door. Pulled him out.

He flashed her a grateful smile. "Thank you, Jennifer! I knew you'd—"

She shoved him away from the patrol car. When he stumbled, she slammed the butt of her gun into the back of his head.

Sam crumpled.

"Nothing personal," she whispered. *Concussion number two.* "If some evil villain is in your head, then I need to make sure he doesn't see anything but darkness." She bit her lip. "I'll pick you up on the way out." Maybe.

She'd let Savannah make the call.

Jennifer hopped back in the car and floored that baby.

***

More guards rushed toward them. Savannah tensed, but those guards just flew right past. Jett lifted his gun to fire after them—

Let's just go. Savannah sent the desperate thought to him. *Leave them.*

She'd had enough death. She and Jett couldn't be seen. They could get out of there and never look back.

He didn't fire. They ran down the hallway. Turned to the right. The left. The place was like a maze, and Savannah had no idea where she was going.

They took another left. Burst into a small room—

And her foot collided with something soft.

"Baby, step back," Jett whispered.

She staggered back.

The lights flashed on. Flew on and had her blinking quickly because it seemed too bright.

Then she looked at the floor and saw that she hadn't tripped on something, but someone. Bennett McNeely lay in a pool of growing blood.

She reached for him.

Jett grabbed her. He pushed her behind his back.

"Jett, he's been shot, he's—"

"*He's* not the threat." Jett's voice was lethal.

Savannah realized someone else was in the room. Someone else had been hiding in the darkness. She peeked around Jett's shoulder and saw Dr. Rowe.

He had a gun in his hand. And the bastard was blocking the door. The only way out of that room.

He was hiding in the shadows behind the door. He waited for us to come inside. To get distracted by McNeely.

Then Dr. Rowe had planned to attack. Only Jett had sensed the guy before Rowe could get a shot off.

"When I fall," Jett told her in his rough, rumbling voice, "don't hesitate. You run out of here, and you get to Sawyer. I'll follow when I rise."

She knew that he was going to shoot Rowe. And Rowe was going to shoot Jett.

They were in a stand-off, and there was only one way for this to end.

Death.

"You're miscalculating," Rowe announced. "You're assuming that I'll just aim for your heart this time, but that won't happen. I'll shoot you in the head. *Are you paying attention, Savannah?*"

Yes, she fucking was. *Prick.*

He laughed. "I'll shoot your lover in the head. He'll shoot me, I'm sure, but my finger is tight around the trigger, and I'll get my hit off before I fall. And if I don't, I've given orders that all of the agents and guards at this facility are to only go for head shots if they see him fleeing. He'll never make it out of here. You might escape, Savannah, but he won't. I guarantee it."

"Jett…" Savannah pressed her left hand to his back. Her right hand still gripped the gun he'd given her in the cell.

"You underestimate us," Jett said softly. "If I'd wanted to fire, I could have done it when I first heard the tap of your footstep. I've just been delaying, waiting on my team to get in position."

Jett had pushed her further behind him. She couldn't see the doctor's face, but she *felt* his sudden tension.

In his lethal voice, Jett continued, "I couldn't risk your bullet going through me and hitting Savannah, so I was waiting. Your dumb move was sliding over so that you blocked the

doorway. You don't even fucking realize it…"
Jett growled. "But my man Sawyer is behind you
right now. You're heard of him, haven't you? The
first Lazarus subject?"

Again, the tension in the air seemed to
deepen.

"Scared to look over your shoulder?" Jett
taunted. "Scared to see your own death?"

"*No one is there!*" Rowe shouted. "No one can
sneak up on me! I can feel everyone coming. I felt
Savannah coming to this room. I felt you. I
guided you to me when you didn't even realize
it! No one is—"

"Boo," a masculine voice drawled. Sawyer's
voice.

Then things happened very fast.

Jett didn't fire a shot at Rowe. Instead, he
whirled and grabbed Savannah, pulling her with
him to the floor. But her hand was up. Her gun
was aimed. And she saw Dr. Rowe as he spun to
confront Sawyer. Sawyer who was, indeed,
standing in the doorway. As Dr. Rowe turned
toward the new threat, she knew he'd shoot
Sawyer.

In that instant, Savannah's finger squeezed
the trigger. The bullet flew, and it thudded into
the doctor's side. He staggered, and his attention
whipped back toward her.

He gaped at her in shock.

She fired again. A hit to his chest. He jerked back, like a marionette on a string. He was gasping, shuddering.

Blood soaked him as he fell.

"Savannah?" Jett's fingers stroked her cheek.

She was still holding the gun. Her fingers felt like claws around the weapon. "I want to fire again."

Sawyer leaned over the doctor. He whistled. "No need. He's dead. That was some *excellent* shooting."

Her heart thundered in her chest.

Jett pulled her closer. She kept her gun, just in case. She'd be keeping that gun until they were out of there. Far away from this nightmare.

"God, I love you," Jett whispered into her ear.

"I love you, too," she told him.

His hold tightened.

"*This* one is still alive," Sawyer announced.

Her head turned. She saw that he was leaning over McNeely.

"Leave him? Finish him?" Sawyer asked, not seeming very concerned either way.

Jett's body tensed. "Bring him. He can answer our questions before I kill the bastard."

"Fair enough." Sawyer slung the bleeding agent over his shoulder. "Let's get the hell out of here. Jay took the security system off-line. Our ride is waiting right outside."

"Our ride?" Savannah asked.

"Yeah, the same van you guys arrived in." He was already heading out of what looked like some kind of control room. Monitors everywhere. Monitors currently only showing gray screens. "Jay's in my ear, giving me directions to the garage. He's got schematics on this place. So just follow me."

She started to follow, but stopped, glancing down at Rowe. She'd killed him. Hadn't even hesitated.

Because he'd threatened Jett. Because he'd threatened her family.

Killing had been easier than she'd suspected it would be.

Jett scooped her into his arms. "Just in case," he whispered before he kissed her. "I'm carrying you. If any guards come out, I'll make sure no bullets hit you."

But Dr. Rowe had said that he'd given orders for his men to shoot Jett in the head. *He* needed protection, not her.

So, as they ran through the twisting corridors, she kept her gun close. If a guard appeared to threaten Jett, Savannah knew what choice she'd make. She *would* fire. She'd protect him, at all costs.

But she didn't have to fire. Sawyer took out two men before the guys could even get their weapons up. Left them in unconscious piles. No one else appeared.

An alarm began to blare. And... "Evacuate," a robotic voice announced. "Clear the premises immediately. Evacuate."

"That's Jay's work! He's hacking the system, making it seem as if the place is about to explode!" Sawyer threw back at them. "Thanks to the alarm, everyone is busy covering their own asses."

They burst into what had to be a garage. The van was there. They all got inside as fast as possible. For super soldiers, it was *very* fast. Jett wired the vehicle. Savannah hopped in the passenger seat and hooked the safety belt. The van growled to life and surged them forward. Jett drove right through the garage door, a metal sheet that gave way beneath the impact of the van's front bumper, and then they were hurtling forward.

"Who the hell is that?" Sawyer thundered.

Someone was up ahead. Aiming a gun at the van.

"Stop!" Savannah yelled. "That's Jennifer!"

Jett jerked the van to the side. The brakes squealed.

Jennifer bounded toward them. She yanked open the passenger side door. "Savannah?" Relief flooded her features. "Oh, God, I thought—"

"If she's on our side, get her in the van," Sawyer yelled to Savannah from the back. An instant later, he was sliding open one of the van's side doors. "She can help me with this guy. He's bleeding all over the place."

Jennifer pulled back, lifting her gun toward Sawyer. "Who the hell are you?"

"A friend," Savannah said quickly. "Get in, Jennifer, come on!"

Jennifer jumped in. The van took off.

"This is Special Agent McNeely!" Jennifer cried from the back of the van as she spied the injured man. "What happened to him?"

"Better question is…" Jett muttered. "What *will* happen to him?"

Savannah shivered.

"Um, hey, you might want to stop near the end of the dirt road. Or not," Jennifer added nervously. "Your cousin is there, Savannah. I think he's got, uh, a concussion. Or two."

Savannah glanced back at her.

But Jennifer wasn't looking at her. She'd put her hands over McNeely's wounds and was applying pressure.

"Savannah?" Jett asked. "Want me to stop for Sam or keep going?"

She still had her gun. She was afraid to let it go.

"Savannah?" he prompted.

She could see Sam's slumped form up ahead.

"He led me to you," Jennifer called from the back, her voice tense. "I think he's a traitorous bastard, but he took me out here."

Dammit. "Get him."

Jett braked. A few moments later, he'd dumped Sam's unconscious form into the back of the van. None-too-gently. "Where the hell am I going?" Jett shouted back at Sawyer as he got the van moving again.

"Turn right at the main road," Sawyer barked back, apparently still getting directions in his ear-piece. "Keep driving until you see the helicopter."

"The helicopter?" Savannah repeated, already leaning forward to peer out of the windshield.

"Yeah, Jay says they're going to find us. As soon as they get a visual, the chopper will land in the middle of the freaking road."

And a few minutes later, that's exactly what it did.

CHAPTER TWENTY-ONE

"Savannah Jacobs is dead," Jett said those words flatly as he stared at the man in the hospital bed.

Pale as the sheets around him, Agent Bennett McNeely swallowed at Jett's announcement. The machines around him beeped faster. "I am so freaking sorry."

"You should be. You worked for a lying psychopath who wanted to destroy the people I care about. You *killed* me three times, and you will pay." He stalked toward the bed.

The hospital door opened behind him. Jett caught the sweet, familiar scent even as he watched the shock flash on McNeely's face.

"Wh-what? Savannah?"

She came to Jett's side. He wrapped his arm around her shoulders. "Savannah Jacobs is dead," Jett said again. "She died in a fire at her shop in Biloxi. That's what you're going to tell anyone who asks. That's what you'll tell the local cops and any reporters. You'll back up Detective

Jennifer Adams's story, and if anyone from the US government ever asks…"

McNeely released a slow breath. "Savannah Jacobs is dead."

Jett nodded. "Now you get the picture."

McNeely glanced around the hospital room. "Where am I?"

"A private place just outside of Jackson, Mississippi. There will be no records of your stay here." Because money could make almost anything happen. Since Jay Maverick had money to burn, he was using those assets to help the team.

"I'm sorry, Savannah," McNeely said, and it sounded as if the jerk meant those words. "I didn't realize how far gone Rowe was, and when I did finally see the truth, I knew that *I* had to stop him. But he was protected, insulated. I had to get a one-on-one meeting with him, and the only way to get the guy to come out from behind his cloud of protection—"

"Was to serve us up to him," Jett finished.

Miserably, McNeely nodded. "I was going to kill him. Then I was going to let you both go, I swear it. I went to the control room to end him—and to get access to all of the files he had on the other cases we'd worked. I wanted to make sure no other innocents had ever been taken."

"One of our associates hacked into the not-so-good doctor's system. I'll make sure the guy gives you a copy of everything he finds." Jett had quickly learned that Jay Maverick never met a system he couldn't hack. "And you'd better make sure *all* innocents are safe."

"I will—"

"The Lazarus team will be helping you. Because we really don't like when people are put in cages for no good reason." He offered a cold smile to McNeely.

"You're going to kick my ass, aren't you?" McNeely asked miserably.

Jett opened his mouth to reply—

"You killed him," Savannah cut in, and there was a hot fury in her voice. "You can say that you were trying to do the right thing, that your target was Rowe, but I had to watch the life drain from the eyes of the man I love."

Jett pulled her closer. *I'm right here, baby.*

Where he'd always be.

"So, yes," she added, voice seething. "You're getting an ass-kicking as soon as you can walk. Then you're helping all of the people Rowe hurt. Here's a word for you to focus on, *agent,* and that word is atonement."

His head sagged. "I will atone, I swear it." His breathing seemed ragged. "Are you and the baby okay?"

Jett's fingers slid to her stomach.

"We're fine," Savannah answered, the rage still cracking in her voice.

They were Jett's world.

"I can't believe you didn't just leave me to die," McNeely rasped. "You should have. I don't deserve—"

"They aren't the monsters," Savannah cut in. "That's not who Jett and his friends are."

McNeely's stare drifted between them. "It's not who I want to be, either."

"Then don't make me regret giving you another chance," Jett warned him. Because Savannah was wrong. He *could* be a monster. If she was ever threatened again, the monster would come out in a wave of darkness.

Savannah twined her fingers with Jett's. "One more question." She exhaled slowly. "When we searched you, we found my baby's yellow blanket in your pocket. What the hell was that doing there?"

McNeely winced. "Found it…at your place. In the middle of freaking chaos. I just—it was wrong. Everything was so wrong. It was the only thing that wasn't destroyed, and I just wanted to save it." His gaze slid over her. Seemed to linger on her stomach. "Just wanted to save…" He cleared his throat. "I'm sorry."

The guy sounded as if he actually meant those words. Only time would reveal the truth, though. Would he be a changed man? Or an asshole who needed to be put down?

Without another word, Jett and Savannah left McNeely's room. The hospital corridor was empty. Jay had flown in nurses and doctors he trusted, and there was only one other patient in the whole place.

But they didn't go into the next room. Not yet. They didn't go see that second patient.

Jett stilled beside Savannah. Her head tipped back as she stared up at him. "Baby…" He brushed back a lock of her hair. "You don't have to go in there and face him. You don't have to ever see Sam again."

"I do."

"He sold you out. Jennifer said she can toss him into a jail cell. He kidnapped her, and she can press charges against him that will last—"

"I need to see him." Her smile almost broke his heart. "And then we're done. One chapter closed. A whole other life waiting."

About that other, precious life. "Did Elizabeth run her tests?"

Savannah had told McNeely that she and the baby were fine, but Jett knew she wouldn't have told that guy anything else. Just a flat, easy answer.

She smiled at him. "She started, but I didn't want her to run the ultrasound just yet. I wanted you there for that part."

It was hard to breathe.

"She said that the baby may be completely normal. No Lazarus side effects. No psychic powers from my side."

"I will love the baby." That was it. Full stop. Savannah's child would always be loved by him, no matter what.

"Then let's finish this with Sam, and then go see our baby."

His heart was racing faster. And he was damn eager. So, when they entered Sam's room, he might have shoved open the door too hard. It flew back, hitting the wall.

Sam gave a quick, sharp cry. His arms jerked up — but his right hand was cuffed to the hospital bed, so it didn't jerk far.

"Settle your ass down," Jennifer advised him with a roll of her eyes. She sat near the bed, guarding her prisoner.

"Savannah!" Relief flashed on Sam's face. "You're okay! Oh, Vannie, I am so sorry! So sorry! That Rowe bastard was in my head. Been in there since I was a kid. I tried to shut him out but never could. Phillip said the guy would help me, the way he'd helped you." The man's words just tumbled out. "I thought he'd shut down the voices, but he made things worse for me. He got —"

"He's dead," Savannah cut in softly.

Sam drew in a ragged breath. "I know." His left hand rose. His fingers touched his temple. "He's not in here any longer."

Savannah walked closer to the bed. "Jennifer said you were trying to help me."

Yeah, well, Jennifer had *also* told them that Sam had been in on Patrick Zane's abduction of Savannah. Jett wasn't ready to embrace the guy in a warm, family hug.

He's someone else who will be getting an ass-kicking.

Sam gazed at Savannah with guilt-ridden eyes. "I never wanted you hurt. The minute he started putting you in his sights, God, when he worked the kidnapping with Patrick — it was too much. I was sick, desperate to get you back home."

And Jett remembered how frantic the guy had seemed when he and Savannah had walked into Phillip's mansion. How relieved to see Savannah alive again.

"Patrick Zane was some for-hire thug," Sam explained in his strained voice. "That guy — he *killed* people for money, and Rowe hired him to take you."

Jett felt fury surge within him once again.

"But Patrick, I think he fell for you, Savannah. Something happened. Because suddenly, he was changing the plan. He stopped talking to Rowe and went silent. I knew where you were," Sam continued in a choked voice. "I could feel your fear. I fed the details of your location to Rowe, and he—"

"He arranged for me and my team to go in with guns blazing," Jett finished. Yeah, he knew how this story ended.

"I'm so sorry," Sam said. "It...*it wasn't me.* It was like I was a puppet, and Rowe was pulling the strings."

"You're not a puppet any longer," Jett snapped at him.

Sam shook his head. "Savannah..."

"Rowe is gone," Savannah said with a quick roll of her shoulders. "I think I'd like to see what you're like, without someone else always being in your head."

"I'm not...I'm not going to jail?" He seemed stunned. He should have been stunned. And grateful.

"I think jail would do him some good," Jennifer argued with a huff. "Let's not be too hasty with this decision."

Sam turned toward her. "I love you."

"What?" Her jaw dropped.

"I do. Couldn't ever tell you because I didn't want him to make you a target. Rowe always targeted the things his enemies cared about." His gaze cut back to Jett. "That's how he was going to bring down Jett's team. But in the end, they were stronger than he ever suspected."

"Savannah is the one who killed him." Jett glanced at the woman *he* loved. "She's the one who's strong."

Savannah focused on Jett. Her gaze softened as she stared at him. "He made a mistake. He tried to take you from me."

Jett bent toward her. Pressed his lips to hers. *I will never leave you again.*

She smiled against his lips. *I think it's time you met our baby.*

He pulled back. The woman owned him, heart and soul. Without looking away from her, he said, "Sam, lucky bastard, you get to keep living. Now work at convincing Jennifer that you're an asshole who *doesn't* belong in jail."

Jett's fingers twined with Savannah's as they left the room. Behind them, he heard...

"You do *not* love me. Don't feed me some BS line because you think it will help your case—"

"That's why I love you. Because you don't accept my BS. Jennifer—"

The door shut.

Jett stared down at Savannah.

"He'll spread the story that I'm dead," she said. "Everyone will believe a senator, right?"

No, but they could try it. Folks would be more likely to believe Jennifer and Agent McNeely.

"When we start our new life, where will we go?" Savannah asked him as they headed down the hallway.

"Anywhere you want." They slipped into the elevator.

Savannah hit the button for the next floor. "I like the beach."

"Then get ready to feel the sand between your toes." He lifted her hand to his mouth. Kissed her knuckles.

She smiled at him. "We're going to start over?"

"We're going to do anything you want."

"I like that." She leaned close. Pressed her lips to his. "I like that a lot."

***

Savannah stared over at the monitor, watching as the dark swirls and shadows took shape.

Elizabeth was staring at the screen. And she was frowning.

Unease slithered through Savannah. "What's happening? When we talked earlier, you said I seemed fine…"

Elizabeth leaned closer to the screen.

Jett's hold tightened on Savannah's hand.

But Elizabeth just tapped the screen. "Right here…this is your baby. See this flutter? That's the heartbeat." She moved the ultrasound wand over Savannah's abdomen. "And you see this…this is your baby, too."

Wait…Too? *Two?*

Elizabeth looked at them with a wide smile on her face. "I wanted the ultrasound so I could be sure, and now it is a definite thing. You have two babies in there, Savannah. Two babies who have very strong heartbeats."

Savannah's gaze latched onto the swirling screen. All of those shadows there…

"Two?" Jett repeated.

His ragged voice had Savannah turning to him. Tears gleamed in his eyes. He blinked them away, but Savannah had seen them. Her own tears were about to fall.

They were safe. They were together.

They were a family.

"It's going to be a whole new world for you," Elizabeth said softly as she patted Savannah's shoulder.

A whole new world for *everyone.*

The Lazarus subjects were here to stay. Her children were coming, and nothing would ever be the same.

Jett kissed Savannah.

Are you ready for this? She sent the thought to him.

I've never wanted anything more.

It was going to be wild ride, and she couldn't wait.

The End

A NOTE FROM THE AUTHOR

Thank you so much for reading HOLD ON TIGHT! If you enjoyed Jett's story, please consider leaving a review. Reviews help new readers to find great books.

I had such a wonderful time writing the "Lazarus Rising" series — the series allowed me to blend my two favorite romance sub-genres, romantic suspense and paranormal romance. I hope you enjoyed going on the twists and turns with me. And who knows...maybe there will be more super soldiers in the future!

If you'd like to stay updated on my releases and sales, please join my newsletter list.

http://www.cynthiaeden.com/newsletter/

Again, thank you for reading HOLD ON TIGHT.

Best,
Cynthia Eden
www.cynthiaeden.com

ABOUT THE AUTHOR

Award-winning author Cynthia Eden writes dark tales of paranormal romance and romantic suspense. She is a New York Times, USA Today, Digital Book World, and IndieReader best-seller. Cynthia is also a three-time finalist for the RITA® award. Since she began writing full-time in 2005, Cynthia has written over eighty novels and novellas.

For More Information

- *www.cynthiaeden.com*
- *http://www.facebook.com/cynthiaedenfanpage*
- *http://www.twitter.com/cynthiaeden*

HER OTHER WORKS

Romantic Suspense
- Secret Admirer
- Don't Trust A Killer

Lazarus Rising
- Never Let Go (Book One, Lazarus Rising)
- Keep Me Close (Book Two, Lazarus Rising)
- Stay With Me (Book Three, Lazarus Rising)
- Run To Me (Book Four, Lazarus Rising)
- Lie Close To Me (Book Five, Lazarus Rising)
- Hold On Tight (Book Six, Lazarus Rising)

Dark Obsession Series
- Watch Me (Dark Obsession, Book 1)
- Want Me (Dark Obsession, Book 2)
- Need Me (Dark Obsession, Book 3)

- Beware Of Me (Dark Obsession, Book 4)
- Only For Me (Dark Obsession, Books 1 to 4)

Mine Series

- Mine To Take (Mine, Book 1)
- Mine To Keep (Mine, Book 2)
- Mine To Hold (Mine, Book 3)
- Mine To Crave (Mine, Book 4)
- Mine To Have (Mine, Book 5)
- Mine To Protect (Mine, Book 6)
- Mine Series Box Set Volume 1 (Mine, Books 1-3)
- Mine Series Box Set Volume 2 (Mine, Books 4-6)

Other Romantic Suspense

- First Taste of Darkness
- Sinful Secrets
- Until Death
- Christmas With A Spy

Paranormal Romance
Bad Things

- The Devil In Disguise (Bad Things, Book 1)
- On The Prowl (Bad Things, Book 2)
- Undead Or Alive (Bad Things, Book 3)
- Broken Angel (Bad Things, Book 4)

- Heart Of Stone (Bad Things, Book 5)
- Tempted By Fate (Bad Things, Book 6)
- Bad Things Volume One (Books 1 to 3)
- Bad Things Volume Two (Books 4 to 6)
- Bad Things Deluxe Box Set (Books 1 to 6)
- Wicked And Wild (Bad Things, Book 7)
- Saint Or Sinner (Bad Things, Book 8)

Bite Series

- Forbidden Bite (Bite Book 1)
- Mating Bite (Bite Book 2)

Blood and Moonlight Series

- Bite The Dust (Blood and Moonlight, Book 1)
- Better Off Undead (Blood and Moonlight, Book 2)
- Bitter Blood (Blood and Moonlight, Book 3)
- Blood and Moonlight (The Complete Series)

Purgatory Series

- The Wolf Within (Purgatory, Book 1)
- Marked By The Vampire (Purgatory, Book 2)
- Charming The Beast (Purgatory, Book 3)
- Deal with the Devil (Purgatory, Book 4)

- The Beasts Inside (Purgatory, Books 1 to 4)

Bound Series

- Bound By Blood (Bound Book 1)
- Bound In Darkness (Bound Book 2)
- Bound In Sin (Bound Book 3)
- Bound By The Night (Bound Book 4)
- Forever Bound (Bound, Books 1 to 4)
- Bound in Death (Bound Book 5)

Made in the USA
Middletown, DE
27 August 2018